PENGUIN BOOKS

The Lair of the White Worm

Bram Stoker was born in Dublin in 1847, the son of a civil servant. He overcame a long childhood illness to attend Trinity College, Dublin, where he distinguished himself in athletics, becoming president of both Philosophical and Historical Societies and graduated in science. From 1870 to 1877 he worked as a civil servant in Dublin Castle, publishing *The Duties of Clerks of Petty Sessions in Ireland* in 1879. During this period he also wrote dramatic criticism, and in 1878 his strong admiration for, and burgeoning friendship with, Henry Irving led the actor to appoint him acting (business) manager at London's Lyceum Theatre, an experience that produced *Personal Reminisces of Henry Irving* (1906). Apart from *Dracula* (1897), Stoker's other novels and stories have declined in popularity since their original publication, an *oeuvre* which includes *The Mystery of the Sea* (1902), *The Jewel of Seven Stars* (1903), *The Man* (1905), and *The Lair of the White Worm* (1911). A collection of Stoker's short stories, *Dracula's Guest and Other Weird Stories* was published post-humously in 1914 by his widow, Florence Stoker.

BRAM STOKER

The Lair of the White Worm

PENGUIN BOOKS

PENGUIN BOOKS

Published by the Penguin Group
Penguin Books Ltd, 80 Strand, London WC2R ORL, England
Penguin Group (USA) Inc., 375 Hudson Street, New York, New York 10014, USA
Penguin Group (Canada), 90 Eglinton Avenue East, Suite 700, Toronto, Ontario,
Canada M4P 2Y3 (a division of Pearson Penguin Canada Inc.)
Penguin Ireland, 25 St Stephen's Green, Dublin 2, Ireland
(a division of Penguin Books Ltd)
Penguin Group (Australia), 250 Camberwell Road, Camberwell, Victoria 3124, Australia
(a division of Pearson Australia Group Pty Ltd)
Penguin Books India Pvt Ltd, 11 Community Centre, Panchsheel Park,
New Delhi – 110 017, India
Penguin Group (NZ), 167 Apollo Drive, Roseland, North Shore 0632,
New Zealand (a division of Pearson New Zealand Ltd)
Penguin Books (South Africa) (Pty) Ltd, 24 Sturdee Avenue, Rosebank,
Johannesburg 2196, South Africa

Penguin Books Ltd, Registered Offices: 80 Strand, London WC2R ORL, England

www.penguin.com

First published by William Rider and Son Ltd 1911
Published as a Penguin Red Classic 2008

2

All rights reserved

Typeset by Palimpsest Book Production Limited, Grangemouth, Stirlingshire
Printed in England by Clays Ltd, St Ives plc

978-0-141-03875-9

TO

MY FRIEND

BERTHA NICOLL

WITH AFFECTIONATE ESTEEM

Contents

I

Adam Salton Arrives

When Adam Salton arrived at the Great Eastern Hotel he found awaiting him a letter in the hand-writing of his grand-uncle, Richard Salton, which he knew so well from the many kind letters which he had received from him in West Australia. The first of them had been written less than a year before, in which the old gentleman, who had in it claimed kinship, stated that he had been unable to write earlier because until then he did not know even of his existence, and it had taken him some time to find out his address. The last, sent after him, had only just arrived, and conveyed a most cordial invitation to stop with him at Lesser Hill for as long a time as he could spare. 'Indeed,' his grand-uncle went on, 'I am in hopes that you will make your permanent home here. You see, my dear boy, that you and I are all that remain of our race, and it is but fitting that you should succeed me when the time comes, which cannot be long now. I am getting close on eighty years of age, and though we have been a long-lived race, the span of life cannot be prolonged beyond reasonable bounds. I am prepared to like you and to make your home with me as happy a one as I can achieve. So do come at once on receipt of this and find the welcome I am waiting to give you. I send, in case such may make matters easy for you, a banker's draft for £500. Come soon, so that we may both of us have such happy days as are still possible to us. For me this is all-important, as the sands of my life are fast running out; but for you I trust there are many happy years to come. If you are able to give me the pleasure of seeing you, send me as soon as you can a letter telling me to expect you. Then when you arrive at Plymouth or Southampton (or whatever port you are bound for), send me a telegram, and I shall come to meet you at the earliest hour possible.'

On Monday, Adam Salton's letter arrived by the morning post, saying that he hoped to travel by the boat which carried it, and that he would therefore be ready to meet his grand-uncle so soon after the arrival of the letter in Mercia as he should be able to reach London. 'I shall wait your arrival, sir, on the ship. By this means we may avoid any cross purposes.'

Mr Salton took it for granted that, no matter how fast he might travel, his guest would be awaiting him; so he gave instructions to have ready a carriage at seven the next morn-ing to start for Stafford, where he would catch the 11.40 for Euston, arriving at 2.10. Thence, driving to Waterloo, he could catch the 3 P.M., due at Southampton at 5.38. He would that night stay with his grand-nephew, either on the ship, which would be a new experience for him, or, if his guest should prefer it, at a hotel. In either case they would start in the early morning for home. He had given instructions to his bailiff to send the postillion carriage on to Southampton to be ready for their journey home, and to arrange for relays of his own horses to be sent on at once. He intended that his grand-nephew, who had been all his life in Australia, should see something of central England on the drive. He had plenty of young horses of his own breeding and breaking, and could depend on a journey memorable to the young man. The luggage would be sent on by rail the same day to Stafford, where one of his own carts would meet it. Mr Salton, during the journey to Southampton, often wondered if his grand-nephew was as much excited as he was at the idea of meeting so near a relation for the first time; and it was with an effort that he controlled himself. The endless railway lines and switches round the Southampton Docks fired his anxiety afresh.

As the train drew up on the dockside, he was getting his

hand traps together, when the carriage door was wrenched open and a young man jumped in, saying as he came:

'How are you, uncle? I wanted to meet you as soon as I could, but everything is so strange to me that I didn't quite know what to do. However, I took chance that the railway people knew something of their own business – and here I am. I am glad to see you, sir. I have been dreaming of the happiness for thousands of miles; and now I find that the reality beats all the dreaming!' As he spoke the old man and the young one were heartily wringing each other's hands. He went on: 'I think I knew you the moment I set eyes on you. I am glad that that dream was only enhanced by the reality!'

The meeting so auspiciously begun proceeded well. Adam, seeing that the old man was interested in the novelty of the ship, suggested timidly that he should stay the night on board, and that he would himself be ready to start at any hour and go anywhere that the other suggested. This affectionate willingness to fall in with his own plans quite won the old man's heart. He warmly accepted the invitation, and at once they became not only on terms of affectionate relationship, but almost as old friends. The heart of the old man, which had been empty for so long, found a new delight. So, too, the young man found on landing in the old country a welcome and a surrounding in full harmony with all his dreams of such matters throughout all his wanderings and solitude, and the promise of a fresh and adventurous life. It was not long before the old man accepted him to full relationship by calling him by his Christian name. The other accepted the proffer with such heartiness that he was soon regarded as the future companion, almost the child, of his old age. After a long talk on affairs of interest, they retired to the cabin, which the elder was to share. Richard Salton, putting his hands affectionately on the boy's shoulders – though Adam was in his twenty-seventh year, he was a boy, and always would be, to his grand-uncle, – said warmly:

'I am so glad to find you as you are, my dear boy – just such a young man as I had always hoped for as a son in the days when I still had such hopes. However, dear boy, that is all past. But thank God there is a new life to begin for both of us. To you must be the larger part – but there is still time for some of it to be shared in common. I have waited till we should have seen each other to enter upon the subject; for I thought it better not to tie up your young life to my old one till we should have both sufficient personal knowledge to justify such a venture. Now I can (so far as I am concerned) enter into it freely, since from the moment my eyes rested on you I saw my son – as he shall be, God willing – if he chooses such a course himself.'

'Indeed I do, sir – with all my heart!'

'Thank you, Adam, for that.' The old man's eyes filled and his voice trembled. Then, after a long silence between them, he went on: 'When I heard you were coming I made my will. It was well that your interests should be protected from that moment on. Here is the deed – keep it, Adam. All I have shall belong to you; and if love and good wishes or the memory of them can make life sweeter, yours shall be a happy one. And now, my dear boy, let us turn in. We start early in the morning and have a long drive before us. I hope you don't mind carriage driving? I was going to have sent down the old travelling carriage in which my grandfather, your great-grand-uncle, went to Court when William IV was king. It is all right – they built well in those days – and it has been kept in perfect order. But I think I have done better: I have sent the carriage in which I travel myself. The horses are of my own breeding, and relays of them shall take us all the way. I hope you like horses? They have long been one of my greatest interests in life.'

'I love them, sir, and I am happy to say I have many of my own. My father gave me a horse farm for myself when I was sixteen. I devoted myself to it, and it has gone on. Before I came away, my steward gave me a memorandum that we have in my own places more than a thousand, nearly all good.'

'I am glad, my boy. Another link between us.'

'Just fancy what a delight it will be, sir, to see so much of middle England – and with you!'

'Thank you again, my boy. I shall tell you all about your future home and its surroundings as we go. We shall travel in old-fashioned state, I tell you. My grandfather always drove four-in-hand; and so shall we.'

'Oh, thanks, sir, thanks. May I take the ribbons some-times?'

'Whenever you choose, Adam. The team is your own. Every horse we use to-day is to be your own.'

'You are too generous, uncle!'

'Not at all. Only an old man's selfish pleasure. It is not every day that an heir to the old home comes back. And – oh, by the way . . . No, we had better turn in now – I shall tell you the rest in the morning.'

II

The Caswalls of Castra Regis

Mr Salton had all his life been an early riser, and necessarily an early waker. But early as he woke on the next morning, and although there was an excuse for not prolonging sleep in the constant whirr and rattle of the 'donkey' engine winches of the great ship, when he waked he met the eyes of Adam fixed on him from his berth. His grand-nephew had given him the sofa, occupying the lower berth himself. The old man, despite his great strength and normal activity, was somewhat tired by his long journey of the day before and the prolonged and exciting interview which followed it. So he was glad to lie still and rest his body, whilst his mind was actively exercised in taking in all he could of his strange surroundings. Adam, too, after the pastoral habit to which he had been bred, woke with the dawn, if not before it, and was ready to enter on the experiences of the new day whenever it might suit his elder companion. It was little wonder, then, that so soon as each realised the other's readiness, they simultaneously jumped up and began to dress. The steward had by previous instructions early breakfast prepared, and it was not long before they went down the gangway on shore in search of the carriage.

They found Mr Salton's bailiff waiting on the dock, and he brought them at once to where the carriage was waiting in the street. Richard Salton pointed out with pride to his young companion the suitability of the trap to every need of travel. It was a sort of double gig, excellently made, and with every appliance adapted for both speed and safety. To it were harnessed four fine, useful horses, with a postillion to each pair.

'See,' said the old man proudly, 'how it has all the luxuries of useful travel – silence and isolation as well as speed. There is nothing to obstruct the view of those travelling and no one to overhear what they may say. I have used that trap for a quarter of a century, and I never saw one more suitable for travel. You shall test it shortly. We are going to drive through the heart of England; and as we go I shall tell you what I was speaking of last night. Our route is to be by Salisbury, Bath, Bristol, Cheltenham, Worcester, Stafford; and so home.'

After remaining silent a few minutes, what time he seemed all eyes, for he perpetually ranged the whole circle of the horizon, Adam said:

'Has our journey to-day, sir, any special relation to what you said last night that you wanted to tell me?'

'Not directly; but indirectly, everything.'

'Won't you tell me now – I see we cannot be overheard – and if anything strikes you as we go along, just run it in. I shall understand.'

So old Salton spoke:

'To begin at the beginning, Adam. That lecture of yours on "The Romans in Britain" set me thinking – in addition to telling me where you were. I wrote to you at once and asked you to come home, for it struck me that if you were fond of historical research – as seemed a fact – this was exactly the place for you, in addition to its being the place of your own forbears. If you could learn so much of the British Romans so far away in West Australia, where there cannot be even a tradition of them, what might you not make of the same amount of study on the very spot. Where we are going is in the real heart of the old kingdom of Mercia, where there are traces of all the various nationalities which made up the conglomerate which became Britain.'

After a slight pause Adam said:

7

'I rather gathered that you had some more definite – more personal reason for my hurrying. After all, history can keep – except in the making!'

'Quite right, my boy. I had a reason such as you very wisely guessed at. I was anxious for you to be here when a rather important phase of our local history occurred.'

'What is that, if I may ask, sir?'

'Certainly. The great owner of all this part of the county – of several of the counties – is on his way home, and there will be a great home-coming, which you may care to see. The fact is, that for more than a century the various owners in the succession here, with the exception of a short time, lived abroad.'

'How is that, sir, if I may again ask?'

'By all means. That is why I wished you to be here – so that you might learn. We have a good stretch without incident before us till we get in sight of Salisbury, so I had better begin now:

'Our great house and estate in this part of the world is Castra Regis, the family seat of the Caswall family. The last owner who lived here was Edgar Caswall, great-grand-uncle of the man who is coming here – and he was the only man who stayed even a short time. His grandfather, also named Edgar – they keep the tradition of the family Christian name – quarrelled with his family and went to live abroad, not keeping up any relations, good or bad, with his relatives. His son was born and lived and died abroad. His son, the latest inheritor, was also born and lived abroad till he was over thirty, – his present age. This was the second line of absentees. The great-great-grandfather of the present Edgar also cut himself off from his family and went abroad, from which sojourn he never returned. The consequence has been that the great estate of Castra Regis has had no knowledge of its owner for six generations – covering more than a hundred years. It has been well administered, however, and no tenant or other connected with it has had anything to complain of. All the same, there has been much natural anxiety to see the new owner, and we are all excited about the event of his coming. Even I am, though I own my own estate, which, though adjacent, is quite apart from Castra Regis. – Here we are now in new ground for you. That is the spire of Salisbury Cathedral, and when we leave that we shall be getting close to the old Roman county and you will naturally want your eyes. So we shall shortly have to keep our minds on old Mercia. However, you need not be disappointed. My old friend, Sir Nathaniel de Salis, who, like myself, is a freeholder near Castra Regis, though not on it – his estate, Doom Tower, is over the border of Derbyshire, on the Peak – is coming to stay with me for all the festivities to welcome Edgar Caswall. He is just the sort of man you will like. He is devoted to history, and is President of the Mercian Archæological Society. He knows more of our own part of the country, with its history and its people, than anyone else. I expect he will have arrived before us, and we three can have a long chat after dinner. He is also our local geologist and natural historian. So you and he will have many interests in common. Amongst other things he has a special knowledge of the Peak and its caverns, and knows all the old legends of the days when prehistoric times were vital.'

From this on till they came to Stafford, Adam's eyes were in constant employment on matters of the road; and it was not till Salton had declared that they had now entered on the last stage of their journey that he referred back to Sir Nathaniel's coming.

As the dusk was closing down they drove on to Lesser Hill, Mr Salton's house. It was now too dark to see detail of their surrounding. Adam could just see that it was on the top of a hill, not quite so high as that which was covered by the Castle, on whose tower flew the flag, and which was all ablaze with moving lights, manifestly used in the preparations for the festivities on the morrow. So Adam deferred his curiosity till daylight. His grand-uncle was met at the door by a fine old man, who said as he greeted him warmly:

'I came over early as you wished me to. I suppose this is your grand-nephew – I am glad to meet you, Mr Adam Salton. I am Nathaniel de Salis, and your uncle is the oldest of my friends.'

Adam, from the moment of their eyes meeting, felt as if they were already old friends. The meeting was a new note of welcome to those that had already sounded in his ears.

The cordiality with which Sir Nathaniel and Adam met made the imparting of the former's information easy both to speak and to hear. Sir Nathaniel was quite a clever old man of the world, who had travelled much and within a certain area studied deeply. He was a brilliant conversationalist, as was to be expected from a successful diplomatist, even under unstimulating conditions. But he had been touched and to a certain extent fired by the younger man's evident admiration and willingness to learn from him. Accordingly the conversation, which began on the most friendly basis, soon warmed to an interest above proof as the old man spoke of it next day to Richard Salton. He knew already that his old friend wanted his grand-nephew to learn all he could of the subject in hand, and so had during his journey from the Peak put his thoughts in sequence for narration and explanation. Accordingly, Adam had only to listen and he must learn much that he wanted to know. When dinner was over and the servants had withdrawn, leaving the three men at their wine, Sir Nathaniel began:

'I gather from your uncle – by the way, I suppose we had better speak of you as uncle and nephew, instead of going into exact relationship? In fact, your uncle is so old and dear a friend, that, with your permission, I shall drop formality with you altogether and speak of you and to you as Adam, as though you were his son.'

'I would wish, sir,' answered the young man, 'nothing better in the world!'

The answer warmed the hearts of both the old men who heard. All the men felt touched, but, with the usual avoidance of Englishmen of emotional subjects personal to themselves, they instinctively moved from the previous question. Sir Nathaniel took the lead:

'I understand, Adam, that your uncle has posted you regarding the relationships of the Caswall family?'

'Partly, sir; but I understood that I was to hear minuter details from you – if you would be so good.'

'I shall be delighted to tell you anything so far as my knowledge goes. Well, we have to remember, in connection with the events of to-morrow, that not less than ten generations of that family are involved. And I really believe that for a true understanding of the family ramifications you cannot begin better than having the list as a basis. Everything which we may consider as we go along will then take its natural place without extra trouble. The present branch of affairs begins only about something more than a hundred and fifty years ago. Later we may have to go further back, for the history of the Caswall family is coeval with that of England – we need not trouble ourselves with dates; the facts will be more easily grasped in a general way.

'The first Caswall in our immediate record is Edgar, who was head of the family and owner of the estate, who came into his kingdom just about the time that George III did. He had one son of about twenty-four. There was a violent quarrel between the two. No one of this generation has any idea of the cause of it; but, considering the family characteristics, we may take it for granted that though it was deep and violent, it was on the surface trivial.

'The result of the quarrel was that the son left the house without approaching a reconciliation or without even telling his father where he was going. He never came back to the house again. A few years after, he died without having in the meantime exchanged a word or a letter with his father. He married abroad and left one son, who seems to have been brought up in ignorance of all belonging to him. The gulf between them appears to have been unbridgeable; for in time this son married and in turn had a son, but neither joy nor sorrow brought the sundered together. Under such conditions no *rapprochement* was to be looked for, and an utter indifference, founded at best on ignorance, took the place of family affection – even on community of interests. It was only due to the watchfulness of the lawyers that the birth and death of a new heir was ever made known. In time a second son appeared, but without any effect of friendly advance.

'At last there arose a dim hope of some cessation of hostility, for though none of the separated made mention of the fact – knowledge of which was again due to the lawyers – a son was born to this youngest member of the voluntary exiles – the great-grandson of the Edgar whose son had left him. After this the family interest merely rested on heirship of the estate – any outside interest being submerged in the fact of a daughter being born to the grandson of the first Edgar. Some twenty years afterwards, the interest flickered up when it was made known – again through the lawyers – that the last two born had been married, thus shutting off any possibility of disputed heirship. As no other child had been born to any of the newer generations in the intervening twenty years, all hopes of heritage were now centred in the son of this last couple – the heir whose home-coming we are to celebrate to-morrow. The elder generations had all died away, and there were no collaterals, so there was no possibility of the heirship being disputed.

'Now, it will be well for you to bear in mind the prevailing characteristics of this race. These were well preserved and unchanging; one and all they are the same: cold, selfish, dominant, reckless of consequences in pursuit of their own will. It was not that they did not keep faith, though that was a matter which gave them little concern, but that they took care to think beforehand of what they should do in order to gain their ends. If they should make a mistake someone else should bear the burthen of it. This was so perpetually recurrent that it seemed to be a part of a fixed policy. It was no wonder indeed that whatever changes took place they were always ensured in their own possessions. They were absolutely of cold, hard nature. Not one of them – so far as we have any knowledge – was ever known to be touched by the softer sentiments, to swerve from his purpose, or hold his hand in obedience to the dictates of his heart. Part of this was due to their dominant, masterful nature. The aquiline features which marked them seemed to justify every personal harshness. The pictures and effigies of them all show their adherence to the early Roman type. Their eyes were full; their hair, of raven blackness, grew thick and close and curly. Their figures were massive and typical of strength.

'The thick black hair growing low down on the neck told of vast physical strength and endurance. But the most remarkable characteristic is the eyes. Black, piercing, almost unendurable, they seem to contain in themselves a remarkable will power which there is no gainsaying. It is a power that is partly racial and partly individual: a power impregnated with some mysterious quality, partly hypnotic, partly mesmeric, which seems to take away from eyes that meet them all power of resistance, nay, deeper, all power of wishing to resist. With eyes like those set in that aquiline, all-commanding face one would need to be strong indeed to even think of resisting the inflexible will that lay beyond. Even the habit and the exercise of power which they implied was a danger to anyone who was conscious of a weakness on his own part.

'You may think, Adam, that all this is imagination on my part, especially as I have never seen any belonging to the generation I have spoken of. So it is. But imagination based on deep study. I have made use of all I know or can surmise logically regarding this strange race. And with this data, however received, I have thought out logical results, correcting, amending, intensifying accepted conclusions, till at times

I see as though various members of the race had always been under my observation – that they are even under it still. With such strange compelling qualities, is it any wonder that there is abroad an idea that in the race there is some demoniac possession, which tends to a more definite belief that certain individuals have in the past sold themselves to the Devil? The Devil, I may say in this connection, is seldom mentioned *in propria persona*, but generally under some accepted guise, "The Powers of Evil," "The Enemy of Mankind," "The Prince of the Air," etc. I don't know what it is in other places; but along this eastern coast it is not considered polite to speak the truth plainly, baldly, in such matters, but to cover up the idea with a veil of obscurity in which safety or security may be hidden.

'But I think we had better go to bed now. We have a lot to go through to-morrow, and I want you to have your brain clear, and all your susceptibilities fresh. Moreover, I want you to come with me in an early walk in which we may notice, whilst the matter is fresh in our minds, the peculiar disposition of this place – not merely your grandfather's estate, but the lie of the country around it. There are many things on which we may seek – and perhaps find – enlightenment. The more we know at the start, the more things which may come into our view will develop themselves.'

So they all went off to bed.

III

Diana's Grove

Curiosity took Adam Salton out of bed in the early morning, but when he had dressed and gone downstairs, he found that, early as he was, Sir Nathaniel de Salis was ahead of him. The old gentleman was quite prepared for a long walk if necessary, and they started at once. Sir Nathaniel, without speaking, led the way a little to the east down the hill. When they had descended and risen again, they found themselves on the eastern brink of a steep hill. It was of lesser height than that on which the Castle was seated; but it was so placed that it commanded the various hills that crowned the ridge. All along the ridge the rock cropped out, bare and bleak, but broken in rough formed natural castellation. The form of the ridge was segment of a circle, with the higher points inland to the west. In the centre rose the Castle on the highest point of all. Between the various rocky excrescences were groups of trees of various sizes and heights, amongst some of which were what in the early morning light looked like ruins. These – whatever they were – were of massive grey stone, probably limestone rudely cut – if indeed they were not shaped naturally. The largest of these clumps was of oak trees of great age. They crossed the least of the hills, that which lay to the eastward. The fall of the ground was steep all along the ridge, so steep that here and there both trees and rocks and buildings seemed to overhang the level plain far below. Through this level ran many streams, and there was a number of blue pools, where was evidently fairly deep water.

Sir Nathaniel stopped and looked all around him, as though to lose nothing of the effect. The sun had climbed the eastern sky and was making all details clear. Sir Nathaniel pointed all round him with a sweeping gesture, as though calling Adam's attention to the wideness of the view. He did so so rapidly as to suggest that he wished the other to take, in the first survey, rather the *coup d'œil* than any detail. Having done so, he covered the ground in a similar way, but more slowly, as though inviting attention to detail. Adam was a willing and attentive pupil, and followed his motions exactly, missing – or trying to miss – nothing. When they had made the rough survey round the whole sweep of the eastern horizon, Sir Nathaniel spoke:

'I have brought you here, Adam, because it seems to me that this is the spot on which to begin our investigations. You have now in front of you almost the whole of the ancient kingdom of Mercia. In fact, we see, theoretically if not practically, the whole of it except that furthest part which is covered by the Welsh Marches and those parts which are hidden from where we stand by the high ground of the immediate west. We can see – again theoretically if not practically – the whole of the eastern bound of the kingdom which ran south from the Humber to the Wash. I want you to bear in mind the trend of the ground, for some time, sooner or later, we shall do well to have it in our mind's eye when we are considering the ancient traditions and even superstitions and are trying to find the *rationale* of them. I think we had better not try to differentiate between these, but let them naturally take their places as we go on. Each legend, each superstition which we receive will help in the understanding and possible elucidation of the others. And as all such have a local basis, we can come closer to the truth – or the probability – by knowing the local conditions as we go along. It will help us to bring to our aid even such geological truth as we may have between us. For instance, the building materials used in various ages can afford their own lessons to understanding eyes. The very heights and shapes and materials of these hills, nay, even of the wide plain that lies between us and the sea, have in themselves the materials of enlightening books.'

'For instance, sir?' said Adam, venturing a question.

'Well, for instance, look at those hills which surround the main one where the site for the Castle was wisely chosen – on the highest ground. Take the others. There is something ostensible in each of them, and in all probability something unseen and unproved, but to be imagined, also.'

'For instance?' continued Adam.

'Let us take them *seriatim*. That to the east, where the trees are, lower down. That was once the location of a Roman temple, possibly founded on a pre-existing Druidical one. Its name implies the former, and the grove of ancient oaks suggests the latter.'

'Please explain.'

'The old name translated means "Diana's Grove." Then the next one higher than it, but just beyond it, is called *"Mercy."* In all probability a corruption or perhaps a familiarisation of the word *Mercia* with a Roman pun included. We learn from early manuscripts that the place was called *Vilula Misericordiæ*. It was originally a nunnery founded by Queen Bertha, but done away with by King Penda, the reactionary to Paganism after St Augustine. Then comes your uncle's place – Lesser Hill. Though it is so close to the Castle, it is not connected with it. It is a freehold, and, so far as we know, of equal age. It has always belonged to your family.'

'Then there only remains the Castle!'

'That is all; but its history contains the histories of all the others – in fact, the whole history of early England.'

Sir Nathaniel, seeing the expectant look on Adam's face, went on:

'The history of the Castle has no beginning so far as we know. The furthest records or surmises or inferences simply accept it as existing. Some of these – guesses let us call them – seem to show that there was some sort of structure there when the Romans came, therefore it must have been a place of importance in Druid times – if indeed that was the beginning. Naturally the Romans accepted it, as they did everything of the kind that was, or might be, useful. The change is shown or inferred in the name Castra. It was the highest protected ground, and so naturally became the most important of their camps. A study of the map will show you that it must have been a most important strategetic centre. It both protected the advances already made to the north, and it helped to dominate the sea coast to the east. It sheltered the western marches, beyond which lay savage Wales – and danger. It provided a means of getting to the Severn, round which lay the great Roman roads then coming into existence, and made possible the great waterway to the heart of England – through the Severn and its tributaries. And it brought the east and the west together by the swiftest and easiest ways known to those times. And, finally, it provided means of descent on London and all the expanse of country watered by the Thames.

'With such a centre, already known and organised, we can easily see that each fresh wave of invasion – the Angles, the Saxons, the Danes, and the Normans – found it a desirable possession and so ensured its upholding. In the earlier centuries it was merely a vantage ground. But when the victorious Romans brought with them the heavy solid fortifications impregnable to the weapons of the time, its commanding position alone ensured its adequate building and equipment. Then it was that the fortified camp of the Cæsars developed into the castle of the king. As we are as yet entirely ignorant of even the names of the first kings of Mercia, no historian has been able to even guess what king made it his ultimate defence; and I suppose we shall never know now. In process of time, as the arts of war developed, it increased in size and strength, and although recorded details are lacking, the history is written in not merely the stone of its building, but is inferred in the changes of structure. Then the general sweeping changes which followed the Norman Conquest wiped out all lesser records than its own. To-day we must accept it as one of the earliest castles of the Conquest, probably not later than the time of Henry I. Roman and Norman were both wise in their retention of places of approved strength or utility. So it was that these surrounding heights, already established and to a certain extent proved, were retained. Indeed, such characteristics as already pertained to them were preserved and to-day afford to us lessons regarding things which have themselves long since passed away.

'So much for the fortified heights; but the hollows too have their own story. But how the time passes! We must hurry home, or else your uncle will wonder what has become of us.' As he spoke he was hurrying with long steps towards Lesser Hill, and Adam was furtively running to be able to keep up with him. When they had arrived close to the house, Sir Nathaniel said:

'I am sorry to cut short our interesting conversation. But it will be only postponed. I want to tell you, and I am sure you want to know, all that I know of this place. And, if I am not mistaken, our next instalment of history will be even more interesting than the first.'

IV

The Lady Arabella March

Breakfast had just begun when Mr Salton said:

'Now, there is no hurry, but so soon as you are both ready we shall start. I want to take you first to see a remarkable relic of Mercia, and then we shall go down to Liverpool through what is called "The Great Vale of Cheshire." You may be disappointed, but take care not to prepare your mind' – this to Adam – 'for anything stupendous or heroic. You would not think the place you are going through was a vale at all, unless you were told it beforehand, and had confidence in the veracity of the teller. We should get to the Landing Stage in time to meet the *West African*. We ought to meet Mr Caswall as he comes ashore. We want to do him honour – and, besides, it will be more pleasant to have the introductions over before we go to his *fête* at the Castle.'

The carriage was ready, the same as was used the previous day. The postillions, too, were the same, but there were two pairs of different horses – magnificent animals, and keen for work. Breakfast was soon over, and they shortly took their places. The postillions had their orders, and they were soon on their way at an exhilarating pace.

Presently, in obedience to Mr Salton's signal, the carriage drew up near Stone, opposite a great heap of stones by the wayside. 'Here,' he said, 'is something that you of all men should not pass by unnoticed. That heap of stones brings us at once to the dawn of the Anglian kingdom. It was begun more than a thousand years ago, in the latter part of the seventh century, in memory of a murder. Wulfere, King of Mercia, nephew of Penda, here murdered his two sons for embracing Christianity. As was the custom of the time, each passer-by added a stone to the memorial heap. Penda represented heathen reaction after St Augustine's mission. Sir Nathaniel can tell you as much as you want about this, and put you, if you wish, on the track of such accurate knowledge as there is.'

Whilst they were looking at the heap of stones, they noticed that another carriage had drawn up beside them, and the passenger – there was only one – was regarding them curiously. The carriage was an old heavy travelling one, with arms blazoned on it gorgeously. The coronet was an earl's, and there were many quarterings. Seeing then the occupant was a lady, the men took off their hats. The occupant spoke:

'How do you do, Sir Nathaniel? How do you do, Mr Salton? I hope none of you has met with any accident. Look at me!'

As she spoke she pointed where one of the heavy springs was broken across, the broken metal showing bright. Adam spoke up at once:

'Oh, that will be soon put right.'

'Soon? I shall have to wait till we get to Wolverhampton. There is no one near who can mend a break like that.'

'I can.'

'You!' She looked incredulously at the dapper young gentleman who spoke. 'You – why, it's a workman's job.'

'All right, I am a workman – though that is not the only sort of work I do. Let me explain. I am an Australian, and, as we have to move about fast, we are all trained to farriery and such mechanics as come into travel – and I am quite at your service.'

She said sweetly: 'I hardly know how to thank you for your kindness, of which I gladly avail myself. I don't know what else I can do. My father is Lord Lieutenant of the County, and he asked me to take his carriage – he is abroad himself – and meet Mr Caswall of Castra Regis, who arrives home from Africa to-day. It is a notable home-coming; his predecessor in the event made his entry more than a century ago, and all the countryside want to do him honour.' She looked at the old men and quickly made up her mind as to the identity of the stranger. 'You must be Mr Salton – Mr Adam Salton of Lesser Hill. I am Lady Arabella March of Diana's Grove.' As she spoke she turned slightly to Mr Salton, who took the hint and made a formal introduction.

So soon as this was done, Adam took some tools from his uncle's carriage, and at once began work on the broken spring. He was an expert workman, and the breach was soon made good. Adam was gathering the tools which he had been using, and which, after the manner of all workmen, had been scattered about, when he noticed that several black snakes had crawled out from the heap of stones and were gathering round him. This naturally occupied his mind, and he was not thinking of anything else when he noticed Lady Arabella, who had opened the door of the carriage, slip from it with a quick gliding motion. She was already among the snakes when he called out to warn her. But there seemed to be no need of warning. The snakes had turned and were wriggling back to the mound as quickly as they could. He laughed to himself behind his teeth as he whispered, 'No need to fear there. They seem much more afraid of her than she of them.' All the same he began to beat on the ground with a stick which was lying close to him, with the instinct of one used to such vermin. In an instant he was alone beside the mound with Lady Arabella, who appeared quite unconcerned at the incident. Then he took a long look at her. She was certainly good to look at in herself, and her dress alone was sufficient to attract attention. She was clad in some kind of soft white stuff, which clung close to her form, showing to the full every movement of her sinuous figure. She was tall and exceedingly thin. Her eyes appeared to be weak, for she wore large spectacles which seemed to be of green glass. Certainly in the centre they had the effect of making her naturally piercing eyes of a vivid green. She wore a close-fitting cap of some fine fur of dazzling white. Coiled round her white throat was a large necklace of emeralds, whose profusion of colour quite outshone the green of her spectacles – even when the sun shone on them. Her voice was very peculiar, very low and sweet, and so soft that the dominant note was of sibilation. Her hands, too, were peculiar – long, flexible, white, with a strange movement as of waving gently to and fro.

She appeared quite at ease, and, after thanking Adam, said that if any of his uncle's party were going to Liverpool she would be most happy to join forces. She added cordially:

'Whilst you are staying here, Mr Salton, you must look on the grounds of Diana's Grove as your own, so that you may come and go just as you do in Lesser Hill. There are some fine views and not a few natural curiosities which are sure to interest you. There are some views in the twilight which are, they say, unique. And if you are a student of natural history – specially of an earlier kind, when the world was younger – you shall not have your labour of discovery in vain.'

The heartiness with which she spoke and warmth of her words – not of her manner, which was abnormally cold and distant – repelled him, made him suspicious. He felt as if he was naturally standing on guard. In the meantime both his uncle and Sir Nathaniel had thanked her for the invitation – of which, however, they said they were unable to avail themselves. Adam had a sort of suspicion that though she answered regretfully, she was in reality relieved. When he had got into the carriage with the two old men and they had driven off, he was not surprised when Sir Nathaniel said:

'I could not but feel that she was glad to be rid of us. She can play her game better alone!'

'What is her game, sir?' asked Adam unthinkingly, but the old man answered without comment:

'All the county knows it, my boy. Caswall is a very rich man. Her husband was rich when she married him – or seemed to be. When he committed suicide it was found that

23

he had nothing at all. Her father has a great position and a great estate – on paper. But the latter is mortgaged up to the hilt, and is held in male tail only, so that her only hope is in a rich marriage. I suppose I need not draw any conclusion. You can do that as well as I can.'

Adam remained silent nearly all the time they were travelling through the alleged Vale of Cheshire. He thought much during that journey and came to several conclusions, though his lips were unmoved. One of these conclusions was that he would be very careful about paying any attention to Lady Arabella. He was himself a rich man, how rich not even his uncle had the least idea, and would have been surprised had he known. The other resolution was that he would be very careful how he went moonlighting in Diana's Grove, especially if he were unattended.

At Liverpool they went aboard the *West African*, which had just come to the landing-stage. There his uncle introduced himself to Mr Caswall, and followed this up by introducing Sir Nathaniel and then Adam. The new-comer received them all very graciously, and said what a pleasure it was on coming home after so long an absence of his family from their old seat, and hoped they would see much of each other in the future. Adam was much pleased at the warmth of the reception; but he could not avoid a feeling of repugnance at the man's face. He was trying hard to overcome this when a diversion was caused by the arrival of Lady Arabella. The diversion was welcome to all; the two Saltons and Sir Nathaniel were shocked at Caswall's face – so hard, so ruthless, so selfish, so dominant. 'God help any,' was the common thought, 'who is under the domination of such a one!'

But presently his African servant approached him, and at once their thoughts changed to a larger toleration. For by comparison with this man his face seemed to have a certain nobility hitherto lacking. Caswall looked indeed a savage – but a cultured savage. In him were traces of the softening civilisation of ages – of some of the higher instincts and education of man, no matter how rudimentary these might be. But the face of Oolanga, as his master at once called him, was pure pristine, unreformed, unsoftened savage, with inherent in it all the hideous possibilities of a lost, devil-ridden child of the forest and the swamp – the lowest and most loathsome of all created things which were in some form ostensibly human.

V

Home-coming

As Lady Arabella and Oolanga arrived almost simultaneously, Adam began to surmise what effect their appearance would have on each other. They were exactly opposite in every quality of appearance, and, so far as he could judge, of mental or moral gifts or traits. The girl of the Caucasian type, beautiful, Saxon blonde, with a complexion of milk and roses, high-bred, clever, serene of nature. The other negroid of the lowest type; hideously ugly, with the animal instincts developed as in the lowest brutes; cruel, wanting in all the mental and moral faculties – in fact, so brutal as to be hardly human. If Adam expected her to show any repugnance he was disappointed. If anything, her pride heightened into disdain. She seemed as if she would not – could not – condescend to exhibit any concern or interest in such a creature. On the other hand, his bearing was such as in itself to justify her pride. He treated her not merely as a slave treats his master, but as a worshipper would treat a deity. He knelt before her with his hands outstretched and his forehead in the dust. So long as she remained he did not move; it was only when she went over to Caswall and spoke that he relaxed his attitude of devotion and simply stood by respectfully. His dress, which was a grotesque mixture, more than ever seemed absurd. He had on evening dress of an ill cut, an abnormally efflorescent white shirt with exaggerated cuffs and collar, all holding mock jewels of various colours. In his nose was a silver ring, and in his ears large ornaments composed of trophies of teeth. He wore a tall hat, which had once been of a shape of *some* kind, with a band of gold lace. Altogether he looked like a horrible distortion of a gentleman's servant. All those around grinned or openly jeered. One of the stewards, who was carrying some of Mr Caswall's lighter luggage and making himself important, after the manner of stewards to debarking passengers, was attentive even to him.

Adam spoke to his own bailiff, Davenport, who was standing by, having arrived with the bailiff of Lesser Hill, who had followed Mr Salton in his own pony trap. As he spoke he pointed to the attentive ship's steward, and presently the two men were conversing.

After a little time Mr Salton said to Adam:

'I think we ought to be moving. I have some things to do in Liverpool, and I am sure that both Mr Caswall and Lady Arabella would like to get under weigh for Castra Regis.' To which said Adam:

'I too, sir, would like to do something. I want to find out where Ross, the animal merchant, lives – you know, the local Jamrach. I want to take a small animal home with me, if you don't mind. He is only a little thing, and will be no trouble.'

'Of course not, my boy. Whatever you like. What kind of animal is it that you want?'

'A mongoose.'

'A mongoose! What on earth do you want it for?'

'To kill snakes.'

'Good!' The old man remembered the mound at Stone. No explanation was needed.

Ross, the animal merchant, had had dealings with Adam chiefly in the way of mongooses. When he heard what was wanted he asked:

'Do you want something special, or will an ordinary mongoose do?'

'Well, of course I want a good one. But I see no need for anything special. It is for ordinary use.'

'I can let you have a choice of ordinary ones. I only asked because I have in stock a very special one which I got lately from Nepaul. He has a record of his own. He killed a king cobra that had been seen in the Rajah's garden. But I don't suppose we have any snakes of the kind in this cold climate – I daresay an ordinary one will do.'

The bargain was effected. When Adam was coming away with the box under his arm, he said to Ross:

'I don't know anything of the snakes here. I wouldn't have believed there are any at all, only I saw some to-day. I shall try this mongoose, and if he is any good I shall be glad to keep him. But don't part with the other yet. I shall send you word if I want him.'

When Adam got back to the carriage, carefully carrying the box with the mongoose, Sir Nathaniel said:

'Hullo! what have you got there?'

'A mongoose.'

'What for?'

'To kill snakes!'

Sir Nathaniel laughed. 'Well, even as yet, it seems you have come to the right place.'

'How do you mean? Why "as yet"?'

'Remember the snakes yesterday. But that is only a beginning.'

'A beginning! How so?'

'That, my boy, belongs to the second section of our inquiry. It will have a direct bearing on it.'

'You mean about the legends?'

'We shall begin on them.'

'And then?'

'I heard Lady Arabella's invitation to you to come to Diana's Grove in the twilight.'

'Well, what on earth has that got to do with it?'

'Nothing directly that I know of. But we shall see.'

Adam waited, and the old man went on:

'Have you by any chance heard the other name which was given long ago to that place?'

'No, sir.'

'It was called – Look here, this subject wants a lot of talk-

28

ing over and listening. Suppose we wait till after dinner to-night, when we shall be alone and shall have lots of time before us.'

'All right, sir. Let us wait!' Adam was filled with curiosity, but he thought it better not to hurry matters. All would come in good time.

His attention was then claimed by the events of the day. Shortly the Lesser Hill party set out for Castra Regis, and for the time he thought no more of Diana's Grove or of what mysteries it had contained – or might still contain.

The guests were crowding in and special places were marked for important guests. Some little time was occupied in finding their seats. Adam, seeing so many persons of varied degree, looked round for Lady Arabella, but could not locate her. It was only when he saw the old-fashioned travelling carriage approach and heard the sound of cheering which went with it, that he realised that Edgar Caswall had arrived. Then, on looking more closely, he saw that Lady Arabella, dressed as he had seen her last, was seated beside him. When the carriage drew up at the great flight of steps, the host jumped down and gave her his hand and led her up to the great daïs table, and placed her in the seat to the right of that kept for himself.

It was evident to all that she was the chief guest at the festivities. It was not long before the seats on the daïs were filled and the tenants and guests of lesser importance had occupied all the coigns of vantage not reserved. The order of the day had been carefully arranged by the committee. There were some speeches, happily neither many nor long; and then festivities were suspended till the time for feasting had arrived. In the interval Caswall walked among his guests, speaking to all in a friendly manner and expressing a general welcome. The other guests came down from the daïs and followed his example, so there was unceremonious meeting and greeting between gentle and simple. Adam Salton naturally followed with his eyes all that went on within their scope, taking note of all who seemed to afford any interest. He was young and a man and a stranger from a far distance; so on all these accounts he naturally took stock rather of the women than of the men, and of these, those who were young and attractive. There were lots of pretty girls among the crowd who had seemingly no dislike to be looked at; and Adam, who was a handsome young man and well set up, got his full share of admiring glances. These did not concern him much, and he remained unmoved until there came along a group of three, by their dress and bearing, of the farmer class. One was a sturdy old man; the other two were good-looking girls, one of a little over twenty, the other not quite grown – seventeen at most. So soon as Adam's eyes met those of the younger girl, who stood nearest to him, some sort of electricity flashed – that divine spark which begins by recognition and ends in obedience. Men call it 'Love.'

Both the elders of the party noticed how much Adam was taken by the pretty girl, and both spoke of her to him in a way which made his heart warm to them.

'Did you notice that party that passed? The old man is Michael Watford, one of the tenants of Mr Caswall. He occupies Mercy Farm, which Sir Nathaniel tells me he pointed out to you to-day. The girls are his grand-daughters, the elder, Lilla, being the only child of his eldest son, who died when she was less than a year old. His wife died on the same day – in fact at the same time. She is a good girl – as good as she is pretty. The other is her first cousin, the daughter of Watford's second son. He went for a soldier when he was just over twenty, and was drafted abroad. He was not a good correspondent, though he was a good enough son. A few letters came, and then his father heard from the colonel of his regiment that he had been killed by dacoits in Burmah. He heard from the same source that his boy had been married to a Burmese, and that there was a daughter only a year old. Watford had the child brought home, and she grew up beside Lilla. The only thing that they heard of her birth was that her name was Mimi. The two children adored each other, and do to this day. Strange how different they are! Lilla all fair, like the old Saxon stock she is sprung from; Mimi almost as dark as the darkest of her mother's race. Lilla is as gentle as a dove, but Mimi's black eyes can glow whenever she is upset. The only thing that upsets her is when anything happens to injure or threaten or annoy Lilla. Then her eyes glow as do the eyes of a bird when her young are threatened.'

VI

The White Worm

Mr Salton introduced Adam to Mr Watford and his grand-daughters, and they all moved on together. Of course people, neighbours, in the position of the Watfords knew all about Adam Salton, his relationship, circumstances, and prospects. So it would have been strange indeed if both girls did not see or dream of possibilities of the future. In agricultural England, eligible men of any class were rare. This particular man was specially eligible, for he did not belong to a class in which barriers of caste were strong. So when it began to be noticed that he walked beside Mimi Watford and seemed to desire her society, all their friends seemed to give the promising affair a helping hand. When the gongs sounded for the banquet, he went with her into the tent where her father had seats. Mr Salton and Sir Nathaniel noticed that the young man did not come to claim his appointed place at the daïs table; but they understood and made no remark, or indeed did not seem to notice his absence. Lady Arabella sat as before at Edgar Caswall's right hand. She was certainly a very beautiful woman, and to all it seemed fitting from her rank and personal qualities that she should be the chosen partner of the heir on his first appearance. Of course nothing was said openly by those of her own class who were present; but words were not necessary when so much could be expressed by nods and smiles. It seemed to be an accepted thing that at last there was to be a mistress of Castra Regis, and that she was present amongst them. There were not lacking some who, whilst admitting all her charm and beauty, placed her in only the second rank of beauty, Lilla Watford being marked as first. There was sufficient divergence of type as well as of individual beauty to allow of fair commenting; Lady Arabella represented the aristocratic type, and Lilla that of the commonalty.

When the dusk began to thicken, Mr Salton and Sir Nathaniel walked home – the trap had been sent away early in the day, leaving Adam to follow in his own time. He came in earlier than was expected, and seemed upset about something. Neither of the elders made any comment. They all lit cigarettes, and, as dinner-time was close at hand, went to their rooms to get ready. Adam had evidently been thinking in the interval. He joined the others in the drawing-room, looking ruffled and impatient – a condition of things seen for the first time. The others, with the patience – or the experience – of age trusted to time to unfold and explain things. They had not long to wait. After sitting down and standing up several times, Adam suddenly burst out:

'That fellow seems to think he owns the earth. Can't he let people alone! He seems to think that he has only to throw his handkerchief to any woman, and be her master.'

This outburst was in itself enlightening. Only thwarted affection in some guise could produce this feeling in an amiable young man. Sir Nathaniel, as an old diplomatist, had a way of understanding, as if by foreknowledge, the true inwardness of things, and asked suddenly, but in a matter-of-fact, indifferent voice:

'Was he after Lilla?'

'Yes. And he didn't lose any time either. Almost as soon as they met he began to butter her up, and to tell her how beautiful she is. Why, before he left her side he had asked himself to tea to-morrow at Mercy Farm. Stupid ass! He might see that the girl isn't his sort! I never saw anything like it. It was just like a hawk and a pigeon.'

As he spoke, Sir Nathaniel turned and looked at Mr Salton – a keen look which implied a full understanding. Then the latter said quietly:

'Tell us all about it, Adam. There are still ten minutes before dinner, and we shall all have better appetites when we have come to some conclusion on this matter.'

Adam spoke with an unwonted diffidence:

'There is nothing to tell, sir; that is the worst of it. I am bound to say that there was not a word said that a human being could object to. He was very civil, and all that was proper – just what a landlord might be to a tenant's daughter ... And yet – and yet – well, I don't know how it was, but it made my blood simply boil.'

'How did the hawk and the pigeon come in?' Sir Nathaniel's voice was soft and soothing, nothing of contradiction or overdone curiosity in it – a tone eminently suited to win confidence.

'I can hardly explain it. I can only say that he looked like a hawk and she like a dove – and, now that I think of it, that is what they each did look like; and do look like in their normal condition.'

'That is so!' came the soft voice of Sir Nathaniel.

Adam went on:

'Perhaps that early Roman look of his set me off. But I wanted to protect her; she seemed in danger.'

'She seems in danger, in a way, from all you young men. I couldn't help noticing the way that even you looked, as if you wished to absorb her.'

Here the kindly, temperate voice of Mr Salton came in:

'I hope both you young men will keep your heads cool. You know, Adam, it won't do to have any quarrel between you, especially so soon after his home-coming and your arrival here. We must think of the feelings and happiness of our neighbours; mustn't we?'

'I hope so, sir. And I assure you that, whatever may happen, or even threaten, I shall obey your wishes in this as in all things.'

'Silence!' whispered Sir Nathaniel, who heard the servants in the passage bringing dinner.

After dinner, over the walnuts and the wine, Sir Nathaniel returned to the subject of the local legends, saying: 'It will perhaps be a less dangerous topic for us to discuss than more recent ones.'

'All right, sir,' said Adam heartily. 'I think you may depend on me now with regard to any topic. I can even discuss with Mr Caswall. Indeed, I may meet him to-morrow. He is going, as I said, to call at Mercy Farm at three o'clock – but I have an appointment at two.'

'I notice,' said Mr Salton, 'that you do not lose any time.'

'No, sir. Perhaps that is the reason why the part I came from has for its motto – "Advance, Australia!"'

'All right, my boy. Advance is good – so long as you take care where you are going and how. There is a line in one of Shakespeare's plays, "They stumble that run fast." It is worth bearing in mind.'

'All right again, sir; but I don't think you need fear me now I have had my kick.'

The two old men once more looked at each other steadily. It was as much as to say, 'Good! The boy has had his lesson. He will be all right!' Then, lest the mood of his listener should change with delay, Sir Nathaniel began at once:

'I don't propose to tell you all the legends of Mercia, or even to make a selection of them. It will be better, I think, for our purpose if we consider a few facts – recorded or unrecorded – about this neighbourhood. I shall try to remember, and you, Adam, shall ask me questions as we go along. We all want stimulation to memory. When we have nothing amongst us to remember it will be time enough to invent. I propose to go on where we left off yesterday morning, about the few places round here that we spoke of. I think we might begin with Diana's Grove. It has roots in the different epochs of our history, and each has, be sure, its special crop of legend. The Druid and the Roman are too far off for matters of detail; but it seems to me the Saxon and the Angles are near enough

35

to yield material for legendary lore. If there were anything well remembered of an earlier period, we may take it that it had some beginning in what was accepted as fact. We find that this particular place had another name or sobriquet besides Diana's Grove. This was manifestly of Roman origin, or of Grecian accepted as Roman. The former is more pregnant of adventure and romance than the Roman name. In Mercian tongue it was "The Lair of the White Worm." This needs a word of explanation at the beginning.

'In the dawn of the language, the word "worm" had a somewhat different meaning from that in use to-day. It was an adaptation of the Anglo-Saxon "wyrm," meaning primarily a dragon or snake; or from the Gothic "waurms," a serpent; or the Icelandic "ormur," or the German "wurm." We gather that it conveyed originally an idea of size and power, not as now in the diminutive of both these meanings. Here legendary history helps us. We have the well-known legend of the "Worm Well" of Lambton Castle, and that of the "Laidly Worm of Spindleston Heugh" near Bamborough. In both these legends the "worm" was a monster of vast size and power – a veritable dragon or serpent, such as legend attributes to vast fens or quags where there was illimitable room for expansion. A glance at a geological map will show that whatever truth there may have been of the actuality of such monsters in the early geologic periods, at least there was plenty of possibility. In the eastern section of England there were originally vast plains where the naturally plentiful supply of water could gather. There the streams were deep and slow, and there were holes of abysmal depth, where any kind and size of antediluvian monster could find a habitat. In places, which now we can see from our windows, were mud-holes a hundred or more feet deep. Who can tell us when the age of the monsters which flourished in slime came to an end? If such a time there was indeed, its limits could only apply to the vast number of such dangers. There must have been times and places and conditions which made for greater longevity, greater size, greater strength than was usual. Such overlappings may have come down even to our earlier centuries. Nay, are there not now creatures of a vastness of bulk regarded by the generality of men as impossible? Even in our own day there are here and there seen the traces of animals, if not the animals themselves, of stupendous size – veritable survivals from earlier ages, preserved by some special qualities in their habitats. I remember meeting a distinguished man in India, who had the reputation of being a great shikaree, who told me that the greatest temptation he had ever had in his life was to shoot a giant snake which he had literally come across in the Terai of Upper India. He was on a tiger-shooting expedition, and as his elephant was crossing a nullah it squealed. He looked down from his howdah and saw that the elephant had stepped across the body of a snake which was dragging itself through the jungle. "So far as I could see," he said, "it must have been eighty or one hundred feet in length. Fully forty or fifty feet was on each side of the track, and though the weight which it dragged had thinned it to its least, it was as thick round as a man's body. I suppose you know that when you are after tiger, it is a point of honour not to shoot at anything else, as life may depend on it. I could easily and with safety have spined this monster, but I felt that I must not – and so with regret I had to let it go."

'Just imagine such a monster anywhere in this country, and at once we could get a sort of idea of the "worms," which possibly did frequent the great morasses which spread round the mouths of any of the great European rivers.'

Adam had been thinking; at last he spoke:

'I haven't the least doubt, sir, that there may have been such monsters as you have spoken of still existing at a much later period than is generally accepted. Also, that if there were such things, that this was the very place for them. I have tried to think over the matter since you pointed out the configuration of the ground. But if you will not be offended

37

by my expressing – not indeed a doubt, but a difficulty – it seems to me that there is a hiatus somewhere.'

'Where? What kind? Tell me frankly, where is your difficulty. You know I am always glad of an honest opinion in any difficulty.'

'Well, sir, all that you say may be, probably is, true. But are there not mechanical difficulties?'

'As how?'

'Well, our antique monster must have been mighty heavy, and the distances he had to travel were long and the ways difficult. From where we are now sitting down to the level of the mud-holes even the top of them is a distance of several hundred feet – I am leaving out of consideration altogether for the present lateral distance. Is it possible that there was a way by which a monster such as you have spoken of could travel up and down, and yet no chance recorder have ever seen him? Of course we have the legends; but is not some more exact evidence necessary in a scientific investigation?'

'My dear Adam, all you say is perfectly right, and, were we starting on just such an investigation, we could not do better than follow your reasoning. But, my dear boy, you must remember that all this took place thousands of years ago. You must remember, too, that all records of the kind that would help us are lacking. Also, that the places to be considered were absolutely desert so far as human habitation or population are considered. In the vast desolation of such a place as complied with the necessary conditions there must have been such profusion of natural growth as would bar the progress of men formed as we are. The lair of such a monster as we have in mind would not have been disturbed for hundreds – or thousands – of years. Moreover, these creatures must have occupied places quite inaccessible to man. A snake who could make himself comfortable in a quagmire a hundred feet deep would be protected even on the outskirts by such stupendous morasses as now no longer exist, or which, if they exist anywhere at all, can be on very few places on the earth's surface. Far be it from me to say, or even to think for a moment, that in more elemental times such things could not have been. The condition of things we speak of belongs to the geologic age – the great birth and growth of the world, when natural forces ran riot, when the struggle for existence was so savage that no vitality which was not founded in a gigantic form could have even a possibility of survival. That such a time was we have evidences in geology, but there only. We can never expect proofs such as this age demands. We can only imagine or surmise such things – or such conditions and such forces as overcame them.'

'Come, let us get to bed,' said Mr Salton. 'Like you both, I enjoy the conversation. But one thing is certain: we cannot settle it before breakfast.'

VII

Hawk and Pigeon

At breakfast-time next morning Sir Nathaniel and Mr Salton were seated when Adam came hurriedly into the room.

'Any news?' asked his uncle mechanically.

'Four.'

'Four what?' asked Sir Nathaniel.

'Snakes,' said Adam, helping himself to a grilled kidney.

'Four snakes. How? I don't understand.'

'Mongoose,' said Adam, and then added explanatorily: 'I was out with the mongoose just after three.'

'Four snakes in one morning! Why, I didn't know there were so many on the Brow' – the local name for the western cliff. 'I hope that wasn't the consequence of our talk of last night?'

'It was, sir. But not directly.'

'But, God bless my soul, you didn't expect to get a snake like the Lambton worm, did you? Why, a mongoose to tackle a monster like that – if there were one – would have to be bigger than a haystack.'

'These were ordinary snakes, only about as big as a walking-stick.'

'Well, it's well to be rid of them, big or little. That is a good mongoose, I suppose; he'll clear out all such vermin round here,' said Mr Salton.

Adam went quietly on with his breakfast. Killing a few snakes in a morning was no new experience to him. He left the room the moment breakfast was finished and went to the study that his uncle had arranged for him. Both Sir Nathaniel and Mr Salton took it that he wanted to be by himself as so to avoid any questioning or talk of the visit that he was to make that afternoon. He stayed by himself either in the house or walking, till about half an hour before dinner-time. Then he came quietly into the smoking-room, where Mr Salton and Sir Nathaniel were sitting together ready dressed. He too was dressed, and the old diplomatist noticed that his hand was, if possible, more steady than usual. He had actually shaved himself when making his toilet, but there was no sign of a cut or even of a quiver of the hand. Sir Nathaniel smiled to himself quietly as he said under his voice:

'He is all right. That is a sign there is no mistaking – for a man in love. He certainly was in love yesterday; and one way or another, if he can get rid of, or overcome, troubles of the heart like that, I think we needn't have any special apprehension about him.' So he resumed the magazine which he had been reading.

After a few minutes of silence all round, Adam gave further evidence of his *aplomb*. He suddenly said, looking at the others:

'I suppose there is no use waiting. We had better get it over at once.'

His uncle, thinking to make things easier to him, said:

'Get what over?'

There was a sign of shyness about him at this. He stammered a little at first, but his voice became more even as he went on:

'My visit to Mercy Farm.'

Mr Salton waited eagerly. The old diplomatist simply smiled easily.

'I suppose you both know that I was much interested yesterday in the Watfords?' There was no denial or fending off the question. Both the old men smiled acquiescence. Adam went on: 'I meant you to see it – both of you. You, uncle, because you are my uncle and the nearest thing to me on earth – of my own kin, and, moreover, you couldn't have been more kind to me or made me more welcome if you had been my own father.' Mr Salton said nothing. He simply held out his hand, and the other took it and held it for a few seconds. 'And you, sir, because you have shown me something of the same affection which in my wildest dreams of home I had no right to expect.' He stopped for an instant, much moved.

Sir Nathaniel said softly, laying his hand on the boy's shoulder:

'You are right, my boy; quite right. That is the proper way to look at it. And I may tell you that we old men, who have no children of our own, feel our hearts growing warm when we hear words like those.'

Then Adam hurried on, speaking with a rush, as if he wanted to come to the crucial point:

'Mr Watford had not come in, but Lilla and Mimi were at home, and they made me feel very welcome. They have all a great regard for my uncle. I am glad of that any way, for I like them all – much. We were having tea when Mr Caswall came to the door, attended by the Christy Minstrel.'

'The Christy Minstrel!' repeated Sir Nathaniel. His voice sounded simply as an acknowledgment, not as a comment of any kind.

'Lilla opened the door herself. The window of the living-room at the farm, as of course you know, is a large one, and from within you cannot help seeing anyone coming. Mr Caswall said he ventured to call, as he wished to make the acquaintance of all his tenants in a less formal way and more individually than had been possible to him on the previous day. The girls made him very welcome. They are very sweet girls those, sir. Someone will be very happy some day there – with either of them.'

'And that man may be you, Adam,' said Mr Salton heartily.

A sad look came over the young man's eyes, and the fire his uncle had seen there died out. Likewise the timbre had left his voice, making it sound dreadfully lonely as he spoke:

'Such might crown my life. But that happiness, I fear, is not for me, or not without pain and loss and woe.'

'Well, it's early days yet!' said Sir Nathaniel heartily.

The young man turned on him his eyes, which had now grown excessively sad, as he answered:

'Yesterday – a few hours ago – that remark would have given me new hope – new courage; but since then I have learned too much.'

The old man, skilled in the human heart, did not attempt to argue in such a matter. He simply varied the idea and went on:

'Too early to give in, my boy.'

'I am not of a giving-in kind,' said the young man earnestly. 'But, after all, it is wise to realise a truth. And when a man, though he is young, feels as I do – as I have felt ever since yesterday, when I first saw Mimi's eyes – his heart jumps. He does not need to learn things. He knows.'

There was silence in the room, during which the twilight stole on imperceptibly. It was Adam who again broke the silence as he asked his uncle:

'Do you know, uncle, if we have any second sight in our family?'

'Second sight? No, not that I ever heard of. Why?'

'Because,' he answered slowly, 'I have a conviction over me which seems to answer all the conditions of second sight that I have ever heard of.'

'And then?' asked the old man, much perturbed.

'And then the usual inevitable. What in the Hebrides and other places, where the Sight is a cult – a belief – is called "the doom" – the court from which there is no appeal. I have often heard of second sight – you know we have many western Scots in Australia; but I have realised more of its true inwardness in an instant of this afternoon than I did in the whole of my life previously – a granite wall stretching up to the very heavens, so high and so dark that the eye of God

43

Himself cannot see beyond. Well, if the Doom must come, it must. That is all.'

The voice of Sir Nathaniel broke in, smooth and sweet and grave, but very, very stern:

'Can there not be a fight for it? There can for most things.'

'For most things, yes. But for the Doom, no. What a man can do I shall do. There will be – must be – a fight. When and where and how I know not. But a fight there will be. But, after all, what is a man in such a case?'

'*A* man! Adam, there are three of us.' He looked at his old friend as he spoke, and that old friend's eyes blazed.

'Ay, three of us,' he said, and his voice rang.

There was again a pause, and Sir Nathaniel, anxious to get back to less emotional and more neutral ground, said quietly:

'Tell us of the rest of the meeting. Omit no detail. It may be useful. Remember we are all pledged to this. It is a fight *à l'outrance*, and we can afford to throw away or forgo no chance.'

Adam said quietly, looking at him:

'We shall throw away or lose nothing that we can help. We fight to win, and the stake is a life – perhaps more than one – we shall see.' Then he went on in a conversational tone, such as he had used when he spoke of the coming to the farm of Edgar Caswall: 'When Mr Caswall came in the Christy Minstrel touched his ridiculous hat and went away – at least, he went a short distance and there remained. It gave one the idea that he expected to be called and intended to remain in sight, or within hail. Then Mimi got another cup and made fresh tea, and we all went on together.'

'Was there anything uncommon – were you all quite friendly?' asked Sir Nathaniel quietly.

Adam answered at once:

'Quite friendly. There was nothing that I could notice out of the common – except,' he went on, with a slight harden-

44

ing of the voice, 'except that he kept his eyes fixed on Lilla in a way which was quite intolerable to any man who might hold her dear.'

'Now, in what way did he look?' asked Sir Nathaniel. 'I am not doubting. I only ask for information.'

'I can hardly say,' was the answer. 'There was nothing in itself offensive; but no one could help noticing it.'

'You did. Miss Watford herself, who was the victim, and Mr Caswall, who was the offender, are out of range as witnesses. Was there anyone else who noticed?'

'Mimi did. I tell you her face flamed with anger as she saw the look.'

'What kind of look was it? Over-ardent or too admiring, or what? Was it the look of a lover or one who fain would be? You understand?'

'Yes, sir, I quite understand. Anything of that sort I should of course notice. It would be part of my preparation for keeping my self-control – to which I am pledged.'

'If it were not amatory, was it threatening? Where was the offence?'

Adam smiled kindly at the old man:

'It was not amatory. Even if it was, such was to be expected. I should be the last man in the world to object, since I am myself an offender in that respect. Moreover, not only have I been taught to fight fair, but by nature I really believe I am just. I would be as tolerant of and as liberal to a rival if he were one as I should expect him to be to me. No, the look I mean was nothing of that kind. And so long as it did not lack proper respect I should not of my own part condescend to notice it. I shall try to describe it to you. Did you ever seriously study the eyes of a hound?'

'At rest?'

'No, when he is following his instincts! Or, better still,' Adam went on, 'the eyes of a bird of prey when he is following his instincts. Not when he is swooping, but merely when he is watching his quarry?'

'No,' said Sir Nathaniel, 'I don't know that I ever did. Why, may I ask?'

'That was the look. Certainly not amatory or anything of that kind – and yet it was, it struck me, more dangerous, if not so deadly as an actual threatening.'

Again there was a silence, which Sir Nathaniel broke as he stood up:

'I think it would be well if we all thought over this by ourselves. Then we can renew the subject.'

VIII

Oolanga

Mr Salton had an appointment for six o'clock at Walsall. When he had driven off, Sir Nathaniel took Adam by the arm and said to him:

'May I come with you for a while to your study? I want to speak to you privately without your uncle knowing about it, or even what the subject is. You don't mind, do you? It is not any idle curiosity. No, no. It is on the subject to which we are all committed.'

Adam said with some constraint:

'Is it necessary to keep my uncle in the dark about it? He might be offended.'

'It is not necessary; but it is advisable. It is for his sake that I asked. My friend is an old man, and it might concern him unduly – even alarm him. I promise you there shall be nothing that could cause him anxiety in our silence, or at which he could take umbrage.'

'Go on, sir!' said Adam simply.

When they were locked into the study he spoke:

'You see, your uncle is now an old man. I know it, for we were boys together. He has led an uneventful and somewhat self-contained life, so that any such condition of things as has now arisen is apt to perplex him from its very strangeness. In fact, any new matter is trying to old people. It has its own disturbances and its own anxieties, and neither of these things are good for lives that should be restful. Your uncle is a strong man with a very happy and placid nature. Given health and ordinary conditions of life, there is no reason why he should not live to be a hundred. You and I therefore, who both love

47

him, though in different ways, should make it our business to protect him from all disturbing influences. Such care shall undoubtedly add to the magnitude of his span of life and the happiness of his days. I am sure you will agree with me that any labour to this end would be well spent. All right, my boy! I see your answer in your eyes; so we need say no more of that. And now,' here his voice changed, 'tell me all that took place at that interview. You cannot be too exhaustive. Nothing is too trivial. There are strange things in front of us – how strange we cannot at present even guess. Doubtless some of the difficult things to understand which lie behind the veil will in time be shown to us to see and understand. In the meantime, all we can do is to think and work patiently, fearlessly, and unselfishly to an end that we think is right. Tell me as well as you can – I shall try to help you. You had just got so far as where Lilla opened the door to Mr Caswall, and the Christy Minstrel, who had followed him, went a little distance away and lurked. You also observed that Mimi was disturbed in her mind at the way Mr Caswall looked at her cousin.'

'Certainly – though "disturbed in her mind" is only a poor way of expressing her objection.'

'Can you remember well enough to describe Caswall's eyes, and how Lilla looked, and what Mimi said and did? Also of the Christy Minstrel, who is, I take it, Oolanga, Caswall's West African servant. When you have said all you know of these things I want you to tell me what you have heard in any way about the "Christy Minstrel." I take it this will be the most humorous way of bringing him in. Though indeed I doubt his being in any conceivable way a subject of humour. Tragedy would more probably be a follower in his train.'

'I'll do what I can, sir. All the time Mr Caswall was staring he kept his eyes fixed and motionless – but not as if he was dead or in a trance. His forehead was wrinkled up as it is when one is trying to see through or into something. At the best of times his face is not of very equable or of gentle

48

expression; but when it was screwed up like that it was almost diabolical. It frightened poor Lilla so that she trembled, and after a bit got so pale that I thought she had fainted. However, she held up and tried to stare back, but in a feeble kind of way. Then Mimi came close and held her hand. That braced her up, and – still, never ceasing her return stare – she got colour again and seemed more like herself.'

'Did he stare too?'

'More than ever. The weaker Lilla seemed the stronger he seemed to get, just as if he was feeding on her strength. All at once she turned round, threw up her hands, and fell down in a faint. I could not see what else happened just then, for Mimi had thrown herself on her knees beside her and hid her from me. Then there was something like a black shadow between us, and there was the pleasing form of the Christy Minstrel, looking more like a malignant devil than ever. He had better look out. I am not usually a patient man, and the sight of that ugly devil is enough to make an Eskimo's blood boil. When he saw my face he seemed to realise danger – immediate danger – and he slunk out of the room as noiselessly as if he had been blown out. I learned one thing, however. He is an enemy, if ever a man had one.'

'That still leaves us three to two!' – this from Sir Nathaniel.

'Then Caswall slunk out much as the nigger had done. When he had gone, Lilla recovered at once. I hope I won't see Mr Christy look at Lilla again!' As he spoke he took a nickel-plated revolver from his pocket and put it back again with an ominous remark: 'I don't know if he wishes to be buried on English soil. He can have his choice if he likes. Ordinarily speaking, he isn't worth a cartridge; but when there is a lady in the case –' The revolver clicked.

'Now,' said Sir Nathaniel, anxious to restore peace, 'have you found out anything yet regarding your friend the Christy Minstrel? I am anxious to be posted regarding him. I fear there will be, or may be, grave trouble with him.'

'Yes, sir, I've heard a good deal about him – of course it is not official; but then hearsay may guide us at first. You know my man Davenport, I think. He really is my *alter ego* – private secretary, confidential man of business, and general factotum. He came with me in a journey of exploration across the desert. He saved my life many times. He is devoted to me, and has my full confidence. I asked him to go on board the *West African* and have a good look round, and find out what he could about Mr Caswall. Naturally, he was struck with the aboriginal savage. He found one of the ship's stewards who had been on the regular voyages to South Africa. He knew Oolanga and had made a study of him. He is a man who gets on well with niggers, and they opened their hearts to him. It seems that this Oolanga is quite a great person in the nigger world of the African West Coast. He has the two things which men of his own colour respect: he can make them afraid, and he is lavish with money. I don't know whose money – but that does not matter. They are always ready to trumpet his greatness. Evil greatness it is – but neither does that matter. Briefly, this is his history. He was originally a witch-finder – about as low an occupation as exists amongst even aboriginal savages, amongst the mangrove swamps. Then he got up in the world and became an Obi-man, which gives an opportunity to wealth *via* blackmail. Finally, he reached the highest honour in hellish service. He became a user of Voodoo, which seems to be a service of the utmost baseness and cruelty. I was told some of his deeds of cruelty, which are simply sickening. They made me long for an opportunity of helping to drive him back to hell. You might think to look at him that you could measure in some way the extent of his vileness; but it would be a vain hope. Monsters such as he is belong to an earlier and more rudimentary stage of barbarism. Whoever kills him when the time comes will not have to fear punishment, but to expect praise. He is in his way a clever fellow – for a nigger; but is none the less danger-ous or the less hateful for that. The men in the ship told me that he was a collector: some of them had seen his collections. Such collections! All that was potent for evil in bird or beast, or even in fish. Beaks that could break and rend and tear. All the birds represented were of a predatory kind. Even the fishes are those which are born to destroy, to wound, to torture. The collection, I assure you, was an object lesson in human malignity. This being has enough evil in his face to frighten even a strong man. It is little wonder that the sight of it unexpectedly put that poor girl into a dead faint! If that other savage intends to keep him round here they may build a new prison at once; for there won't be a decent man or woman in his neighbourhood that won't be a criminal at the very start, if indeed it be a crime to destroy such a thing.'

Adam was up in the early morning and took a smart walk round the Brow. As he was passing Diana's Grove he looked in on the short avenue of trees, and noticed the snakes killed on the previous morning by the mongoose. They all lay in a row, straight and rigid, as if they had been placed by hands. Their skins seemed all damp and sticky, and they were covered all over with ants and all sorts of insects. They looked loathsome, so after a glance he passed on. A little later, when his steps took him, naturally enough, past the entrance to Mercy Farm, he was passed by the Christy Minstrel moving quickly under the trees wherever there was shadow. Laid across one extended arm, and looking like dirty towels across a rail, he had the horrid-looking snakes. He did not seem to see Adam, to the pleasant surprise of the latter. No one was to be seen at Mercy except a few workmen in the farmyard. So, after waiting round on a chance of seeing Mimi, he began to go slowly home. Once more he was passed on the way. This time it was by Lady Arabella, walking hurriedly and so furiously angry that she did not seem to recognise him even to the extent of acknowledging his bow. He wondered, but simply went on his way. When he got to Lesser Hill, he went to the coach-house where the box with the mongoose was kept, and took it with him, intending to finish at the Mound of Stone what he had begun the previous morning with regard to the extermination. He found that the snakes were even more easily attacked than on the previous day; no less than six were killed in the first half-hour. As no more appeared, he took it for granted that the morning's work was over, and went towards home. The mongoose had by this time become accustomed to him, and was willing to let himself be handled freely. Adam lifted him up and put him on his shoulders and walked on. Presently he saw a lady advancing towards him, and as they grew nearer recognised Lady Arabella. Hitherto the mongoose had been quiet, like a playful affectionate kitten; but when the two got close he was horrified to see the mongoose, in a state of the wildest fury, with every hair standing on end, jump from his shoulder and run towards Lady Arabella. It looked so furious and so intent on attack that he called out:

'Look out – look out! The animal is furious and means to attack.'

She looked more than ever disdainful and was passing on; the mongoose jumped at her in a furious attack. Adam rushed forward with his stick, the only weapon he had. But just as he got within striking distance the lady drew out a revolver and shot the animal, breaking his backbone. Not satisfied with this, she poured shot after shot into him till the magazine was exhausted. There was no coolness or hauteur about her now. She seemed more furious even than the animal, her face transformed with hate, and as determined to kill as he had appeared to be. Adam, not knowing exactly what to do, lifted his hat in apology and hurried on to Lesser Hill.

IX

Survivals

At breakfast Sir Nathaniel noticed that Adam was put out about something. But he said nothing. The lesson of silence is better remembered in age than in youth. When they were both in the study, where Sir Nathaniel had followed him, Adam at once began to tell his companion of what had happened. Sir Nathaniel looked graver and graver as the narration proceeded, and when Adam had stopped he remained silent for several minutes. At last he said:

'This is very grave. I have not formed my thought yet; but it seems to me at first impression that this is worse than anything we had thought of.'

'Why, sir?' said Adam. 'Is the killing of a mongoose – no matter by whom – so serious a thing as all that?'

The other smoked on quietly for quite another few minutes before he spoke.

'When I have properly thought it over I may moderate my opinion. But in the meantime it seems to me that there is something dreadful behind all this – something that may affect all our lives – that may mean the issue of life or death to any of us.'

Adam sat up quickly.

'Do tell me, sir, what is in your mind – if, of course, you have no objection to, or do not think it better not.'

'I have no objection, Adam. In fact, if I had, I should have to overcome it. I fear there can be no more hidden or reserved thoughts between us.'

'Indeed, sir, that sounds serious, worse than serious!'

Again they both resumed their cigars, and presently Sir Nathaniel said gravely:

'Adam, I greatly fear the time has come for us – for you and me, at all events – to speak out plainly to one another. Does not there seem something very mysterious about this?'

'I have thought so, sir, all along. The only difficulty one has is what one is to think and where to begin.'

'Let us begin with what you have told me. First take the conduct of the mongoose.'

Adam waited; the other went on:

'He was quiet, even friendly and affectionate with you. He only attacked the snakes, which is, after all, only his business in life.'

'That is so!'

'Then we must try to find out or imagine some reason why he attacked Lady Arabella.'

'I fear we shall have to imagine; there is no logical answer to that question.'

'Then let us imagine. He had not shown any disposition hitherto to attack strangers?'

'No; the opposite. He made friends at once with everyone he came across.'

'Then even if his action is based on instinct, why does he single out one person in such a way?'

'In that, sir, I see a difficulty, or, if you will permit me, it may be only a flaw in your reasoning.'

'Permit! I shall be glad. Go on.'

'It seems to me that you take "instinct" as a definite fixed thing concerning which there can be only one reading – even by the brute creation.'

'Go on, Adam. This is very interesting.'

'We both may have erred in our idea of "instinct." May it not be that a mongoose may have merely the instinct to attack, that nature does not allow or provide him with the fine reasoning powers to discriminate who he is to attack?'

'Good! Of course that may be so. But then, on the other hand, should we not satisfy ourselves why he does wish to attack anything? If for centuries in all parts of the world this particular animal is known to attack only one kind of other animal, are we not justified in assuming that when a case strange to us comes before us, if one of the first class attacks a hitherto unclassed animal, he recognises in that animal some quality which it has in common with the hitherto classed animal?'

'That is a good argument, sir,' Adam went on, 'but a dangerous one. If we followed it out with pure logic it would lead us to believe that Lady Arabella is a snake. And I doubt if we – either of us – are prepared to go so far.'

'So far as I am concerned I am to follow blindly the lead of logic. But before doing so we have a duty to fulfil.'

'What is that duty, sir?'

'The first of all duties, truth. We must be sure before going to such an end that there is no point as yet unconsidered which would account for the unknown thing which puzzles us.'

'As how?'

'Well, suppose the instinct works on some physical basis – sight, for instance, or smell. If there were anything in recent juxtaposition to the accused which would look like the cause or would carry the scent, surely that would supply the missing cause.'

'Of course!' Adam spoke with conviction.

Sir Nathaniel went on:

'Now, from what you tell me, your Christy Minstrel friend had just come from the direction of Diana's Grove carrying the dead snakes, which the mongoose had killed the previous morning. Might not the scent have been carried that way?'

'Of course it might, probably was. I never thought of that. Look here, sir, I really think it will be prudent of us not to draw final conclusions till we know more. At any rate that episode has a suggestive hint for us – one which we can follow up without saying anything to anybody. Then we shall be in a safer position for going on.'

'Good and sensible!' Sir Nathaniel spoke approvingly; and so it was tacitly arranged between the two to wait.

But whilst they were sitting in silence an idea struck Adam, and he thought it wise to make it known to the elder man.

'Two things I want to ask you, if I may. One is a sort of corollary to the other.' Sir Nathaniel listened. He went on: 'Is there any possible way of even guessing approximately how long a scent will remain? You see, this is a natural scent, and may derive from a place where it has been effective for thousands of years. Then, does a scent of any kind carry with it any form or quality of another kind, either good or evil? I ask you because one ancient name of the house lived in by the lady who was attacked by the mongoose was "The Lair of the White Worm." If any of these things be so, our possibilities of knowledge and our difficulties have multiplied indefinitely. They may even change in kind. We may get into even moral entanglements; before we know it it may be even in the midst of a bedrock struggle between good and evil.'

Sir Nathaniel, after a pause, asked:

'Is that the question you wished to ask me?'

'Yes, sir.'

Sir Nathaniel smiled gravely.

'I don't see on what the corollary rests. With regard to the first question – or the first part, though, so far as I know, there are no fixed periods with which a scent may be active – I think we may take it that that period does not run into thousands of years. As to whether any moral change accompanies a physical one, I can only say that I have met no argument or proof or even no assertion of the fact. At the same time, we must remember that "good" and "evil" are terms so wide as to take in the whole scheme of creation and all that is implied by them and by their mutual action and reaction. Generally, I would say that in the scheme of a

56

First Cause anything is possible. So long as the inherent forces or tendencies of any one thing are veiled from us we must expect mystery. This hides from us more than we at first conceive, and as time goes on and *some* light gets into the darker places, we are able to understand that there are other darknesses. And so on, until the time shall come when the full light of understanding beats upon us.'

'Then I presume, sir,' said Adam, 'that it would be at least wise of us to leave these questions alone till we know more.'

'Most certainly. To listen and remember should be our guiding principle in such an inquiry.'

'There is one other question on which I should like to ask your opinion. It is the last of my general questions – for the present. Suppose that there are any permanent forces appertaining to the past, what we may call "survivals," do these belong to good as well as to evil? For instance, if the scent of the primæval monster can so remain in proportion to the original strength, can the same be true of things of good import?'

Sir Nathaniel thought a while, then he answered:

'We must be careful from the beginning not to confuse the physical and the moral, to differentiate the two and to keep them differentiated. I can see that already you have switched on the moral entirely, so perhaps we had better follow it up first. On the side of the moral we have certain justification for belief in the utterances of revealed religion. For instance, "the effectual fervent prayer of a righteous man availeth much" is altogether for good. We have nothing of a similar kind on the side of evil. But if we accept this dictum we need have no more fear of "mysteries": these become thenceforth merely obstacles.'

Adam waited in silence, which was intended to be, and was, respectful. Then he suddenly changed to another phase of the subject.

'And now, sir, may I turn for a few minutes to purely practical things, or rather to matters of historical fact?'

Sir Nathaniel bowed acquiescence. He went on:

'We have already spoken of the history, so far as it is known, of some of the places round us – "Castra Regis," "Diana's Grove" and "The Lair of the White Worm." I would like to ask if there is anything not necessarily of evil import about any of the places?'

'Which?' asked Sir Nathaniel shrewdly.

'Well, for instance, this house and Mercy Farm?'

'Here we turn,' said Sir Nathaniel, 'to the other side, the light side of things. Let us take Mercy Farm first. You have no objection?'

'Thank you, sir.' The young man's comment was complete and illuminative.

'Perhaps we had better remember the history of that particular place. The details may later on help us in coming to some useful, or at all events interesting, conclusion.

'When Augustine was sent by Pope Gregory to Christianise England in the time of the Romans, he was received and protected by Ethelbert, King of Kent, whose wife, daughter of Charibert, King of Paris, was a Christian, and did much for Augustine. She founded a nunnery in memory of Columba, which was named *Sedes misericordiæ*, the House of Mercy, and, as the region was Mercian, the two names became inextricably involved. As Columba is the Latin for dove, the dove became a sort of signification of the nunnery. She seized on the idea and made the newly-founded nunnery a house of doves. Someone sent her a freshly-discovered dove, a sort of carrier, but which had in the white feathers of its head and neck the form of a religious cowl. And so in especial the bird became the symbol of the nuns of Mercy. The nunnery flourished for more than a century, when, in the time of Penda, who was the reactionary of heathendom, it fell into decay. In the meantime the doves, which, protected by religious feeling, had increased mightily, were known in all Catholic communities. When King Offa ruled in Mercia about a hundred and fifty years later, he restored Christianity, and under its protection the nunnery of St Columba was restored and its doves flourished again. In process of time this religious house again fell into desuetude; but before it disappeared it had achieved a great name for good works, and in especial for the piety of its members. I think I see now where your argument leads. I do not know if you started it, having thought it out to the full. But in any case I will venture an opinion; that if deeds and prayers and hopes and earnest thinking leave anywhere any moral effect, Mercy Farm and all around it have almost the right to be considered holy ground.'

'Thank you, sir,' said Adam earnestly, and was silent. Again Sir Nathaniel understood.

X

Smelling Death

Adam Salton, though he made little talk, did not let the grass grow under his feet in any matter which he had undertaken, or in which he was interested. He had agreed with Sir Nathaniel that they should not *do* anything with regard to the mystery of Lady Arabella's fear of the mongoose, but he steadily pursued his course in being *prepared* to do whenever the opportunity might come. He was in his own mind perpetually casting about for information or clues which might lead to such. Baffled by the killing of the mongoose, he looked around for another line to follow. He did not intend to give up the idea of there being a link between the woman and the animal, but he was already preparing a second string to his bow. His new idea was to use the faculties of Oolanga, so far as he could, in the service of discovery. His first move was to send Davenport to Liverpool to try to find the steward of the *West African*, who had told him about Oolanga, and then to get him to try to induce (by bribery or other means) the nigger to come to the Brow. So soon as he himself would have speech of the Voodoo-man he would be able to learn from him something useful. Davenport went away in the early morning, and was successful in both his missions, for he had to get Ross to send another mongoose, and also the one reserved for sending when told; he was able to tell Adam that he had seen the steward, who already told him a lot he wanted to know, and had also arranged to have Oolanga brought to Lesser Hill the following day. At this point Adam saw his way sufficiently clear to adumbrate to Davenport with fair exactness what he wished him to find out. He had come to the conclusion that it would be better – certainly at first – not himself to appear in the matter, with which Davenport was fully competent to deal. It would be time for himself to take a personal part when matters had advanced a little further.

That evening, when Davenport arrived, he had a long interview with Adam, in which he told what he had learned, partly from the ship steward, partly from the other Africans in the ship's service, and partly from Oolanga's own boasting. If what the nigger said was in any wise true, the man had a rare gift which might be useful in the quest they were after. He could, as it were, 'smell death.' If any one was dead, if any one had died, or if a place had been used in connection with death, he seemed to know the broad fact by intuition. Adam made up his mind that to test this faculty with regard to several places would be his first task. Naturally he was anxious for this, and the time passed slowly. The only comfort was the arrival the next morning of a strong packing case, locked, from Ross, the key being in the custody of Davenport. In the case were two smaller boxes, both locked. One of them contained a mongoose to replace that killed by Lady Arabella; the other was the reserved mongoose which had already killed the king-cobra in Nepaul. When both the animals had been safely put under lock and key in the place arranged for them, he felt that he might breathe more freely. Of course no one was allowed to know the secret of their existence in the house, except himself and Davenport. He arranged that Davenport should take Oolanga round the neighbourhood for a walk, stopping at each of the places which he designated. Having gone all along the Brow, he was to return the same way and induce him to touch on the same subjects in talking with Adam, who was to meet them as if by chance at the farthest part – that beyond Mercy Farm. Davenport was never to lose sight of him and was to bring him back to Liverpool safely, and leave him on board the ship, where he was to wait till his master should send for him.

The incidents of the day were just what Adam expected. At Mercy Farm, at Diana's Grove, at Castra Regis, and a few other spots, he stopped and, opening his wide nostrils as if to sniff boldly, said that he smelled death. It was not always in the same form. At Mercy Farm he said there were many small deaths. At Diana's Grove his bearing was different. There was a distinct sense of enjoyment about him, especially when he spoke of many great deaths long ago. Here, too, he sniffed in a strange way, like a bloodhound at check, and looked puzzled. He said no word in either praise or disparagement, but in the centre of the Grove where, hidden amongst ancient oak stumps, was a block of granite slightly hollowed on the top, he bent low and placed his forehead on the ground. This was the only place where he showed distinct reverence. At the Castle, though he spoke of much death, he showed no sign of respect. There was evidently something about Diana's Grove which both interested and baffled him. Before leaving he moved all over the place unsatisfied, and in one spot where, close to the edge of the Brow, was a deep hollow, he appeared to be afraid. After returning several times to this place, he suddenly turned and ran in a panic of fear to the higher ground, crossing as he did so the outcropping rock. Then he seemed to breathe more freely, and even recovered some of his jaunty impudence.

All this seemed to satisfy Adam's expectations. He went back to Lesser Hill with a serene and settled calm upon him.

When he went back to the house, Adam met Sir Nathaniel, who followed him into his study, saying as he closed the door behind him:

'By the way, I forgot to ask you details about one thing. When that extraordinary staring episode of Mr Caswall went on, how did Lilla take it – how did she bear herself?'

'She looked frightened, and trembled just as I have seen a pigeon with a hawk, or a bird with a serpent.'

'Thanks. That will do. It is just as I expected. There have

been circumstances in the Caswall family which lead one to believe that they have had from the earliest times some extraordinary mesmeric or hypnotic faculty. Indeed, a skilled eye could read so much in their physiognomy. That shot of yours, whether by instinct or intention, of the hawk and the pigeon was peculiarly apposite. I think we may settle on that as a fixed trait to be accepted throughout our investigation.'

When the dusk had fallen, Adam took the new mongoose – not the one from Nepaul – and, carrying the box slung over his shoulder, strolled towards Diana's Grove. Close to the gateway he met Lady Arabella, clad as usual in tightly fitting white, which showed off her extraordinarily slim figure.

To his intense astonishment the mongoose allowed her to pet him, take him up in her arms and fondle him. As she was coming in his direction he left him with her and walked on.

Round the roadway between the entrances of Diana's Grove and Lesser Hill were many trees with tall thin trunks with not much foliage except at top. In the dusk this place was shadowy, and the view of anyone was hampered by the clustering trunks. In the uncertain, tremulous light which fell through the tree-tops, it was hard to distinguish anything clearly, and as Adam looked back it seemed to him that Lady Arabella was actually dancing in a fantastic sort of way. Her arms were opening and shutting and winding about strangely; the white fur which she wore round her throat was also twisting about, or seemed to be. Not a sound was to be heard. There was something uncanny in all this silent movement which struck Adam as worthy of notice; so he waited, almost stopping his progress altogether, and walked with lingering steps, so as to let her overtake him. But as the dusk was thickening he could distinguish no more than he could at first. At last somehow he lost sight of her altogether, and turned back on his track to find her. Presently he came across her close to her own gate. She was leaning over the paling of split oak branches which formed the paling of the avenue. He could not see the mongoose, so he asked her where he had gone to.

'He slipt out of my arms while I was petting him,' she answered, 'and disappeared under the hedges.'

As she spoke she was walking back with him looking for the little animal. They found him at a place where the avenue widened so as to let carriages pass each other. The little creature seemed quite changed. He had been ebulliently active; now he was dull and spiritless – seemed to be dazed. He allowed himself to be lifted by either of the pair; but when he was alone with Lady Arabella he kept looking round him in a strange way, as though trying to escape. When they had come out on the roadway Adam held the mongoose tight to him, and, lifting his hat to his companion, moved quickly towards Lesser Hill; he and Lady Arabella lost sight of each other in the thickening gloom.

When Adam got home he put the mongoose in his box, which was left in the room where he had been, and locked the door. The other mongoose – the one from Nepaul – was safely locked in his own box, but he lay quiet and did not stir. When he got to his study Sir Nathaniel came in, shutting the door behind him.

'I have come,' he said, 'while we have an opportunity of being alone, to tell you something of the Caswall family which I think will interest you. Somehow we got switched off when we were within touch of the subject this afternoon.'

Adam prepared himself to listen. The other began at once:

'The point I was coming to to-day, when we were diverted from the subject, was this: there is, or used to be, a belief in this part of the world that the Caswall family had some strange power of making the wills of other persons subservient to their own. There are many allusions to the subject in memoirs and other unimportant works, but I only know of

64

one where the subject is spoken of definitely. It is *Mercia and its Worthies*, written by Ezra Toms more than a hundred years ago. The author more than infers that it was a mesmeric power, for he goes into the question of the close association of the then Edgar Caswall with Mesmer in Paris. He speaks of Caswall being a pupil and the fellow worker of Mesmer, and states that though, when the latter left France, he took away with him a vast quantity of philosophical and electric instruments, he was never known to use them again. He once made it known to a friend that he had given them to his old pupil. The term he used was odd, for it was "bequeathed," but no such bequest of Mesmer was ever made known. At any rate the instruments were missing, and never turned up. I just thought I would call your attention to this, as you might want to make a note of it. We have not come, yet at all events, to the mystery of the "hawk and the pigeon."'

Just as he finished speaking, a servant came into the room to tell Adam that there was some strange noise coming from the locked room into which he had gone when he came in. He hurried off to the place at once, Sir Nathaniel going with him. Having locked the door behind him, Adam opened the packing-case where the boxes of the two mongooses were locked up. There was no sound from one of them, but from the other a queer restless struggling. Having opened both boxes, he found that the noise was from the Nepaul animal, which, however, became quiet at once. In the other box the new mongoose lay dead, with every appearance of having been strangled.

There was nothing to be done that night. So Adam locked the boxes and the room again, taking with him the keys; and both he and Sir Nathaniel went off to bed.

XI

The First Encounter

Adam Salton was up with the dawn, and, taking a fast horse, rode off to Liverpool, bringing with him, slung across his shoulders, the box with the body of the mongoose. He was so early that he had to wake up Mr Ross. From him he, however, got what he wanted, the address of a comparative anatomist, who helped him in dealing with the health of his menagerie. Dr Cleaver lived not far away, and in a very short time Adam was ushered into his study. Unstrapping the box, he took out the body of the mongoose, now as stiff as wood, for the *rigor mortis* had long ago set in. Laying the body on Dr Cleaver's table, he said:

'Last night this was frisky in my arms. Now it is dead. What did it die of?'

The doctor went methodically to work and made a full examination. Then he said gravely:

'It may be necessary to make a more exhaustive examination. But in the meantime, I may say that it has been choked to death. And, considering the nature of its uses and its enemies, I think it was killed by some powerful snake of the constrictor class. Vast pressure must have been exercised, as every bone in its body seems to have been broken.' As the doctor accompanied Adam to the door, he said: 'Of course it is none of my business, but as I am a comparative anatomist, such things are of keen interest to me – I shall be really grateful if some time you will give me details of the death; and if you can possibly do so, supply me with weights and measures of both the animals.'

Adam, on paying his fee, thanked him warmly, gave him

his card, and promised that some time later on he would be happy to tell him all he himself knew. Then he rode back to Lesser Hill and got in just as his uncle and Sir Nathaniel were sitting down to breakfast.

When breakfast was over, Sir Nathaniel went with Adam to the study. When he had closed the door, and Adam had told him all up to the previous night, he looked at the young man with a grave, inquiring glance and said:

'Well?'

Adam told him all that occurred at his visit to Dr Cleaver. He finished up with:

'I am at sea, sir. I am looking for your opinion.'

'So am I for yours,' said Sir Nathaniel. 'This gets worse and worse. It seems to me that the mysteries are only beginning. We have now a detective story added. I suppose there is nothing to do but to wait – as we are doing – for the other parts of the mystery.'

'Do you want me specially for anything this afternoon?' asked Adam, adding, 'Of course I am at your command if you do. If not, I thought of calling at Mercy Farm.' He said this with a diffidence which made the old man's stern features relax.

'I suppose you would not wish me to come with you?' he asked playfully.

Adam at once replied:

'I should love it, sir; but to-day I think it would be better not.' Then, seeing the other's inquiring look, he went on: 'The fact is, sir, that Mr Caswall is going to tea to-day, and I think it would be wiser if I were present.'

'Quite so. Of course you will tell me later if there should take place anything which it would be well for me to know.'

'Certainly. I shall try to see you as soon as I get home.'

They said no more, and a little after four o'clock Adam set out for Mercy.

He was home just as the clocks were striking six. He was

pale and upset, but otherwise looked strong and alert. The old man summed up his appearance and manner thus: 'Braced up for battle.' Realising that Adam wished to talk with him, he quietly went over and locked the door.

'Now!' said Sir Nathaniel, and settled down to listen, looking at Adam steadily and listening attentively that he might miss nothing – even the inflection of a word.

'I found Miss Watford and Mimi at home. Watford had been detained by business on the farm. Miss Watford received me as kindly as before. Mimi, too, seemed glad to see me. Mr Caswall came so soon after I had arrived, that he or someone on his behalf must have been watching for me. He was followed closely by the Christy Minstrel, who was puffing hard as if he had been running – so it was probably he who watched. Mr Caswall was very cool and collected, but there was a more than usually iron look about his face that I did not like. However, both he and I got on very well. He talked pleasantly on all sorts of questions. The nigger waited a while and then disappeared as on the other occasion. Mr Caswall's eyes were as usual fixed on Lilla. True, they seemed to be very deep and earnest, but there was no offence in them. Had it not been for the drawing down of the brows and the stern set of the jaws, I should not at first have noticed anything. But the stare, when presently it began, increased in intensity. I could see that Lilla began to suffer from nervousness, as on the first occasion; but she carried herself bravely. However, the more nervous she grew, the harder Mr Caswall stared. It was evident to me that he had come prepared for some sort of mesmeric or hypnotic battle. After a while he began to throw glances round him and then raised his hand, without letting either Lilla or Mimi see the action. It was evidently intended to give some sign to the Christy Minstrel, for he came, in his usual stealthy way, quietly in by the hall door, which was open. Then Mr Caswall's efforts at staring became intensified, and poor Lilla's nervousness grew greater. Mimi, seeing that her cousin was distressed, came close to her, as if to comfort or strengthen her with the consciousness of her presence. This evidently made a difficulty for Mr Caswall, for his efforts, without seeming to get feebler, seemed less effective. This continued for a little while, to the gain of both Lilla and Mimi. Then there was a diversion. Without word or apology the door opened and Lady Arabella March entered the room. We had seen her coming through the great window. Without a word she crossed the room and stood beside Mr Caswall. It really was very like a fight of a peculiar kind; and the longer it was sustained the more earnest – the fiercer – it grew. That combination of forces – the over-lord, the white woman, and the black man – would have cost some – probably all of them – their lives in the Southern States of America. To us all it was simply horrible. But all that you can understand. This time, to go on in sporting phrase, it was understood by all to be a "fight to a finish," and the mixed group did not slacken a moment or relax their efforts. On Lilla the strain began to tell disastrously. She grew pale – a patchy pallor, which meant that all her nerves were out of order. She trembled like an aspen, and though she struggled bravely, I noticed that her legs would hardly stiffen. A dozen times she seemed about to collapse in a faint, but each time, on catching sight of Mimi's eyes, she made a fresh struggle and pulled through.

'By now Mr Caswall's face had lost its appearance of passiv-ity. No longer was it immobile. His eyes glowed with a red fiery light. He was still the old Roman in inflexibility of purpose; but grafted on the Roman was a new Berserker fury. The statical force of his nature had entered on a new phase. It had become dynamical. His companions in the baleful work seemed to have taken on something of his feeling. Lady Arabella looked like a soulless, pitiless being, not human unless it revived old legends of transformed human beings who had lost their humanity in some transformation or in the sweep of natural savagery. As for the Christy Minstrel, the only comparison I can suggest was a fiend from hell, engaged in the active pursuit of his natural purpose. I think I have already given you my impression of his lofty natural beauty. That I take back, for then I only spoke of possibilities . . . Now that I have seen his devilry in full blast, such a belief is inadequate. I can only say, that it was solely due to the self-restraint which you impressed on me that I did not wipe him out as he stood – without warning, without fair play – without a single one of the graces of life and death. Lilla was silent in the helpless concentration of deadly fear; Mimi was all resolve and self-forgetfulness, so intent on the soul-struggle in which she was engaged that there was no possibility of any other thought. As for myself, the bonds of will which held me inactive seemed like bands of steel which numbed all my faculties, except sight and hearing. I was limited absolutely to the power of waiting. We seemed fixed in an *impasse*. Something must happen, though the power of guessing what was inactive. As in a dream, I saw Mimi's hand move restlessly, as if groping for something. It was like a hand grown blind. Mechanically it touched that of Lilla, and in that instant she was transformed. It was as if youth and strength entered afresh into something already dead to sensibility and intention. As if by inspiration, she grasped the other's hand with a force which blenched the knuckles. Her face suddenly flamed, as if some divine light shone through it. Her form rose and expanded till it stood out majestically. Lifting her right hand, she stepped forward towards Caswall, and with a bold sweep of her arm seemed to drive some strange force towards him. Again and again was the gesture repeated, the man falling back from her at each movement. Towards the door he retreated, she following. There was a sound as of the cooing sob of doves, which seemed to multiply and intensify with each second. The sound from the unseen source rose and rose as he retreated, till finally it swelled out in a triumphant peal, as she, with a fierce sweep of her arm, seemed to hurl something at her foe, and he, moving his hands blindly before his face, appeared to be swept through the doorway and out into the open sunlight. At the same moment as he went, the light of day became suddenly dimmed, as though a mighty shadow had swept over the face of the earth. The air was full of a fierce continuous sound as of whirring wings.

'All at once my own faculties were fully restored; I could see and hear everything, and be fully conscious of what was going on. Even the figures of the baleful group were there, though dimly seen as through a veil – a shadowy veil. I saw Lilla sink down in a swoon, and Mimi throw up her arms in a gesture of triumph. As I saw her through the great window, the sunshine flooded the landscape, which, however, was momentarily becoming eclipsed by an on-rush of a myriad birds.

'Hark to the rushing of their wings!'

XII

The Kite

By the next morning, daylight showed the actual danger which threatened the east side of England. From every part of the eastern counties reports were received concerning the enormous immigration of birds. Experts were sending – on their own account, on behalf of learned societies, and through local and imperial governing bodies – reports dealing with the matter, and suggesting remedies. As might have been expected, the latter were mostly worthless. They were either disguised or undisguised advertisements with some personal object, or else merely the babble of persons desirous of notoriety on a quasi-scientific basis. The long-suffering public showed by its indifference to such reports forced upon them that they were not such fools as they were supposed to be. Of course the reports closer to home were more disturbing, even if more monotonous, for Castra Regis was the very centre of the trouble. All day long, and even all night long, it would seem that the birds were coming thicker from all quarters. Doubtless many were going as well as coming, but the mass seemed never to get less. Each bird seemed to sound some note of fear or anger or seeking, and the whirring of wings never ceased nor lessened. The air was full of a muttered throb. No window or barrier could shut out the sound, till the ears of any listening became partly paralysed by the ceaseless sound. So monotonous it was, so cheerless, so disheartening, so melancholy, that all longed, but in vain, for any variety, no matter how terrible it might be.

The second morning the reports from all the districts round were more alarming than ever. Farmers began to dread the coming of winter as they saw the dwindling of the timely fruitfulness of the earth. And as yet it was only warning of evil, not the evil accomplished; the ground began to look bare whenever some passing sound temporarily frightened the birds.

Edgar Caswall tortured his brain for a long time unavailingly, to think of some means of getting rid of what he as well as his neighbours had come to regard as a plague of birds. At last he recalled a circumstance which promised a solution of the difficulty. The experience was of some years ago in China, far up-country, towards the head-waters of the Yang-tze-kiang, where the smaller tributaries spread out in a sort of natural irrigation scheme to supply the wilderness of paddy-fields. It was at the time of the ripening rice, and the wilderness of birds which came to feed on the coming crop was a serious menace not only to the district, but to the country at large. The farmers, who were more or less afflicted with the same trouble every season, knew how to deal with it. They made a vast kite, which they caused to be flown over the centre spot of the incursion. The kite was shaped like a great hawk; and the moment it rose into the air the birds began to cower and seek protection and then to disappear. So long as that kite was flying overhead the birds lay low. The crop was saved. Accordingly Caswall had his men construct an immense kite, adhering as well as they could to the lines of a hawk. Then he and his men, with a sufficiency of string, began to fly it high overhead. The experience of China was repeated. The moment the kite rose, the birds hid or sought shelter. The following morning, the kite still flying high, no bird was to be seen as far as the eye could reach from Castra Regis. But there followed in turn what proved even a worse evil. All the birds were cowed; their sounds stopped. Neither song nor chirp was heard – silence seemed to have taken the place of the myriad voices of bird life. But that was not all. The silence spread to all animals.

The fear and restraint which brooded amongst the denizens of the air began to affect all life. Not only did the birds cease song or chirp, but the lowing of the cattle ceased in the fields and the myriad sounds of life died away. In the place of these things was only a soundless gloom, more dreadful, more disheartening, more soul-killing than any concourse of sounds, no matter how full of fear and dread. Pious individuals and bodies put up constant prayers for relief from the intolerable solitude. After a little there were signs of universal depression which who ran might read. One and all the faces of men and women seemed bereft of vitality, of interest, of thought, and, most of all, of hope. Men seemed to have lost the power of expression of their thoughts. The soundless air seemed to have the same effect as the universal darkness when men gnawed their tongues with pain.

From this infliction of silence there was no relief. Everything was affected; gloom was the predominant note. Joy appeared to have passed away as a factor of life, and this creative impulse had nothing to take its place. That giant spot in high air was a plague of evil influence. It seemed like a new misanthropic belief which had fallen on human beings, carrying with it the negation of all hope. After a few days, men began to grow desperate; their very words as well as their senses seemed to be in chains. Edgar Caswall again tortured his brain to find any antidote or palliative of this greater evil than before. He would gladly have destroyed the kite, or caused its flying to cease; but he dared not. The instant it was pulled down, the birds rose up in even greater numbers; all those who depended in any way on agriculture sent pitiful protests to Castra Regis.

It was strange indeed what influence that kite seemed to exercise. Even human beings were affected by it, as if both it and they were realities. As for the people at Mercy Farm, it was like a taste of actual death. Lilla felt it most. If she had been indeed a real dove, with a real kite hanging over her in the air, she could not have been more frightened or more affected by the fright this created.

Of course, some of those already drawn into the vortex noticed the effect on individuals. Those who were interested took care to compare their information. They felt that it might be of service later on. Strangely enough, as it seemed to the others, the person who took the ghastly silence least to heart was the Christy Minstrel. By nature he was not a man sensitive to, or afflicted by, nerves. This alone would not have produced the seeming indifference, so they set their minds to discover the real cause. Adam came quickly to the conclusion that there was for him some compensation that the others did not share; and he soon believed that that compensation was in one form or another enjoyment of the sufferings of others. Thus, he had a never-failing source of amusement. The birds alone seemed as if they would satisfy even him. He took delight in the oppression by the predatory birds of the others of their kind. And then, even of them he took the occasion to add to his collection of beaks. Lady Arabella's cold nature rendered her immune to anything in the way of pain or trouble to or of others. And Edgar Caswall was far too haughty a person, and too stern of nature, to concern himself about even poor or helpless people, much less the lower order of mere animals. Mr Watford, Mr Salton, and Sir Nathaniel were all concerned in the issue, partly from kindness of heart – for none of them could see suffering, even of wild birds, unmoved – and partly on account of their property, which had to be protected, or ruin would stare them in the face before long. Lilla suffered acutely. As time went on, her face became pinched, and her eyes dull with watching and crying. Mimi suffered too on account of her cousin's suffering. But as she could do nothing, she resolutely made up her mind to self-restraint and patience. The inhabitants of the district around took the matter with indifference. They had been freed from the noises, and the silence did not trouble them. It is often so; people put a different and more lofty name on their own purposes. For instance, these people probably considered their own view founded on common weal, whereas it was merely indifference founded on selfishness.

XIII

Mesmer's Chest

After a couple of weeks had passed, the kite seemed to give to Edgar Caswall a new zest for life. It appeared to have a satisfying influence on him. He was never tired of looking at its movements. He had a comfortable armchair put out on the tower, wherein he sat sometimes all day long, watching as though the kite was a new toy and he a child lately come into possession of it. He did not seem to have lost interest in Lilla, for he still paid an occasional visit at Mercy Farm.

Indeed, his feeling towards her, whatever it had been at first, had now so far changed that it had become a distinct affection of a purely animal kind. In the change of the kind of affection, the peculiarly impersonal, philosophic, almost platonic, had shed all the finer qualities that had belonged to it. Indeed, it seemed as though the man's nature had become corrupted, and that all the baser and more selfish and more reckless qualities had become more conspicuous. There was not so much sternness apparent in his nature, because there was less self-restraint. Determination had become indifference. Sensitiveness, such as had been, became callousness. Altogether, there did not seem to be in his nature the same singleness of purpose, either in kind or degree. Strangely, as he unconsciously yielded to this demoralising process, he seemed to be achieving a new likeness to Oolanga. Sometimes as Adam – ever on the watch – noticed the growing change, he began to wonder whether the body was answering to the mind or the mind to the body. Accordingly, it was a never-ending thought to him which momentum – the physical or the moral – was antecedent. The thing which puzzled him

76

most was that the forbidding qualities in the African, which had at first evoked his attention and his disgust, remained the same. Had it been that the two men had been affected, one changing with the other by slow degrees – a sort of moral metabolism, – he could have better and more easily understood it. Transmutation of different bodies is, in a way, more understandable than changes in one body that have no equivalent equipoise in the other. The idea was recurrent to him that perhaps when a nature has reached its lowest point of decadence it loses the faculty of change of any kind. However it was, the fact remained. Oolanga preserved all his original brutal decadence, while Caswall slowly deteriorated without any hint of resilience.

The visible change in Edgar was that he grew morbid, sad, silent; the neighbours thought he was mad. He became absorbed in the kite, and watched it not only by day, but often all night long. It became an obsession to him.

Adam kept his eyes and ears open and his mouth shut. He felt that he was learning. And, indeed, he was not mistaken when he acted as if silence was a virtue. He took a certain amount of interest – pleasure would be too smooth a word – in the generally expressed opinions of the neighbours of Castra Regis. It was commonly held regarding Caswall that he was mad. He took a personal interest in the keeping of the great kite flying. He had a vast coil of string efficient for the purpose, which worked on a roller fixed on the parapet of the tower. There was a winch for the pulling in of the slack of the string; the outgoing line was controlled by a racket. There was invariably one man at least, day and night, on the tower to attend to it. At such an elevation there was always a strong wind, and at times the kite rose to an enormous height, as well as travelling for great distances laterally. In fact, the kite became, in a short time, one of the curiosities of Castra Regis and all around it. Edgar began to attribute to it, in his own mind, almost human qualities. It became to him a separate entity, with a mind and a soul of its own.

Being idle-handed all day, he began to apply to what he considered the service of the kite some of his spare time, and found a new pleasure – a new object in life – in the old schoolboy game of sending up 'runners' to the kite. The way this is done is to get round pieces of paper so cut that there is a hole in the centre through which the string of the kite passes. The natural action of the wind-pressure takes the paper thus cut along the string, and so up to the kite itself, no matter how high or how far it may have gone. In the early days of this amusement Edgar Caswall spent hours. Hundreds of such messengers flew along the string, until soon he bethought him of writing messages on these papers so that he could make known his ideas to the kite. It may be that his brain gave way under the opportunities given by his foregone illusion of the entity of the toy and its power of separate thought. From sending messages he came to making direct speech to the kite – without, however, ceasing to send the runners. Doubtless, the height of the tower, seated as it was on the hill-top, the rushing of the ceaseless wind, the hypnotic effect of the lofty altitude of the speck in the sky at which he gazed, and the rushing of the paper messengers up the string till sight of them was lost in distance, all helped to further affect his brain, undoubtedly giving way under the strain of a concatenation of beliefs and circumstances which were at once stimulating to the imagination, occupative of his mind, and absorbing.

The next step of intellectual decline was to bring to bear on the main idea of the conscious identity of the kite all sorts of subjects which had imaginative force or tendency of their own. He had, in Castra Regis, a large collection of curious and interesting things formed in the past by his forebears, of similar likes to his own. There were all sorts of strange anthropological specimens, both old and new, which had been collected through various travels in strange places: ancient Egyptian relics from tombs, and mummies; curios from Australia, New Zealand, and the South Seas; idols and images

– from Tartar ikons to ancient Egyptian, Persian, and Indian objects of worship; objects of death and torture of American Indians; and, above all, a vast collection of lethal weapons of every kind and from every place – Chinese 'high pinders,' double knives, Afghan double-edged scimitars made to cut a body in two, heavy knives from all the Eastern countries, ghost daggers from Thibet, the terrible kukri of the Ghourka and other hill tribes of India, assassins' weapons from Italy and Spain, even the knife which was formerly carried by the slave-drivers of the Mississippi region. Death and pain of every kind were fully represented in that gruesome collection. That it had a fascination for Oolanga goes without saying. He was never tired of visiting the museum in the tower, and spent endless hours in inspecting the exhibits, till he was thoroughly familiar with every detail of all of them. He asked permission to clean and polish and sharpen them – a favour which was readily granted. In addition to the above objects, there were many things of a kind to awaken human fear. Stuffed serpents of the most objectionable and horrid kind; giant insects from the tropics, fearsome in every detail; fishes and crustaceans covered with weird spikes; dried octopuses of great size. Other things, too, there were not less deadly though seemingly innocuous – dried fungi, the touch of which was death and whose poison was carried on the air; also traps intended for birds, beasts, fishes, reptiles, and insects; machines which could produce pain of any kind and degree, and the only mercy of which was the power of producing speedy death. Caswall, who had never seen any of these things, except those which he had collected himself, found a constant amusement and interest in them. He studied them, their uses, their mechanism – where there was such, – and their places of origin, until he had an ample and real knowledge of all belonging to them. Many were secret and intricate, but he never rested till he found out all the secrets. When once he had become interested in strange objects and the way to use them, he began to explore various likely places for similar finds. He began to inquire of his household where strange lumber was kept. Several of the men spoke of old Simon Chester as one who knew everything in and about the house. Accordingly, he sent for the old man, who came at once. He was very old, nearly ninety years of age, and very infirm. He had been born in the Castle, and served its succession of masters – present or absent – ever since. When Edgar began to question him on the subject regarding which he had sent for him, old Simon exhibited much perturbation. In fact, he became so frightened that his master, fully believing that he was concealing something, ordered him to tell at once what remained unseen, and where such was hidden away. Face to face with discovery of his secret, the old man, in a pitiable state of concern, spoke out even more fully than Mr Caswall had expected:

'Indeed, indeed, sir, everything is here in the tower that has ever been imported or put away in my time – except – except' – here he began to shake and tremble – 'except the chest which Mr Edgar – he who was Mr Edgar when I first took service – brought back from France, after he had been with Dr Mesmer. The trunk has been kept in my room for safety; but I shall send it down here now.'

'What is in it?' asked Edgar sharply.

'That I do not know. Moreover, it is a peculiar trunk, without any visible means of opening it.'

'Is there no lock?'

'I suppose so, sir; but I do not know. There is no keyhole.'

'Send it here; and then come to me yourself.'

The trunk, a heavy one with steel bands round it, but no lock or keyhole, was carried in by four men. Shortly afterwards old Simon attended his master. When he came into the room, Mr Caswall himself went and closed the door; then he asked:

'How do you open it?'

'I do not know, sir.'

'Do you mean to say you never opened it?'

With considerable and pathetic dignity, the old man answered:

'Most certainly I do say so, your honour. How could I? It was entrusted to me with the other things by my master. To open it would have been a breach of trust.'

Caswall sneered as he said:

'Quite remarkable! Leave it with me. Close the door behind you. Stay – did no one ever tell you about it – say anything regarding it – make any remark?'

Old Simon turned pale, and put his trembling hands together as though imploring:

'Oh, sir, I entreat you not to touch it. That probably contains secrets which Dr Mesmer told my master. Told them to his ruin!'

'How do you mean? What ruin?'

'Sir, he it was who, men said, sold his soul to the Evil One; I had thought that that time and the evil of it had all passed away.'

'That will do. Go away; but remain in your own room, or within call. I may want you.'

The old man bowed deeply and went out trembling, but without speaking a word.

XIV

The Chest Opened

Left alone in the turret-room, Edgar Caswall carefully locked the door and hung a handkerchief over the keyhole. Next, he inspected the windows, and saw that they were not overlooked from any angle of the main building. Then he carefully examined the trunk, going over it with a magnifying glass. He found it intact: the steel bands were flawless; the whole trunk was compact into unity. After sitting opposite to it for some time, and the shades of evening beginning to melt into darkness, he gave up the task and took himself to his bedroom, after locking the door of the turret-room behind him and taking away the key.

He woke in the morning at daylight, and resumed his patient but unavailing study of the metal trunk. This he continued during the whole day with the same result – humiliating disappointment which overwrought his nerves and made his head ache. The result of the long strain was seen later in the afternoon, when he sat locked within the turret-room before the still baffling trunk, distrait, listless and yet agitated, sunk in a settled gloom. As the dusk was falling he told the steward to send him four men, strong ones. These he told to take the trunk to his bedroom. In that room he then sat on into the night, without pausing even to take any food. His mind was in a whirl, a fever of excitement. The result was that when late in the night he locked himself in his room his brain was full of odd fancies; he was on the high road to mental disturbance. He lay down on his bed in the dark, still brooding over the mystery of the closed trunk.

Gradually he yielded to the influences of silence and darkness. After lying there quietly for some time his mind became active again. But this time there were round him no disturbing influences; his brain was active and able to work freely and to deal with memory. A thousand forgotten – or only half-known – incidents, fragments of conversations or theories long ago guessed at and long forgotten, crowded in on his mind. He seemed to hear again around him the legions of whirring wings to which he had been so lately accustomed. Even to himself he knew that that was an effort of imagination founded on imperfect memory. But he was content that imagination should work, for out of it might come some solution of the mystery which surrounded him. And in this frame of mind, sleep made another and more successful essay. This time he enjoyed peaceful slumber, restful alike to his wearied body and his overwrought brain.

In his sleep in the darkness he arose, and, as if in obedience to some influence beyond and greater than himself, lifted the great trunk and set it on a strong table at one side of the room, from which he had previously removed a quantity of books. To do this, he had to use an amount of strength which was, he knew, far beyond him in his normal state. As it was, it seemed easy enough; everything yielded before his touch. Then he became conscious that somehow – how, he never could remember – the chest was open. Again another wonder. He unlocked his door, and, taking the chest on his shoulder, carried it up to the turret-room, the door of which also he unlocked. Even at the time he was amazed at his own strength, and wondered unavailingly whence it had come. His mind, lost in conjecture, was too far off to realise more immediate things. He knew that the chest was enormously heavy. He seemed, in a sort of vision which lit up the absolute blackness around, to see the four sturdy servant men staggering under its great weight. He locked himself again in the turret-room and laid the opened chest on a table, and in the darkness began to carefully unpack it, laying out the contents, which

83

were mainly of metal and glass – great pieces in strange forms, – on another table. He was conscious of being still asleep, and of acting rather in obedience to some unseen and unknown command than in accordance with any reasonable plan to be followed by results which he understood and was aiming at. This phase completed, he proceeded to arrange in order the component parts of some large instruments formed mostly of glass. His fingers seemed to have acquired a new and exquisite subtlety and even a volition of their own. Then he brought some force to bear – how or where, he knew not, – and soon the room was filled with the whirr of machinery moving at great speed. Through the darkness, in its vicinity, came irregularly quick intermittent flashes of dazzling light. All else was still. Then weariness of brain came upon him; his head sank down on his breast, and little by little everything became wrapped in gloom.

He awoke in the early morning in his bedroom, and looked around him, now clear-headed, in amazement. In its usual place on the strong table stood the great steel-hooped chest without lock or key. But it was now locked. He arose quietly and stole to the turret-room. There everything was as it had been on the previous evening. He looked out of the window where high in air flew, as usual, the giant kite. He unlocked the wicket gate of the turret stair and went out on the roof. Close to him was the great coil of string on its reel. It was humming in the morning breeze, and when he touched the string it sent a quick thrill through hand and arm. There was no sign anywhere that there had been any disturbance or displacement of anything during the night.

Utterly bewildered, he sat down in his room to think. Now for the first time he *felt* that he was asleep and dreaming. Presently he fell asleep again, and slept for a long time. He awoke hungry and made a hearty meal. Then towards evening, having locked himself in, he fell asleep again. When he awoke he was in darkness, and was quite at sea as to his whereabouts. He began feeling about the dark room, and was recalled to the consequences of his position by the breaking of a large piece of glass. This he, having obtained a light, discovered to be a glass wheel, part of an elaborate piece of mechanism which he must have in his sleep taken from the chest, which was opened. He had once again opened it whilst asleep, but he had no sort of recollection of the circumstances. He came to the conclusion that there had been some sort of dual action of his mind which might lead to some catastrophe or some discovery of his secret plans; so he resolved to forgo for a while the pleasure of making discoveries regarding the chest. To this end, he applied himself to quite another matter – an investigation of the other treasures and rare objects in his collections. He went amongst them in simple, idle curiosity, his main object being to discover some strange item which he might use for experiment with the kite. He had already resolved to try some runners other than those made of paper. He had a vague idea that with such a force as the great kite straining at its leash, this might be used to lift to the altitude of the kite itself heavier articles. His first experiment with articles of little but increasing weight was eminently successful. So he added by degrees more and more weight, until he found out that the lifting power of the kite was considerable. He then determined to take a step still further, and to use for sending to the kite some of the articles which lay in the steel-hooped chest. The last time he had opened it in sleep it had not been shut again, so he had inserted a wedge so that he could open it at will. He made examination of the contents, but came to the conclusion that the glass objects were unsuitable. They were too light for testing weight, and they were so frail as to be dangerous to send to such a height. So he looked around for something more solid with which to experiment. His eye caught sight of an object which at once attracted him. This was a small copy of one of the ancient Egyptian gods – that of Bes, who represented the destructive power of nature. It was so bizarre and mysterious as to commend itself to his humour. In lifting it from the cabinet, he was struck by its great weight in proportion to its size. He made accurate examination of it by the aid of some philosophical instruments, and came to the conclusion that it was carven from a lump of lodestone. He remembered that he had read somewhere of an ancient Egyptian god cut from a similar substance, and, thinking it over, he came to the conclusion that he must have read it in Sir Thomas Brown's *Popular Errors*, a book of the seventeenth century. He got the book from the library, and looked out the passage:

'A great example we have from the observation of our learned friend Mr *Graves*, in an Ægyptian idol cut out of Loadstone and found among the *Mummies*; which still retains its attraction, though probably taken out of the mine about two thousand years ago.' – Book II, Chap. VII.

The strangeness of the figure, and its being so close akin to his own nature, attracted him. He made from thin wood a large circular runner and in front of it placed the weighty god, and sent it up to the flying kite along the throbbing string.

XV

Oolanga's Hallucinations

During the last days Lady Arabella had been getting exceedingly impatient. Her debts, always pressing, were growing to an embarrassing amount. The only hope she had of comfort in life was a good marriage; but the good marriage on which she had fixed her eye did not seem to move quickly enough – indeed, it did not seem to move at all – in the right direction. Edgar Caswall was not an ardent wooer. From the very first he seemed *difficile*, but now he had been keeping to his own room ever since his struggle with Mimi Watford. On that occasion she had shown him in an unmistakable way what her feelings were; indeed, she had made it known to him, in a more overt way than pride should allow, that she wished to help and support him. The moment when she had gone across the room to stand beside him in his mesmeric struggle, had been the very limit of her voluntary action. It was quite bitter enough, she felt, that he did not come to her, but now that she had made that advance, she felt that any withdrawal on his part would, to a woman of her class, be nothing less than a flaming insult. Had she not classed herself with his nigger servant, an unreformed savage? Had she not shown her preference for him at the festival of his home-coming? Had she not ... Lady Arabella was cold-blooded, and she was prepared to go through all that might be necessary of indifference and even insult to become chatelaine of Castra Regis. In the meantime, she would show no hurry – she would wait. She would even, in an unostentatious way, come to him again. She knew him now, and could make a keen guess at his desires with regard to Lilla Watford.

With that secret in her possession, she could bring pressure to bear on him which would make it no easy matter to evade her. The great difficulty she had was how to get near him. He was shut up within his Castle, and guarded by a defence of convention which she could not pass without danger of ill repute to herself. Over this question she thought and thought for days and nights. At last she thought she saw a way of getting at him. She would go to him openly at Castra Regis. Her individual rank and position would make such a thing possible if carefully done. She could explain matters afterwards if necessary. Then when they were alone – as she would manage – she would use her arts and her experience to make him commit himself. After all, he was only a man, with a man's dislike of difficult or awkward situations. She felt quite sufficient confidence in her own womanhood to carry her through any difficulty which might arise. From Diana's Grove she heard each day the luncheon-gong from Castra Regis sound, and knew the hour when the servants would be in the back of the house. She would enter the house at that hour, and, pretending that she could not make anyone hear her, would seek him in his own rooms. The tower was, she knew, away from all the usual sounds of the house, and moreover she knew that the servants had strict orders not to interrupt him when he was in the turret chamber. She had found out, partly by the aid of an opera-glass and partly by judicious questioning, that several times lately a heavy chest had been carried to and from his room, and that it rested in the room each night. She was, therefore, confident that he had some important work on hand which would keep him busy for long spells. And so she was satisfied that all was going well with her – that her designs were ripening.

Synchronously, another member of the household at Castra Regis had got ideas which he thought were working to fruition. A man in the position of a servant has plenty of opportunity of watching his betters and forming opinions regarding them. Oolanga, now living at the Castle, was in his

88

way a clever, unscrupulous man, and he felt that with things moving round him in this great household there should be opportunities of self-advancement. Being unscrupulous and stealthy – and a savage – he looked to dishonest means. He saw plainly enough that Lady Arabella was making a dead set at his master, and he was watchful of even the slightest sign of anything which might materialise this knowledge. Like the other men in the house, he knew of the carrying to and fro of the great chest, and had got it into his head that the care exercised in its portage indicated that it was full of great treasure. He was for ever lurking around the turret-rooms on the chance of making some useful discovery. But he was as cautious as he was stealthy, and took care that no one else watched him. It was thus that he became aware of Lady Arabella's venture into the house, as she thought, unseen. He took more care than ever, since he was watching another, that the positions were not reversed. More than ever he kept his eyes and ears open and his mouth shut. Seeing Lady Arabella gliding up the stairs towards his master's room, he took it for granted that she was there for no good, and doubled his watching intentness and caution. She waited patiently, hidden in his room, till Caswall returned upstairs after his lunch. She took care not to frighten or startle him in any way. As she did not know that anyone was watching and listening, her movements were merely a part of caution. She knew that sudden surprise occasions sudden sound, and that by this, in turn, others who were listeners would almost of necessity betray themselves. Oolanga was disappointed, but he dared not exhibit any feeling on the subject lest it should betray that he was hiding. Therefore he slunk downstairs again noiselessly, and waited for a more favourable opportunity of furthering his plans. It must be borne in mind that he thought that the heavy trunk was full of valuables, and that he believed that Lady Arabella had come to try to steal it. His purpose of using for his own advantage the combination of these two ideas was seen later in the day.

When, after some time, Lady Arabella had given up the idea of seeing Caswall that afternoon, she moved quietly out of the Castle, taking care not to be noticed either within the house or outside it. Oolanga secretly followed her. He was an expert at this game, and succeeded admirably on this occasion. He watched her enter the private gate of Diana's Grove and then, taking a roundabout course and keeping altogether out of her sight, by following her at last overtook her in a thick part of the Grove where no one could see the meeting. Lady Arabella was at the moment much surprised. She had not seen him for several days, and had almost forgotten his existence. Oolanga would have been surprised had he known and been capable of understanding the real value placed on him, his beauty, his worthiness, by other persons, and compared it with the value in these matters in which he held himself. But in some cases, if ignorance be bliss, bliss has a dynamic quality which later leads to destruction. Doubtless Oolanga had his dreams like other men. In such cases he doubtless saw himself – or would have done had he had the knowledge with which to make the comparison – as a young sun-god – colour not stated – as beautiful as the eye of dusky or even white womanhood had ever dwelt upon. He would have been filled with all noble and captivating qualities regarded as such in West Africa. Women would have loved him, and would have told him so in the overt and fervid manner usual in affairs of the alleged heart in the shadowy depths of the forest of the Gold Coast. After all, etiquette is a valuable factor in the higher circles of even Africa in reducing chaos to social order and in avoiding mistakes properly ending in lethal violence. Had he known of such an educational influence, the ambitious Oolanga might have regretted its absence from his curriculum. But as it was, intent on his own ends, he went on in blind ignorance of offence. He came close behind Lady Arabella, and in a hushed voice suitable to the importance of his task, and in deference to the respect he had for her and the place, began to unfold the story of his love. Lady Arabella was not usually a humorous person, but no man or woman born with the usual risible faculties of the white race could have checked the laughter which rose spontaneously to her lips. The circumstances were too grotesque, the contrast too violent, for even subdued mirth. The man a debased specimen of one of the most debased races of the earth, and of an ugliness which was simply devil-ish; the woman of high degree, beautiful, accomplished. She thought that her first moment's consideration of the outrage – it was nothing less in her eyes – had given her the full material for thought. But every instant after threw new and varied lights on the affront. Her indignation was too great for passion: only irony or satire would meet the situation. And so her temper was able to stand the test. Calmed by a few moments of irony, she found voice. Her cold, cruel nature helped, and she did not shrink to subject even the poor igno-rant savage to the merciless fire-lash of her scorn. Oolanga was dimly conscious, at most, that he was being flouted in a way he least understood; but his anger was no less keen because of the measure of his ignorance. So he gave way to it as does a tortured beast. He ground his great teeth together, he raved, he stamped, he swore in barbarous tongues and with barbarous imagery. Even Lady Arabella felt that it was well she was within reach of help, or he might have offered her brutal violence – even have killed her.

'Am I to understand,' she said with cold disdain, so much more effective to wound than hot passion, 'that you are offering me your love? *Your* – love?'

For reply he nodded his head. The scorn of her voice in a sort of baleful hiss sounded – and felt – like the lash of a whip.

Then she continued, her passion rising as she spoke:

'And you dared! you – a savage – a slave – the basest thing in the world of vermin! Take care! I don't value your worth-less life more than I do that of a rat or spider. Don't let me ever see your hideous face here again, or I shall rid the earth of you. Have you anything to say for yourself why I should not kill you?'

As she was speaking, she had taken out her revolver and was pointing it at him. In the immediate presence of death his impudence forsook him, and he made a weak effort to justify himself. His speech was short, consisting of single words. To Lady Arabella it sounded mere gibberish, but it was in his own dialect, and meant love, marriage, wife. From the intonation of the words, she guessed, with her woman's quick intuition, at their meaning; but she quite failed to follow when, becoming more pressing, he continued to urge his suit in a mixture of the grossest animal passion and ridiculous threats. In the latter he said that he knew she had tried to steal his master's treasure, and that he had caught her in the act. So if she would be his he would share the treasure with her, and they would live in luxury in the African forests. But if she refused, he would tell his master, who would flog and torture her and then give her to the police, who would kill her.

Altogether it was a fine mixture of opposing base projects, just such as a savage like him might be expected to evolve out of his passions.

XVI

Battle Renewed

The consequences of that meeting in the dusk of Diana's Grove were acute and far-reaching, and not only to the two engaged in it. From Oolanga, this might have been expected by anyone who knew the character of the tropical African savage. To such, there are two passions that are inexhaustible and insatiable – vanity and that which they are pleased to call love. Oolanga left the Grove with an absorbing hatred in his heart. His lust and greed were afire, and his vanity had been wounded to the core. Lady Arabella's icy nature was not so deeply stirred, though she too was in a seething passion. More than ever was she set upon bringing Edgar Caswall to her feet. The obstacles she had encountered, the insults she had endured, were only as fuel to the purpose of revenge which consumed her.

As she sought her own rooms in Diana's Grove, she went over the whole subject again and again, always finding in the face of Lilla Watford a key to a problem which puzzled her – the problem of a way to turn Caswall's powers – his very existence – to aid her purpose.

When in her boudoir, she wrote a note, taking so much trouble over it that she wrote, destroyed, and rewrote, till her dainty waste-basket was half-full of torn sheets of notepaper. When quite satisfied, she copied out the last sheet afresh, and then carefully burned all the spoiled fragments. She put the copied note in an emblazoned envelope, and directed it to Edgar Caswall at Castra Regis. This she sent off by one of her grooms. The letter ran:

'*Dear Mr Caswall*, – *I want to have a little chat with you on a subject in which I believe you are interested. Will you kindly call for me to-day after lunch – say at three or four o'clock, and we can walk a little way together. Only as far as Mercy Farm, where I want to see Lilla and Mimi Watford. We can take a cup of tea at the Farm. Do not bring your African servant with you, as I am afraid his face frightens the girls. After all, he is not pretty, is he? I have an idea you will be pleased with your visit this time. – Yours sincerely,*

'*Arabella March.*'

At half-past three Edgar Caswall called at Diana's Grove. Lady Arabella met him on the roadway outside the gate. She wished to take the servants into confidence as little as possible. She turned when she saw him coming, and walked beside him towards Mercy Farm, keeping step with him as they walked. When they got near Mercy, she turned and looked around her, expecting to see Oolanga or some sign of him. He was, however, not visible. He had received from his master peremptory orders to keep out of sight – an order for which the African scored a new offence up against her. They found Lilla and Mimi at home and seemingly glad to see them, though both the girls were surprised at the visit coming so soon after the other.

The proceedings were a simple repetition of the battle of souls of the former visit. On this occasion, however, Edgar Caswall seemed as if defeated, even before the strife began. This was the more strange, as on this occasion he had only the presence of Lady Arabella to support him – Oolanga being absent. Moreover, Mimi lacked on the present occasion the support of Adam Salton, which had been of such effective service before. This time the struggle for supremacy of will was longer and more determined. Caswall felt that if on this occasion he could not achieve supremacy, he had better give up the idea of trying to settle at Castra Regis, and so all his pride was enlisted against Mimi. When they had been waiting for the door to be opened, Lady Arabella, believing in a sudden attack, had said to him in a low, stern voice which somehow carried conviction:

'This time you should win. She is, after all, only a woman. Show her no mercy. That is weakness. Fight her, beat her, trample on her, kill her if need be. She stands in your way, and I hate her. Never take your eyes off her. Never mind Lilla – she is afraid of you. You are already her master. The other, Mimi, will try to make you look at her cousin. Do not. There lies defeat. Let nothing – no, not death itself, no matter of whom – take your attention from Mimi, and you will win. If she is overcoming you, take my hand and hold it hard whilst you are looking into her eyes. If she is too strong for you, I shall interfere. I shall make a diversion, and under the shade of it you must retire unbeaten, even if not victorious. Hush! silence! they are coming. Be resolute, and still.'

The two girls came to the door together. They had been fixing up an æolian harp which Adam had given Mimi. At the open door they listened for a few moments. Strange sounds were coming up over the Brow from the east. It was the rustling and crackling of the dry reeds and rushes from the low lands on the hither side of the Eastern Sea. The season had been an unusually dry one. Also the sound came from another cause: the strong east wind was helping forward enormous flocks of birds, most of them pigeons with white cowls. Not only were their wings whirring, but their cooing was plainly audible. From such a multitude of birds the mass of sound, individually small, assumed the volume of a storm. Surprised at the influx of birds, to which they had been strangers so long, they all looked towards Castra Regis, from whose high tower the great kite had been flying as usual. But even as they looked the string broke, and the great kite fell headlong in a series of sweeping dives. Its own weight and the aerial force opposed to it which caused it to rise, combined with the strong easterly breeze, had been too much for the great length of cord holding it.

Somehow, the mishap to the kite gave new hope to Mimi. It was as though the side issues had been shorn away, so that the main struggle was thenceforth on simpler lines. She had a feeling in her heart as though some religious chord had been newly touched. It may, of course, have been that with the renewal of the bird voices a fresh courage, a fresh belief in the good issue of the struggle came too. It may also have been that the unaccustomed sounds of the æolian harp woke fresh trains of thought. In the misery of silence, from which they had all for so long suffered, any new train of thought was almost bound to be a boon. As the inrush of birds continued, their wings beating against the crackling rushes, Lady Arabella suddenly grew pale, and almost fainted. With strained ears she listened, and suddenly asked:

'What is that?'

To Mimi, bred in Siam, the sound was strangely like an exaggeration of the sound produced by a snake-charmer. It was doubtless the union of the crackling from the rushes and the weird sound of the harp; but no one asked explanation, and none offered it.

Edgar Caswall was the first to recover from the interruption of the falling kite. After a few minutes he seemed to have quite recovered his *sang froid*, and was able to use his brains to the end which he had in view. Mimi too quickly recovered herself, but from a different cause. With her it was a deep religious conviction that the struggle round her was of the powers of Good and Evil, and that Good was triumphing. The very appearance of the snowy birds, with the cowls of Saint Columba, heightened the impression. With this conviction strong upon her, it is hardly to be wondered at that she continued the strange battle with fresh vigour. She seemed to tower over Caswall, and he to give back before her oncoming. Once again her vigorous passes drove him to the door. He was just going out backward when Lady Arabella, who had been gazing at him with fixed eyes, caught his hand and tried to stop his retrograde movement. She was, however, unable to stop him, and so holding hands they passed out together. As they did so, the strange music which had so alarmed Lady Arabella suddenly stopped. Instinctively they looked toward the tower of Castra Regis, and saw that the workmen had refixed the kite, which had risen again and was beginning to float out to its former station.

As they were looking, the door opened and Michael Watford came into the room. By that time all had recovered their self-possession, and there was nothing out of the common to attract his attention. As he came in, seeing inquiring looks all around him, he said:

'A telegram has come from the Agricultural Department. The new influx of birds is only the annual migration of pigeons from Africa. They say it will soon be over.'

XVII

The Shutting of the Door

The second victory of Mimi Watford made Edgar Caswall more moody than ever. He felt thrown back on himself, and this, superadded to his absorbing interest in the hope of a victory of his will, was now a deep and settled purpose of revenge. The chief object of his animosity was, of course, Mimi, whose will had overcome his, but it was obscured in greater or lesser degree by all who had opposed him. Lilla was next to Mimi in his hate – Lilla, the harmless, tender-hearted, sweet-natured girl, whose heart was so full of love for all things that in it was no room for the passions of ordinary life – whose nature resembled those doves of St Columba, whose colour she wore, whose appearance she reflected. Adam Salton came next – after a gap; for against him Caswall had no direct animosity. He regarded him as an interference, a difficulty in the way to be got rid of or destroyed. The young Australian had been so discreet that the most he had against him was his knowledge of what had been. Caswall did not understand him, and to such a nature as his, ignorance was a cause of alarm, of dread. He resumed his habit of watching the great kite straining at its cord, varying his vigils in this way by a further examination of the mysterious treasures of his house, especially Mesmer's chest. He sat much on the roof of the tower, brooding over all his thwarted hopes. The vast extent of his possessions visible to him at that altitude might, one would have thought, have restored some of his complacency. But not so; the very extent of his ownership thus perpetually brought before him made a fresh sense of grievance. How was it, he thought, that with so much at command that others wished for, he could not achieve the dearest wishes of his heart? It was the very cry of fallible humanity, which, because it yearns for something as yet unattainable, looks on disappointment to his wishes as a personal and malicious wrong done to himself by the powers that be. In this state of intellectual and moral depravity, he found a solace in the renewal of his experiments with the mechanical powers of the kite. This study helped to take him out of himself, to bring his esoteric woes in exoteric thought, even in his bafflements had an element of comfort, though a melancholy one. For quite a couple of weeks he did not see Lady Arabella, who was always on the watch for a chance of meeting him; neither did he see the Watford girls, who studiously kept out of his way. Adam Salton simply marked time, keeping himself ready to deal with anything at his hands that might affect his friends. He heard from Mimi of the last battle of wills, but it had only one consequence of one kind. He got from Ross several more mongooses, including a second king-cobra-killer, which he generally carried with him in its box whenever he walked out.

He constantly saw Sir Nathaniel de Salis, and the two talked over the things that happened, and they remembered all the things that had been before these; so that the two who thought and remembered seemed also to know what would be before it too happened.

Mr Caswall's experiments with the kite went on successfully. Each day he tried the lifting of greater weight, and it seemed almost as if the machine had a sentience of its own, which was increasing with the obstacles placed before it. All this time the kite hung in the sky at an enormous height. The wind was steadily from the north, so the trend of the kite was to the south. All day long, runners of increasing magnitude were sent up. These were only of paper or thin cardboard, or leather, or other flexible materials. The great height at which the kite hung made a great concave curve in the string, so that as the runners went up they made a flapping sound. If one laid a hand or a finger on the string, the sound answered to the flapping of the runner in a sort of hollow intermittent murmur. Edgar Caswall, who was now wholly obsessed by the kite and all belonging to it, found a distinct resemblance between that intermittent rumble and the snake-charming music produced by the pigeons flying through the dry reeds whilst the æolian harp was playing.

One day he made a discovery in Mesmer's chest which he thought he would utilise with regard to the runners. This was a great length of wire 'fine as human hair,' coiled round a finely made wheel, which ran to a wondrous distance freely, and as lightly. He tried this on runners, and found it worked admirably. Whether the runner was alone, or carried something much more weighty than itself, it worked equally well. Also it was strong enough and light enough to easily draw back the runner without undue strain. He tried this a good many times successfully, but it was now growing dusk and he found some difficulty in keeping the runner in sight. So he looked for something heavy enough to keep it still. He placed this, which happened to be the Egyptian image of Bes, on the fine wire which crossed the wooden ledge which protected it. Then the darkness growing, he went indoors and forgot all about it. He had a strange feeling of uneasiness that night – not sleeplessness, for he was conscious of being asleep. At daylight he rose, and as usual looked out for the kite. He did not see it in its usual position in the sky, so took a glass and looked all round the points of the compass. He was more than astonished when presently he saw the missing kite struggling as customary against the controlling string. But it had gone to the further side of the tower, and now hung and strained *against the wind* to the north. He thought it so strange that he determined to investigate the phenomenon, and to say nothing about it in the meantime. In his many travels, Edgar Caswall had been accustomed to use the sextant, and was now an expert in the matter. By the aid of this and other instruments of the kind, he was able to fix the exact position of the kite and the point over which it hung. He was actually startled to find exactly under it – so far as he could ascertain – was Diana's Grove. He had an inclination to take Lady Arabella into his confidence in the matter, but he thought better of it and wisely refrained. For some reason which he did not even try to explain to himself, he was glad of his silence, when on the following morning he found, on looking out, that the point over which the kite then hovered was Mercy Farm. When he had verified this with his instruments, he sat before the window of the tower, looking out and thinking. The new locality was more to his liking than the other; but the why of it puzzled him, all the same. He spent the rest of the day in the turret-room, which he did not leave all day. It seemed to him that he was now drawn by forces which he could not control – of which, indeed, he had no knowledge – in directions which he did not understand, and which were without his own volition. In sheer helpless inability to think the problem out satisfactorily, he called up a servant and told him to tell Oolanga that he wanted to see him at once in the turret-room. The answer came back that the African had not been seen since the previous evening. He was now so irritable that even this small thing upset him. As he was distrait and wanted to talk to somebody, he sent for Simon Chester, who came at once, breathless with hurrying and upset by the unexpected summons. Caswall made him sit down, and when the old man was in a less uneasy frame of mind, he again asked him if he had ever seen what was in Mesmer's chest or heard it spoken of. Chester admitted that he had once in the time of 'the then Mr Edgar' seen the chest open, which, knowing something of its history and guessing more, so upset him that he had fainted. When he recovered, the chest was closed. From that time the then Mr Edgar had never spoken about it again.

When Caswall asked him to describe what he had seen when the chest was open, he got very agitated, and, despite all his efforts to remain calm, he suddenly went off into a dead faint. Caswall summoned servants, who applied the usual remedies. Still the old man did not recover. After the lapse of a considerable time, the doctor who had been summoned made his appearance. A glance was sufficient for him to make up his mind. Still, he knelt down by the old man, and made a careful examination. Then he rose to his feet, and in a hushed voice said:

'I grieve to say, sir, that he has passed away.'

XVIII

On the Track

Those who had seen Edgar Caswall familiarly since his arrival, and had already estimated his cold-blooded nature at something of its true value, were surprised that he took so to heart the death of old Chester. The fact was that not one of them had guessed correctly at his character. Good, simple souls, they had estimated it by their own. They thought, and naturally enough, that the concern which he felt was that of a master for a faithful old servant of his family. They little thought that it was merely the selfish expression of his disappointment that he had lost the only remaining clue to an interesting piece of family history – one which was now and would be for ever wrapped in mystery. Caswall knew enough of the life of his ancestor in Paris to wish to know more fully and more thoroughly all that had been. The period covered by that ancestor's life in Paris was one inviting every form of curiosity. The only one who *seemed* to believe in the sincerity of his sorrow was Lady Arabella, who had her own game to play, and who saw in the *métier* of sympathetic friend a series of meetings with the man she wanted to get hold of. She made the first use of the opportunity the day after old Chester's death; indeed, so soon as ever the news had filtered in through the back door of Diana's Grove. At that meeting, she played her part so well that even Caswall's cold nature was impressed. Oolanga was the only one who did not credit her with at least some sense of fine feeling in the matter. But this was only natural, for he was perhaps the only one who did not know what fine feeling meant. In emotional, as in other matters, Oolanga was distinctly a utilitarian, and as he could not understand anyone feeling grief except for his own suffering pain or for the loss of money, he could not understand anyone simulating such an emotion except for show intended to deceive. He thought that she had come to Castra Regis again for the opportunity of stealing something, and was determined that on this occasion the chance of pressing his advantage over her should not pass. He felt, therefore, that the occasion was one for extra carefulness in the watching of all that went on. Ever since he had come to the conclusion that Lady Arabella was trying to steal the treasure-chest, he suspected nearly everyone of the same design, and, as the night generally is friendly to thieves, he made it a point to watch all suspicious persons and places when night is merging into dawn and dawn into day. At that time, too, the active faculties of the mind are not at their best. Sleep is a factor of carelessness to be counted on, and, as it affects both thief and guardian, may be doubly useful both to learn and to do. The dawn, therefore, generally found him on the watch; and as this was the period also when Adam was engaged on his own researches regarding Lady Arabella, it was only natural that there should be some crossing of each other's tracks. This is what did happen. Nature is a logician, and what does happen is generally what ought to happen if the chances are in its favour. Adam had gone for an early morning survey of the place in which he was interested, taking with him, as usual, the mongoose in its box. He arrived at the gate of Diana's Grove just as Lady Arabella was preparing to set out for Castra Regis on what she considered her mission of comfort. And she, seeing from her window Adam in a mysterious way going through the shadows of the trees round the gate, thought that he must be engaged on some purpose similar to her own. So, quickly making her toilet, she quietly left the house without arousing anybody, and, taking advantage of every shadow and substance which could hide her from him, followed him on his walk. Oolanga, the experienced tracker, followed her, but succeeded in hiding his movements better than she did. He saw that Adam had hung on his shoulder the mysterious box, which he took to contain something valuable. Seeing that Lady Arabella was secretly following him, confirmed this idea. His mind – such as it was – was fixed on her trying to steal, and he credited her at once with making use of this new opportunity. In his walk, Adam went into the grounds of Castra Regis, and Oolanga saw her follow him with great secrecy. He feared to go closer, as now on both sides of him were enemies who might make discovery. Therefore, when he ascertained that Lady Arabella was bound for the Castle, he devoted himself to following her with singleness of purpose. He therefore missed seeing that Adam branched off the track he was following and returned to the high road, and that she, seemingly not interested in his further movements, took her course to the Castle.

That night Edgar Caswall had slept badly. The tragic occurrence of the day was on his mind, and he kept waking and thinking of it. At the early dawn he rose and, wrapping himself in a heavy dressing-gown, sat at the open window watching the kite and thinking of many things. From his room he could see all round the neighbourhood, and as the morning advanced, its revealing light showed him all the little happenings of the place. His life had not had much interest for him in the doings of other people, and he had no distinct idea of how many little things went to make up the sum of an ordinary person's daily life. This bird's-eye view of a community engaged in its ordinary avocations at even this early hour was something new to him. He set himself to watch it as a new interest. His cold nature had no place for sympathy for lesser things than himself; but this was a study to be followed just as he would have watched the movements of a colony of ants or bees or other creatures of little interest individually. He saw, as the light grew more searching, the beginnings of the day for humble people. He saw the movements which followed waking life. He even began to exercise his imagination in trying to understand the why and the wherefore of each individual movement. As soon as he was able to recognise individual houses as they emerged from the mass of darkness or obscurity, he became specially interested in all that went on around him. The two places that interested him most were Mercy Farm and Diana's Grove. At first the movements were of a humble kind – those that belonged to domestic service or agricultural needs – the opening of doors and windows, the sweeping and brushing, and generally the restoration of habitual order. Then the farm servants made preparations for the comfort of the cattle and other animals; the drawing of water, the carrying of food, the alterations of bedding, the removal of waste, and the thousand offices entailed by the needs of living things. To Caswall, self-absorbed, disdainful, selfish egotist, this bird's-eye view was a new and interesting experience of the revolution of cosmic effort. He was so interested with this new experience that the dim hours of the morning slipped by unnoticed. The day was in full flow when he bethought him of his surroundings. He could now distinguish things and people, even at a distance. He could see Lady Arabella, whose blinds had been drawn and windows opened, move about in her room, the white dress which she wore standing out against the darker furniture of her room. He saw that she was already dressed for out of doors. As he looked, he saw her suddenly rise and look out of the window, keeping herself carefully concealed behind the curtain, and, following the direction in which her face was turned, he saw Adam Salton, with a box slung on his shoulder, moving in the shadow of the clump of trees outside her gate. He noticed that she quickly left the room, and in another minute was following Salton down the road in the direction of Castra Regis, carefully avoiding observation as she went. Then he was surprised to see Oolanga's black face and rolling white eyeballs peering out from a clump of evergreens in the avenue. He too was watching.

From his high window – whose height was alone a screen

from the observation of others – he saw the chain of watchers move into his own grounds, and then presently break up, Adam Salton going one way, and Lady Arabella, followed by the nigger, another. Then Oolanga disappeared amongst the trees; but Caswall could see that he was still watching. Lady Arabella, after looking around her, slipped in by the open door, and he could, of course, see her no longer.

Presently, however, he heard a light tap at his door – a tap so light that he only knew it was a tap at all when it was repeated. Then the door opened very, very slowly, and he could see the flash of Lady Arabella's white dress through the opening.

XIX

A Visit of Sympathy

Caswall was genuinely surprised when he saw Lady Arabella, though he need not have been surprised after what had already occurred in the same way. The look of surprise on his face was so much greater than Lady Arabella had expected – though she thought she was prepared to meet anything that might occur – that she stood still, open-eyed in sheer amazement. Cold-blooded as she was and ready for all social emergencies, she was nonplussed how to go on. She was plucky, however, and began to speak at once, although she had not the slightest idea what she was going to say. Had she been told that she was beginning to propose to a man, she would have indignantly denied it.

'I came to offer you my very, very warm sympathy with the grief you have so lately experienced.'

There was a new surprise in his voice as he replied:

'My grief? I am afraid I must be very dull; but I really do not understand.'

Already she felt at a disadvantage, and hesitated as she went on:

'I mean about the old man who died so suddenly – your old . . . retainer.'

Caswall's face relaxed something of its puzzled concentration:

'Oh, him! I hope you don't think he was any source of grief. Why, he was only a servant; and he had overstayed his three-score and ten years by something like twenty years. He must have been ninety, if he was a day!'

'Still, as an old servant . . . !'

Caswall's words were not so cold as their inflection.

'I never interfere with servants. Besides, I never saw or heard of him. He was kept on here merely because he had been so long on the premises, or for some other idiotic reason. I suppose the steward thought it might make him unpopular if he were to be dismissed. All that is nonsense. There is no sentiment in business; if he is a sentimentalist, he has no right to be a steward of another man's property!'

Somehow this tone almost appalled her. How on earth was she to proceed on such a task as hers if this was the utmost geniality she could expect? So she at once tried another tack – this time a personal one:

'I am very sorry I disturbed you. I took a great liberty in the so doing. I am really not unconventional – and certainly no slave to convention. Still there are limits . . . It is bad enough to intrude in this way, and I do not know what you can say or think of the time selected for the intrusion.'

After all, Edgar Caswall was a gentleman by custom or habit, so he rose to the occasion:

'I can only say, Lady Arabella, that you are always welcome at any time when you may deign to honour my house with your presence.'

She smiled at him sweetly as she said:

'Thank you *so* much. You *do* put one at ease. A breach of convention with you makes me glad rather than sorry. I feel that I can open my heart to you about anything.'

Caswall smiled in his turn.

'Such consideration and understanding as yours are almost prohibitive of breach of convention.'

'Try me. If I stand the test it will be another link between us.'

'That, indeed, would be a privilege. Come, I will try you.'

Forthwith she proceeded to tell him about Oolanga and his strange suspicions of her honesty. He laughed heartily and made her explain all the details. He laughed genuinely at her reading of Oolanga's designs, which he did not even dignify with the *sobriquet* of insolence. His final comment was enlightening.

'Let me give you a word of advice: If you have the slightest fault to find with that infernal nigger, shoot him on sight. A swelled-headed nigger with a bee in his bonnet is one of the worst difficulties in the world to deal with. So better make a clean job of it, and wipe him out at once!'

'But what about the law, Mr Caswall?'

'Oh, the law is all right. But even the law doesn't concern itself much about dead niggers. A few more or less of them does not matter. To my mind it's rather a relief!'

'I'm afraid of you,' was her only comment, made with a sweet smile and in a soft voice.

'All right,' he said, 'let us leave it at that. Anyhow, we shall be rid of one of them!'

'I don't love niggers any more than you do,' she said, 'but I suppose one mustn't be too particular where that sort of cleaning up is concerned.'

Then she changed in voice and manner, and asked genially:

'And now tell me, am I forgiven?'

'You are, dear lady – if there be anything to forgive.'

As he spoke, seeing that she had moved to go, he came to the door with her, and in the most natural way accompanied her downstairs. He passed through the hall door with her and down the avenue. As he went back to the house, she smiled to herself and took herself into her own confidence in a whisper:

'Well, that is all right. I don't think the morning has been altogether thrown away.'

And she walked slowly back to Diana's Grove.

When Adam Salton separated from Lady Arabella he continued the walk which he had begun. He followed the line of the Brow, and refreshed his memory as to the various localities. He got home to Lesser Hill just as Sir Nathaniel was beginning breakfast. Mr Salton had gone to Walsall to keep an early appointment; so he was all alone. When breakfast was over, he, seeing in Adam's face that he had something to speak about, followed into the study and shut the door.

When the two men had lighted their pipes, Sir Nathaniel began:

'Since we talked, I have remembered an interesting fact about Diana's Grove that I intended to have mentioned earlier, only that something put it out of my head. It is about the house, not the Grove. There is, I have long understood, some strange mystery about that house. It may be of some interest, or it may be trivial, in such a tangled skein as we are trying to unravel.'

'I am listening. Please tell me all – all you know or suspect, and I shall try to form an opinion. To begin, then, of what sort is the mystery – physical, mental, moral, historical, scientific, occult? Any kind of hint will help me.'

'Well, my dear boy, the fact is, I don't know!'

'Don't know, sir?'

'That is not so strange as it may appear. It may belong to any or all of these categories. Naturally, you are incredulous of such complete ignorance –'

'Oh, sir, I would not doubt you.'

'No, of course not. But all the same, you may not be able to believe or understand. Of course I understand your reluctance to speak of a doubt. But that applies not to the fact, but to the manner of expressing it. Be quite assured. I fully accept your belief in my *bona fides*. But we have difficulties to encounter, barriers to pass; so we must trust each other to speak the truth even if we do not understand it ourselves.'

Adam was silent for a few moments, and then said, with his face brightening:

'I think, sir, the best way we can go on is to tell each other facts. Explanation may bring necessary doubt; but we shall have something to go on!'

'Quite right. I shall try to tell you what I think; but I have not put my thoughts on the subject in sequence, and so you

III

must forgive me if due order is not observed in my narration. I suppose you have seen the house at Diana's Grove?'

'The outside of it; but I have that in my mind's eye, and I can fit into my memory whatever you may call my attention to.'

'Good! Well, I shall just tell you, to begin with, what I know, and I may happen to know more of it than you do.

'The house is very old – probably the first house of some sort that stood there was in the time of the Romans. This was probably renewed – perhaps several times at later periods. The house stands, or, rather, used to stand as it is when Mercia was a kingdom – I do not suppose that the basement was later than the Norman Conquest. Some years ago, when I was President of the Mercian Archæological Society, I went all over it very carefully. This was before it was purchased by Captain March. The house had then been done up so as to be suitable to bring the bride to. The basement is very strange – almost as strong and as heavy as if it was intended to be a fortress. There are a whole series of rooms deep underground. One of them in particular struck me. The room itself is of considerable size, but the masonry is more than massive. In the middle of the room is a sunk well, built up to floor level and evidently going to deep underground. There is no windlass or any trace of there ever having been any – no rope – nothing. Now, we know that even the Romans had wells of immense depth from which the water was lifted by the "old rag rope"; that at Woodhull used to be nearly a thousand feet. Here, then, we have simply an enormously deep well-hole. The door of the room when I saw it was massive, and was fastened with a lock nearly two feet square. It was evidently intended for some kind of protection to something or someone; but no one in those days when I made the visit had ever heard of anyone having been allowed even to see the room. All this is *à propos* of the suggestion of which I have hinted that the well-hole was a way by which the White Worm (whatever it was) went and came. At that time I would have had search made, even excavation if necessary, at my own expense, but all suggestions were met with a prompt and explicit negative. So, of course, I took no further step in the matter. Then it died out of recollection – even of mine.'

'Do you remember, sir,' asked Adam, 'what was the appearance of the room where the well-hole was? And was there furniture – in fact, any sort of thing in the room?'

'I do not remember. It was all very dark – so dark that it was impossible to distinguish anything. The only thing I do remember was a sort of green light – very clouded – very dim, which came up from the well. Not a fixed light, but intermittent and irregular. Quite unlike anything I had ever seen.'

'Do you remember how you got into that room – the well-room? Was there a separate door from outside, or was there any interior room or passage which opened into it?'

'I think there must have been some room with a way into it. I remember going up some steep steps by which I came into the well-room. They must have been worn smooth by long use or something of the kind, for I could hardly keep my feet as I went up. Once I stumbled and nearly fell into the well-hole. I was more careful after that.'

'Was there anything strange about the place – any queer smell, for instance?'

'Queer smell? – yes. Like bilge or a rank swamp.

'It was distinctly nauseating; I remember that when I came out I felt that I had been just going to be physically sick. I shall try back on my visit and see if I can recall any more of what I saw or felt.'

'Then perhaps, sir, later in the day you will kindly tell me anything you may chance to recollect.'

'I shall be delighted, Adam. If your uncle has not returned by then, I shall join you in the study after dinner, and we shall resume this interesting chat.'

XX

The Mystery of 'The Grove'

When Adam, after leaving Lady Arabella, went on his own road outside Castra Regis, Oolanga followed him in secret. Adam had at first an idea, or rather a suspicion, that he was being followed, and looked around a good many times in the hope of making discovery of his pursuer. Not being successful in any of these attempts, he gradually gave up the idea, and accepted the alternative that he had been mistaken. He wondered what had become of the nigger, whom he had certainly seen at first, so kept a sharp look-out for him as he went on his way. As he passed through the little wood outside the gate of Diana's Grove, he thought he saw the African's face for an instant. He knew it must be him; otherwise, there must be a devil wandering loose somewhere in the neighbourhood. So he went deeper into the undergrowth, and followed along parallel to the avenue to the house. He was, in a way, glad that there was no workman or servant about, for he did not care that any of Lady Arabella's people should find him wandering about her grounds at such an hour. Taking advantage of the thickness of the trees, he came close to the house and skirted round it. He was repaid for his trouble, for on the far side of the house, close to where the rocky frontage of the cliff fell away, he saw Oolanga crouched behind the irregular trunk of a great oak. The man was so intent on watching someone, or something, that he did not guard against being himself watched. This suited Adam, for he could thus make scrutiny at will. The thick wood, though the trees were mostly of small girth, threw a heavy shadow, in addition to that made by the early sun being in the east, so that the steep declension, in front of which grew the tree behind which the African lurked, was almost in darkness. Adam drew as close as he could, and was amazed to see a patch of light on the ground before him; when he realised what it was, he was determined more than ever to follow on his quest. The nigger had a dark lantern in his hand, and was throwing the light down the steep incline. The glare showed that the decline, which was in a sort of sunken way, emerged on a series of stone steps, which ended in a low-lying heavy iron door fixed against the side of the house. His mind was in a whirl. All the strange things he had heard from Sir Nathaniel, and all those, little and big, which he had himself noticed, crowded into his mind in a chaotic way, such as marks the intelligence conveyed in a nightmare. Instinctively he took refuge from the possibility of Oolanga seeing him behind a thick oak stem, and set himself down to watch what might occur.

After a very short time it was apparent that the African was trying to find out what was behind the heavy door. There was no way of looking in, for the door fitted tight into the massive stone slabs. The only opportunity for the entrance of light was through a small hole left in the building between the great stones above the door. This hole was much too high up to look through from the ground level. The nigger was so intent on his effort to see beyond this, that Adam found there was no necessity for his own careful concealment, which was a considerable help to him in his task. Oolanga, having tried standing tiptoe on the highest point near, and holding the lantern as high as he could, threw the light round the edges of the door to see if he could find anywhere a hole or a flaw in the metal through which he could obtain a glimpse. Foiled in this, he brought from the shrubbery a plank, which he leant against the top of the door and then climbed up with great dexterity. This did not bring him near enough to the window-hole to look in, or even to throw the light of the lantern through it, so he climbed down and carried the plank back to the place from which he had got it. Then he concealed himself near the iron door and waited, manifestly with the intent of remaining there till someone came near. Presently Lady Arabella, moving noiselessly through the shade, approached the door. When he saw her close enough to touch it, Oolanga stepped forward from his concealment, and said in a whisper, which through the gloom sounded like a hiss:

'I want to see you, missy – soon and secret.'

Her lip curled in scorn as she answered:

'You see me now. What do you want? What is it?'

'You know well, missy. I told you already.'

She turned on him with her eyes blazing, so that the green tint in them shone like emeralds.

'Come, none of that. If there is anything sensible which you may wish to say to me, you can see me here, just where we are, at seven o'clock.'

He made no reply in words, but, putting the backs of his hands together, bent lower and lower still till his forehead touched the earth. She stood stone-still, which seeing, he rose and went slowly away. Adam Salton, from his hiding-place, saw and wondered. In a few minutes he moved from his place and went away home to Lesser Hill, fully determined that seven o'clock would find him in some hidden place behind Diana's Grove.

When he got home he placed the box containing the mongoose in the gun-room. Not having any immediate intention of making use of the animal, it passed quite out of his mind.

At a little before seven Adam stole softly out of the house and took the back-way to the rear of Diana's Grove. The place seemed silent and deserted, so he took the opportunity of concealing himself near the spot whence he had seen Oolanga trying to investigate whatever was concealed behind the iron door. He was quite content when he found himself safely ensconced in his hiding-place. He waited, perfectly still, and at last saw a gleam of white passing soundlessly through the undergrowth. He was not surprised when he recognised the shape and colour of Lady Arabella's dress. She came close and waited, with her face to the iron door. From some place of concealment near at hand Oolanga appeared, and came close to her. Adam noticed with surprised amusement that over his shoulder was his, Adam's, box with the mongoose. Of course the African did not know that he was seen by anyone, least of all by the man whose property he had in possession. Silent-footed as he was, Lady Arabella heard him coming, and turned to meet him. It was somewhat hard to see in the gloom, for, as usual, he was all in black, only his collar and cuffs showing white. The black of his face helped with that of his clothing in eating up what faint light there was. Lady Arabella opened the conversation which ensued between the two:

'I see you are here – what do you want? To rob me, or murder me?'

'No, to lub you!'

This, getting explicit so soon, frightened her a little, and she tried to change the tone:

'Is that a coffin you have with you? If so, you are wasting your time. It would not hold me.'

When a nigger suspects he is being laughed at, all the ferocity of his nature comes to the front; and as the man was naturally of the lowest kind, the usual was to be expected:

'Dis ain't no coffin for nobody. Quite opposite. Dis box is for you. Somefin you lub. Me give him to you!'

Still anxious to keep off the subject of affection, on which she believed him to have become crazed, she made another effort to keep his mind elsewhere:

'Is this why you want to see me?'

He nodded.

She went on: 'Then come round to the other door. And be quiet. I have no particular desire to be seen so close to my own house in conversation with a – a – a nigger like you!'

She had chosen the word of dishonour deliberately. She wished to meet his passion with another kind. Such would, at all events, help to keep him quiet. In the deep gloom she could not see the anger which suffused his face. Rolling eyeballs and grinding teeth are, however, sufficient indices of anger to be decipherable in the dark. She moved round the corner of the house to her right hand. Oolanga was following her, when she stopped him by raising her hand:

'No, not that door,' she said: 'that is not for niggers. The other door will do well enough for that!'

There was such scorn in her voice – scorn carried to a positive quality with malignity added – that the African writhed. Suddenly he stopped as if turned into stone, and said in a voice, whose very quietude was dangerous:

'Gib me your gun.'

Unthinkingly, she pulled out the revolver, which was in her breast, and handed it to him:

'Do you want to kill me?' she said. 'Go on. I am not afraid of you; but, remember, you will swing for it. This is not Benin or Ashantee – this is England!'

He answered in an even voice:

'Don't fear, missee. Gun no to kill nobody. Only to protect myself.'

He saw the wonder in her face, and explained:

'I heard this morning what master said in his room. You no thought I heard. He say, "If you have any fault to find with that infernal nigger" – he said that – "shoot him on sight." Now you call me nigger, speak to me like a dog. And you want me to go into your house by door which I not know. Gun safer now with me. Safer for Oolanga if gun wanted to hurt him.'

'What have you in that box?'

'That is treasure for you, missee. I take care of it, and give it to you when we get in.'

Lady Arabella took in her hand a small key which hung at the end of her watch-chain, and moved to a small door, low down, round the corner, and a little downhill from the edge of the Brow. Oolanga, in obedience to her gesture, went back to the iron door. Adam looked carefully at the mongoose box as the African went by, and was glad to see that it was locked. Unconsciously, as he looked, he fingered the key that was in his waistcoat pocket. When Oolanga was out of sight, Lady Arabella, who had waited quite still, said to him:

'Mr Salton, will you oblige me by coming with me for a few minutes? I have to see that – that coloured person – on a matter of business, and I do not care to see him alone. I shall be happier with a witness. Do you mind obliging me, and coming? It will be very kind of you.'

He bowed, and walked with her to the door round the corner.

XXI

Exit Oolanga

The moment they got out of sight of the nigger, Adam said to Lady Arabella:

'One moment whilst we are alone. You had better not trust that nigger!'

Her answer was crisp and concise:

'I don't.'

'Forewarned is forearmed. Tell me if you will – it is for your own protection. Why do you mistrust him?'

'It is an odd story, but I had better tell you, though, in truth, it is somewhat humiliating – disturbing – to my *amour propre*. He is a thief – at least, so I gather from his readiness to commit a felony. Then you saw that he took my pistol practically under threat. Again he wants to blackmail me – oh I have lots of reasons to distrust him.'

'*He* blackmail *you*! The scoundrel! But how could he hope to do such a thing?'

'My friend, you have no idea of that man's impudence. Would you believe that he wants me to marry him?'

'No!' said Adam incredulously, amused in spite of himself.

'Yes, and wanted to bribe me to do it by sharing a chest of treasure – at least, he thought it was – stolen from Mr Caswall. Why do you yourself distrust him, Mr Salton?'

'I shall give you an instance. Did you notice that box he had slung on his shoulder? That belongs to me. I left it in the gun-room when I went to lunch. He must have crept in and stolen it. Doubtless he thinks that it, too, is full of treasure.'

'He does!'

'How on earth do you know?' asked Adam.

'A little while ago he offered to give it to me – another bribe to accept him. Faugh! I am ashamed to tell you such a thing. The beast!'

'You say he has an appointment to see you?' asked Adam.

'Yes, that was his reason for taking my revolver. He thought perhaps, naturally enough, that I should want to shoot him.'

'You would be all right for anything of that sort with him – if I were on the jury.'

'Oh, he isn't worth it. After all, even a bullet is of *some* little value.'

'Don't alarm yourself, Lady Arabella. You shan't have to do any dirty work. I have a gun!' As he spoke, he took from his pistol pocket a revolver carrying an ounce ball. 'I mention this now to make and keep your mind at rest. Moreover, I am a good and a quick shot.'

'Thanks!'

'By the way, in case there should be any need to know later, what revolver do you use?'

'Weiss of Paris, No. 3,' she answered. 'And you?'

'Smith and Wesson, "The Ready!"'

'You noticed, I suppose, how deftly he stole it?'

Adam was astonished – with quite a new astonishment. It had been so dark that he himself had only been able to see the general movement as Oolanga had annexed the pistol. And yet, this woman had seen the smallest details. She must have wonderful eyes to see in the dark like that!

Whilst they had been speaking, she had opened the door, a narrow iron one well hung, for it had opened easily and closed tightly without any creaking or sound of any kind. Within all was dark; but she entered as freely and with as little misgiving or restraint as if it had been broad daylight. For Adam, there was just sufficient green light from somewhere to see that there was a broad flight of heavy stone steps leading upward; but Lady Arabella, after shutting the door behind her, when it closed tightly without a clang, tripped up the steps lightly and swiftly. For an instant all was dark again, but there came again the faint green light which enabled him to see the outlines of things. Another iron door, narrow like the first and fairly high, led into another large room, the walls of which were of massive stones so closely joined together as to exhibit only one smooth surface. This too presented the appearance of having at one time been polished. On the far side, also smooth like the walls, was the reverse of a great wide but not high iron door. Here there was a little more light, for the high-up aperture over the door opened to the air. Lady Arabella took from her girdle another small key, which she inserted in a tiny keyhole in the centre of a massive lock, which seemed the counterpart and reverse of the lock of some two feet square which Adam had noted on the outside of the door. The great bolt seemed wonderfully hung, for the moment the small key was turned the bolts of the great lock moved noiselessly and the iron doors swung open. On the stone steps outside stood Oolanga with the mongoose box slung over his shoulder. Lady Arabella stood a little on one side and moved back a few feet, and the African, accepting the movement as an invitation, entered in an obsequious way. The moment, however, that he was inside, he gave a quick look around him, and in an oily voice, which made Adam shudder, said with a sniff:

'Much death here – big death. Many deaths. Good, good!'

He sniffed round as if he was enjoying a scent. The matter and manner of his speech were so revolting that instinctively Adam's hand wandered to his revolver, and, with his finger on the trigger, rested satisfied that he was ready for any emergency.

Oolanga seemed more 'crawly' than ever in his movements. He unslung the box from his shoulder and put it on a stone ledge which ran along the side of the room to the right of the iron door, saying as he looked towards Adam:

'I have brought your box, master, as I thought you would want it. Also the key which I got from your servant.'

He laid this beside the box, and began to sniff again with an excellent pretence of enjoyment, raising his nose as he turned his head round as if to breathe all the fragrance he could.

There was certainly opportunity for such enjoyment, for the open well-hole was almost under his nose, sending up such a stench as almost made Adam sick, though Lady Arabella seemed not to mind it at all. It was like nothing that Adam had ever met with. He compared it with all the noxious experiences he ever had – the drainage of war hospitals, of slaughter-houses, the refuse of dissecting rooms. None of these were like it, though it had something of them all, with, added, the sourness of chemical waste and the poisonous effluvium of the bilge of a water-logged ship whereon a multitude of rats had been drowned. However, he was content not to go any further in a search for analogy; it was quite bad enough to have to endure even for a moment, without thinking of it. Besides, he was lost in wonder at a physical peculiarity of Lady Arabella. She seemed to be able to see as well in the dark as in the light. In the gloom under the trees, she had followed every movement of Oolanga. In the Cimmerian darkness of the inner room she had not been for a moment at a loss. It was wonderful. He determined to watch for developments of this strange power – when such should arrive. In the meantime, he had plenty of use for his eyesight to notice what was going on around him. The movements of Oolanga alone were enough to keep his eyes employed. Since the African had laid down the box and the key, Adam had only taken his eyes off it to watch anything seemingly more pressing. He had an idea or an intuition that before long that box would be of overwhelming importance. It was by an intuition also that he grasped his revolver and held it tight. He could see that Oolanga was making up his mind to take some step of which he was at present doubtful.

All in a moment it explained itself. He pulled out from his breast Lady Arabella's pistol and shot at him, happily missing. Adam was himself usually a quick shot, but this time his mind had been on something else and he was not ready. However, he was quick to carry out an intention, and he was not a coward. In another second both men were in grips. Beside them was the dark well-hole, with that horrid effluvium stealing up from its mysterious depths. Adam and Oolanga both had pistols. Lady Arabella, who had not one, was probably the most ready of them all in the theory of shooting, but that being impossible, she made her effort in another way. Gliding forward with inconceivable rapidity, she tried to seize the African; but he eluded her grasp, just missing, in doing so, falling into the mysterious hole. As he swayed back to firm foothold, he turned her own gun on her and shot. Instinctively Adam leaped at her assailant; clutching at each other, they tottered on the very brink. Lady Arabella's anger, now fully awake, was all for Oolanga. She moved forward towards him with her bare hands extended, and had just seized him when the catch of the locked box from some movement from within flew open, and the king-cobra-killer flew at her with a venomous fury impossible to describe. As it seized her throat she caught hold of it, and, with a fury superior to its own, actually tore it in two just as if it had been a sheet of paper. The strength used for such an act must have been terrific. In an instant, it seemed to spout blood and entrails, and was hurled into the well-hole. In another instant she had seized Oolanga, and with a swift rush had drawn him, her white arms encircling him, with her down into the gaping aperture. As the forms flashed by him Adam saw a medley of green and red lights blaze in a whirling circle, and as it sank down into the well a pair of blazing green eyes became fixed, sank lower and lower with frightful rapidity, and disappeared, throwing upward the green light which grew more and more vivid every second. As the light sank into the noisome depths, there came a shriek which chilled Adam's very blood – a prolonged agony of pain and terror which seemed to have no end.

Adam Salton felt that he would never be able to free his mind from the memory of those last dreadful moments. The gloom which surrounded that horrible charnel pit, which seemed to go down to the very bowels of the earth, conveyed from far down the sights and sounds of the nethermost hell. The ghastly fate of the African as he sank down to his terrible doom, his black face growing grey with terror, his white eyeballs, now like veined bloodstone, rolling in the helpless extremity of fear. The mysterious green light was in itself a *milieu* of horror. And through it all the awful cry came up from that fathomless pit, whose entrance was flooded with gouts of fresh blood. Even the death of the fearless little snake-killer – so fierce, so frightful, as if stained with a ferocity which told of no living force above earth, but only of the devils of the pit – was only an incident. Adam was in a state of intellectual tumult, which had no peer in his existence. He tried to rush away from the horrible place; even the baleful green light thrown up through the gloomy well-shaft was dying away as its source sank deeper into the primeval ooze. The darkness was closing in on him in overwhelming density. Darkness in such a place and with such a memory of it! He made a wild rush forward – slipt on the steps in some sticky, acrid-smelling mass that felt and smelt like blood, and, falling forward, felt his way into the inner room, where the well-shaft was not. A faint green light began to grow around him until it was sufficient to see by. And then he rubbed his eyes in sheer amazement. Up the stone steps from the narrow door by which he had entered, glided the thin white-clad figure of Lady Arabella, the only colour to be seen on her being blood-marks on her face and hands and throat. Otherwise, she was calm and unruffled, as when earlier she stood aside for him to pass in through the narrow iron door.

XXII

Self-justification

Adam Salton went for a walk before returning to Lesser Hill; he felt that it might be well, not only to steady his nerves, shaken by the horrible scene, but to get his thoughts into some sort of order, so as to be ready to enter on the matter with Sir Nathaniel. He was a little embarrassed as to telling his uncle, for already affairs had so vastly progressed beyond his original view that he felt a little doubtful as to what would be the old gentleman's attitude when he should hear of the strange events for the first time. He might take umbrage that he had not been consulted or, at least, told of the earlier happenings. At first there had only been inferences from circumstances altogether outside his uncle and his household. Now there were examples of half the crimes in the calendar, of which there was already indisputable proof, together with dark and bloody mysteries, enough to shake the nerves of the whole country-side. Mr Salton would certainly not be satisfied at being treated as an outsider with regard to such things, most of which had points of contact with the interior of his own house. It was with an immense sense of relief that Adam heard that he had telegraphed to the housekeeper that he was detained by business at Walsall, where he would remain for the night; and that he would be back in the morning in time for breakfast. When Adam got home after his walk, he found Sir Nathaniel just going to bed. He did not say anything to him then of what had happened, but contented himself with arranging that they would walk together in the early morning, as he had much to say that would require serious attention.

Strangely enough he slept well, and awoke at dawn with his mind clear and his nerves in their usual unshaken condition. The maid brought up, with his early morning cup of tea, a note which had been found in the letter-box. It was from Lady Arabella, and was evidently intended to put him on his guard as to what he should say about the previous evening. He read it over carefully several times before he was satisfied that he had taken in its full import.

'DEAR MR SALTON, – I cannot go to bed until I have written to you, so you must forgive me if I disturb you, and at an unseemly time. Indeed, you must also forgive me if, in trying to do what is right, I err in saying too much or too little. The fact is that I am quite upset and unnerved by all that has happened in this terrible night. I find it difficult even to write; my hands shake so that they are not under control, and I am trembling all over with memory of the horrors we saw enacted before our eyes. I am grieved beyond measure that I should be, however partially or remotely, a cause of this shock and horror coming on you. Forgive me if you can, and do not think too hardly of me. This I ask with confidence, for since we shared together the danger – the very pangs – of death, I feel that we should be to one another something more than mere friends, that I may lean on you and trust you, assured that your sympathy and pity are for me. A common danger draws, they say, even men together. How close, then, must be the grasp of a poor, weak woman to you, a brave, strong man, and we have together looked into the eyes of Death. You really must let me thank you for the friendliness, the help, the confidence, the real aid at a time of deadly danger and deadly fear which you showed me. That awful man – I shall see him for ever in my dreams. His black, malignant face will shut out all memory of sunshine and happiness. I shall eternally see his evil eyes as he threw himself into that well-hole in a vain effort to escape from the inevitable consequences of his own misdoing. The more I think of it, the more apparent it seems to me that he had premeditated the whole thing – of course, except his own horrible death. He must have intended to murder me, else why *did he take away from me my pistol, the only weapon I had? He probably intended to murder you too. If he had known you had a revolver, he would have tried to get that also, I am sure. You know that women do not reason – we know – that he meant to seize that occasion also for stealing my emeralds.'*

When next Adam saw her he asked:

'How did it all come about?'

She explained simply, sweetly, and seeming to say what she could in the man's favour, but doubly damning him whilst she did so.

'Perhaps you have noticed – of course, I do not blame if you have not; men are not supposed to remember such trivial things – a fur collar I occasionally wear – or rather wore, it is now. It is one of my most valued treasures – an ermine collar studded with emeralds. They are very fine ones, if that is any justification to anything. It is an old collar, with hanging pieces as well as those of the collar proper. I had often seen the nigger's eyes gleam covetously when he looked at it. Unhappily, I wore it yesterday. That may have been the last cause that lured the poor man to his doom. I hope you do not think me altogether hard-hearted. Of course, as a Christian, I ought to forgive my enemies, and this individual was my enemy – he tried to murder me, and did rob me; but it is above my nature to forgive him stealing my emeralds, which were an heirloom, and, though valuable, in themselves of greater value to me from historical association. I mention these things now, for I may not have an opportunity of referring to them again.'

The letter went on:

'I saw a look on your face as the nigger sank into that terrible pit which I – probably wrongly – mistook; but it seemed to me you were surprised at seeing what seemed to be my arms round his neck. The fact is, on the very brink of the abyss he tore the collar from my neck and threw it over his own shoulder. That was the

last thing of him that I saw. When he sank into the hole, I was rushing from the iron door, which I pulled behind me. I am glad to say I did, for it shut out from me the awful sight. When I heard that soul-sickening yell, which marked his disappearance in the deep, darkling chasm, I was more glad than I can say that my eyes were spared the pain and horror which my ears had to endure. Even with the fear and horror which I had so recently endured, and the last awful moments which, although it was through his own act, he had to suffer, I could not forgive him – I have prayed ever since, and will ever pray, for forgiveness of my unchristian spirit. And it may one day come in God's mercy. I have endured the punishment; the sweetness of forgiveness of such an error may come in time. Won't you pray for me too?

'When I tore myself out of the villain's grasp as he sank into the well-hole, I flew upstairs to be safe with you again. But it was not till I was out in the night, and saw the blessed stars gleaming and flashing above me in their myriad beauty, that I could realise what freedom meant. Freedom! Freedom! Not only from that noisome prison-house, which has now such a memory, but from the more noisome embrace of that hideous monster. Whilst I live I shall always thank you for my freedom. You must let me. A woman must sometimes express her gratitude; otherwise it is too great to bear. I am not a sentimental girl who merely likes to thank a man. I am a woman who knows all, of bad as well as good, that life can give. I have known what it is to love and to lose. But there, you must not let me bring any unhappiness into your life. I must live on – as I have lived – alone, and, in addition, bear with other woes the memory of this latest insult and horror. I hardly know which is greatest or worst. In the meantime, I must get away as quickly as possible from Diana's Grove. In the morning I shall go up to town, where I shall remain for a week – I cannot stay longer, as certain business affairs demand my presence here after that time. I think, however, that a week in the rush of busy London, surrounded with multitudes of busy, commonplace people, will help to wear out – I cannot expect total obliteration – the terrible images of the bygone night. When I can sleep easily – which will be, I expect, after a day or two – I shall be fit to return home and take up again the burden which will, I suppose, be always with me.

'I shall be most happy to see you on my return – or earlier, if my good fortune sends you on any errand to London. I shall be in the Great Eastern Hotel. In that busy spot we may forget some of the dangers and horrors we have already shared together. Adieu, and thank you, again and again, for all your kindness and consideration to me.'

Adam was naturally somewhat surprised by this effusive epistle, but he determined to say nothing of it to Sir Nathaniel until he should have thought it well over.

XXIII

An Enemy in the Dark

When Adam Salton met Sir Nathaniel de Salis at breakfast, he was glad that he had taken the time to turn things over in his mind. The result had been that not only was he familiar with the facts of everything, but he had already so far differentiated them that he was now able to arrange them in his own mind according to their values. Thus he was in a position to form his own opinions, and to accept any fact or any reading of it if at all credible; whatever was mysterious, or seemed to be mysterious, he frankly accepted as such, and held it apart in his own mind for future investigation and discussion. The utility of this course was apparent to him when he began to talk to Sir Nathaniel, which was so soon as breakfast was over and they had withdrawn to the study. They were alone, for Mr Salton was not expected home till noon. Breakfast had been a silent function, so it did not interfere in any way with the process of thought.

So soon as the door was closed, Sir Nathaniel began:

'I see, Adam, that much has occurred, and that you have much to tell me and to consult about.'

'That is so, sir. I suppose I had better begin by telling you all I know – all that has happened since I left you last evening?'

'Quite right. Tell me *all*. It will be time enough to look for meanings when we know facts – that is, know them as we understand them to be.'

Accordingly Adam began, and gave him details of all that had been during the previous evening. He confined himself rigidly to the narration of circumstances, taking care not to colour events, even impliedly, by any comment of his own, or any opinion of the meaning of things which he did not fully understand. At first, Sir Nathaniel seemed disposed to ask some questions, but shortly gave this over when he recognised that the narration was well thought over, concise and self-explanatory. Thenceforth, he contented himself with quick looks and glances, easily interpreted or by some acquiescent motions of his hands, when such could be convenient, to emphasise his idea of the correctness of inference. He was so evidently *en rapport* with Adam, that the latter was helped and emboldened when the time came for his statement of beliefs or inferences as to the meanings of things. This suited Adam exactly – and also Sir Nathaniel came to a quicker, more concise, and more thorough understanding than he could otherwise have done. Until Adam ceased speaking, having evidently come to an end of what he had to say with regard to this section of his story, the elder man made absolutely no comment whatever, remaining silent, except on a very few occasions asking an elucidatory question now and then. Even when Adam, having finished the purely narrative part of what he had seen and heard, took from his pocket Lady Arabella's letter, with manifest intention of reading it, he did not make any comment. Finally, when Adam folded up the letter and put it, in its envelope, back in his pocket, as an intimation that he had now quite finished, the old diplomatist carefully made a few notes in his pocket-book. After a careful reconsideration of these, he spoke:

'That, my dear Adam, is altogether admirable. It is a pity that your duty in life does not call for your writing either political or military despatches or judicial reports. For in all of these branches of work you would probably make a name for yourself. I think I may now take it that we are both well versed in the actual facts, and that our further conference had better take the shape of mutual exchange of ideas. Let us both ask questions as they may arise; and I do not doubt that we shall arrive at some enlightening conclusions.'

'Carried *nem. con.* Will you kindly begin, sir? and then we shall have all in order. I do not doubt that with your experience you will be able to dissipate some of the fog which envelops certain of the things which we have to consider.'

'I hope so, my dear boy. For the beginning, then, let me say that Lady Arabella's letter makes clear some things which she intended – and also some things which she did not intend. But, before I begin to comment and draw deductions, let me ask you a few, a very few questions. I know that this is not necessary; but as two men of full age, talking of matters of a peculiarly intimate kind and which may bring in considerations of other persons, it will be as well to have a thorough understanding, leaving nothing to chance or accident!'

'Good again, sir! Please ask away what you will. I shall keep nothing back.'

'Right, my boy. That is the spirit in which to begin a true conference, if it is to have any result.'

The old man pondered a few moments, and then asked a question which had manifestly been troubling him all along, and which he had made up his mind to ask:

'Adam, are you heart-whole, quite heart-whole, in the matter of Lady Arabella?'

He answered at once, each looking the other straight in the eyes during question and answer:

'Lady Arabella, sir, is a very charming woman, and I have hitherto deemed it a privilege to meet her – to talk to her – even – since I am in the confessional – to flirt a little with her. But if you mean to ask if my affections are in any way engaged, I can emphatically answer "No!" – as indeed you will understand when presently I give you the reason.'

'Could you – would you mind giving me the reason now? It will help us to understand what is before us in the way of difficulty, and what to rely on.'

'Certainly, sir. I can speak at once – should like to. My reason, on which I can fully depend, is that I love another woman!'

'That clinches it. May I offer my good wishes, and, I hope, my congratulations?'

'I am proud of your good wishes, sir, and I thank you for them. But, it is too soon for congratulations – the lady does not even know my wishes yet. Indeed, I hardly knew them myself, as definite, till this moment. Under the circumstances, it may be wiser to wait a little.'

'Quite so. A very wise precaution. There can never be any harm in such delay. It is not a check, remember, but only wise forethought. I take it then, Adam, that at the right time I may be allowed to know who the lady is?'

Adam laughed a low, sweet laugh, such as ripples from a happy heart.

'In the matter there need not be an hour's, a minute's delay. I shall be glad to share my little secret with you, sir. We two are, I take it, tiled. So that there come no wrong or harm to anyone else in the enlargement of the bounds of our confidence!'

'None. As for me, I promise absolute discretion and, unless with your own consent, silence.'

Both men smiled and bowed.

'The lady, sir, whom I am so happy as to love and in whom my dreams of life-long happiness are centred, is Mimi Watford!'

'Then, my dear Adam, I need not wait to offer hopes and congratulations. She is indeed a very charming lady. I do not think I ever saw a girl who united in such perfection the qualities of strength of character and sweetness of disposition. With all my heart, I congratulate you. Then I may take it that my question as to your heart-wholeness is answered in the affirmative?'

'Yes; and now, sir, may I ask in turn why the question?'

'Certainly! I asked because it seems to me that we are coming to a point where such questions would be painful – impossible, no matter how great friends we may be.'

Adam smiled.

'You will now understand why I spoke so positively. It is not merely that I love Mimi, but I have reason to look on Lady Arabella as her enemy!'

'Her enemy?'

'Yes. A rank and unscrupulous enemy who is bent on her destruction.'

Sir Nathaniel paused.

'Adam, this grows worse and worse. I do not contradict you; do not doubt. I only want to be sure.'

He went on with an infinite sadness in his tone. 'I wish to God, my dear young friend, that I could disagree with you. I wish also that she or you – if not both – could be kept completely outside this question. But that, I fear, is impossible. Now for a moment let me hark back to your story of last night. It is better that we clear up an important matter right here; we can then get on more easily.'

Adam said nothing, but he looked interrogatively.

The other went on: 'It is about Lady Arabella's letter in connection with last night. And indeed, I almost fear to approach it – not on her account, but on yours and Mimi's.' Adam, when his friend mentioned Mimi so familiarly, felt his heart warm at once from the chill that accompanied the ominous opening of his speech. Sir Nathaniel saw the look and smiled. Then he went over to the door, looked outside it and returned, locking it carefully behind him.

XXIV

Metabolism

'Am I looking grave?' asked Sir Nathaniel inconsequently when he re-entered the room.

'You certainly are, sir.'

'Yes. I ought to be, I feel as if I had on the Black Cap!' Then he went on more calmly: he felt that he should remain calm if he could. Calmness was a necessary condition of what he had to say. 'This is in reality a black-cap affair. We little thought the day we met, only a few days ago, that we should be drawn into such a vortex. Already we are mixed up in robbery, manslaughter, and probably murder, but, a thousand times worse than all the crimes in the calendar, in an affair of gloom and mystery which has no bottom and no end – with magic and demonology, and even with forces of the most unnerving kind, which had their origin in an age when the world was different from the world which we know. We are going back to the origin of superstition – to the age when dragons of the prime tore each other in their slime. I shall come back to all these things presently. We must fear nothing – no conclusion, however improbable, almost impossible it may be. Life and death is at the present moment hanging on our judgment. Life and death not only for ourselves, but for others whom we love. Therefore we must think accurately, go warily, and act boldly. Remember, I count on you as I hope you count on me.'

'I do, with all confidence.'

'Then,' said Sir Nathaniel, 'let us think justly and boldly and fear nothing, however terrifying it may seem. I suppose I am to take as exact in every detail your account of all the strange things which happened whilst you were in Diana's Grove?'

'So far as I know, yes. Of course I may be mistaken in recollection or appreciation, at the time, of some detail or another, but I am certain that in the main what I have said is correct.'

'Then you will not be offended if I ask you, if occasion demands it, to reiterate?'

'I am altogether at your service, sir, and proud to serve.'

'We have one account of what happened from an eye-witness whom we do believe and trust – that is you. We have also another account written by Lady Arabella under her own hand. These two accounts do not agree. Therefore we must take it that one of the two is lying.'

'Apparently, sir.'

'And Lady Arabella is the liar!'

'Apparently – as I am not.'

'We must, therefore, try to find a reason for her lying. She has nothing to fear from Oolanga, who is dead. Therefore the only reason which could actuate her would be to convince someone else that she was blameless. This "someone" could not be you, for you had the evidence of your own eyes. There was no one else present; therefore it must have been an absent person.'

'That seems beyond dispute, sir.'

'There is only one other person whose good opinion she could wish to keep – that person we know to be Edgar Caswall. He is the only one who fills the bill.'

The old man smiled and went on:

'Her lies point to other things besides the death of the African. She evidently wanted it to be accepted that Oolanga had killed the mongoose, but that his falling into the well was his own act. I cannot suppose that she expected to convince you, the eye-witness; but if she wished later on to spread the story, it was at least wise of her to try to get your acceptance of it.'

'That is so!'

Again Sir Nathaniel smiled. He felt that his argument was convincing.

'Then there were other matters of untruth. That, for instance, of the ermine collar embroidered with emeralds. If an understandable reason be required for this, it would be to draw attention away from the green lights which were seen in the room, and especially in the well-hole. Any unprejudiced person would accept the green lights to be the eyes of a great snake such as tradition pointed to living in the well-hole. In fine, therefore, Lady Arabella wanted the general belief to be that there was no snake of the kind in Diana's Grove. Let us consider this. For my own part, I don't believe in a partial liar. This art does not deal in veneer; a liar is a liar right through. Self-interest may prompt falsity of the tongue; but if one prove to be a liar, nothing that he says can ever be believed. This leads us to the conclusion that because she said or inferred that there was no snake, we should look for one – and expect to find it, too.

'Now let me here digress. I live, and have for many years lived, in Derbyshire, a county more celebrated for its caves than any other county in England. I have been through them all, and am familiar with every turn of them; as also with other great caves in Kentucky, in France, in Germany, and a host of places – with all, in fact, of these very deep caves of narrow aperture which are so valued by intrepid explorers, who descend narrow gullets of abysmal depth and sometimes never return. In many of the caverns in the Peak I am convinced that some of the smaller passages were used in primeval times as the lairs of some of the great serpents of legend and tradition. It may have been that such caverns were formed in the usual geologic way – bubbles or flaws in the earth's crust – which were later used by the monsters of the period of the young world. It may have been, of course, that some of them at least were worn originally by water; but in time they all found a use when suitable for living monsters. Such may be – I only give it as a suggestion for thought.

'This brings us to another point more difficult to accept and understand than any other requiring belief in a base not usually accepted or indeed entered on: whether such abnormal growths, as must have been in the case of the earlier inhabitants, could have ever changed in their nature. Some day the study of metabolism may progress so far as to enable us to accept structural changes proceeding from an intellectual or moral base. If such ever be probable, we may lean towards a belief that great animal strength may be a sound base for changes of all sorts. If this be so, what could be a more fitting subject than primeval monsters whose strength was such as to allow a survival of thousands of years? Mind, I do not assert, but only suggest it as a subject for thought. We do not know yet if brain can increase and develop independently of other parts of living structure. This again I only suggest as a subject for thought. My reason for doing so will be presently touched on.

'After all, the mediæval belief in the Philosopher's Stone which could transmute metals has its counterpart in the accepted theory of metabolism which changes living tissue. Why, the theory has been put forward by a great scientist that the existence of radium and its products proves the truth of the theory of transmutation of metal. In an age of investigation like our own, when we are returning to science as the base of wonders – almost of miracles, – we should be slow to refuse to accept facts, however impossible they may seem to be. We are apt to be hide-bound as to theory when we begin to learn. In a more enlightened age, when the base of knowledge has not only been tested but broadened, perhaps we shall come to an understanding of that marvellous definition of "faith" by St Paul: "the substance of things hoped for; the evidence of things unseen."

'Now, my dear Adam, pardon these digressions into matters which are as far from that with which we are concerned as are the Poles from each other; but even these may help us to accept, even if they cannot help to elucidate. We are in a quagmire, my boy, as vast and as deep as that in which the monsters of the geologic age found shelter and perhaps advance.

'Now, I think we have talked enough for the present of many things hard to understand. It will be better, perhaps, if we lay them aside for the present. When you and I resume this chat we shall be more clear-headed to accept evident deductions, more resolute and better satisfied to act on them. Let us adjourn till to-morrow.'

XXV

The Decree

When after breakfast the next morning Sir Nathaniel and
Adam met, the elder man, after inquiring how his companion
had slept, and satisfying him as to his own experiences in the
same matter, said:

'I think we may take it that we are both calm of nerve
and brain, and that we are fit to resume so momentous a
subject as that deferred. Suppose we begin by taking a problematical case of fact based on our conclusions of yesterday.
Let us suppose a monster of the early days of the world – a
dragon of the prime – of vast age running into thousands of
years, to whom had been conveyed in some way – it matters
not – a brain of even the most rudimentary kind – some
commencement, however small, just sufficient for the beginning of growth. Suppose the monster to be of incalculable
size and of a strength quite abnormal – a veritable incarnation
of animal strength. Suppose this animal was allowed to remain
in one place, thus being removed from accidents of interrupted development: might not, would not this creature in
process of time – ages, if necessary – have that rudimentary
intelligence developed? There is no impossibility in all this. It
is only the natural process of evolution; not taken from genii
and species, but from individual instances. Atmosphere, which
is the condition of life – vegetable and animal, – is an immediate product of size. In the beginning, the instincts of animals
are confined to alimentation, self-protection, and the multi-
plication of their species. As time goes on and the needs of
life become more complex, power follows need. Here let me
make another digression. We are prepared already for abnor-

mal growth – it is the corollary of normal growth. We have been long accustomed to consider growth as applied almost exclusively to size in its various aspects. But Nature, who has no doctrinaire ideas, may equally apply it to concentration. A developing thing may expand in any given way or form. Now, it is a scientific law that increase implies gain and loss of various kinds; what a thing gains in one direction it may lose in another. In mechanics direction is a condition of the increase or limitation of speed or force. Why not apply this more widely? May it not be that Mother Nature may deliberately encourage decrease as well as increase – that it may be an axiom that what is gained in concentration is lost in size? Take, for instance, monsters tradition has accepted and localised, such as the Worm of Lambton or that of Spindleston Heugh. If such a one were, by its own process of metabolism, to change much of its bulk for a little intellectual growth, we should at once arrive at a new class of creature, more dangerous, perhaps, than the world has ever had any experience of – a force which can think, which has no soul and no morals, and therefore no acceptance of responsibility. A worm or snake would be a good illustration of this, for it is cold-blooded and therefore removed from the temptations which often weaken or restrict warm-blooded creatures. If, for instance, the Worm of Lambton – if such ever existed – were guided to its own ends by an organised intelligence capable of expansion, what form of creature could we imagine which would equal it in potentialities of evil? Why, such a being would devastate a whole country. Now, all these things require much thought, and we want to apply the knowledge usefully, and we should therefore be exact. Would it not be well to have another "easy," and resume the subject later in the day?'

'I quite agree, sir. I am all in a whirl already; and I want to attend carefully to what you say; so that I may try to digest it.'

Both men seemed fresher and better for the 'easy,' and

when they met in the afternoon each of them had, out of his thought, something to contribute to the general stock of information. Adam, who was by nature of a more militant disposition than his elderly friend, was glad to see that the conference at once assumed a practical trend. Sir Nathaniel recognised this, and, like an old diplomatist, turned it to present use.

'Tell me now, Adam, what is the outcome, in your own mind, of our previous conversations?'

He answered at once:

'That the whole difficulty already assumes practical shape; but with added dangers that at first I did not dream of.'

'What is the practical shape, and what are the added dangers? I am not disputing, but only trying to clear my own ideas by the consideration of yours –'

Sir Nathaniel waited, so he went on:

'Will it bore you, sir, if I put in order of an argument your own ideas as seen by me?'

'Not at all; I should like it if it will help to clear my own mind.'

'Then I will begin with your argument – only in general, not in detail. And please bear in mind, sir, that I am trying to state not so much what you said as the ideas conveyed to my mind – possibly erroneously, – but in the honest belief to comprehend thoroughly.'

'Go on, my dear boy, do not fear. I shall understand and, if necessary, make allowance.'

So Adam went on:

'In the past, in early days of the world, there were monsters who were so vast that they could exist thousands of years. Some of them must have overlapped the Christian era. They may have progressed intellectually in process of time. If they had in any way so progressed, or got even the most rudimentary form of brain, they would be the most dangerous things that ever were in the world. Tradition says that one of these monsters lived in the Marsh of the East and came up to a cave in Diana's Grove which was also called the Lair of the White Worm. Such creatures may have grown down (small) as well as up (long). They *may* have grown into, or something like, human beings. Lady Arabella March is of snake nature. She has committed crimes to our knowledge. She retains something of the vast strength of her primal being – can see in the dark – has eyes of a snake. She used the nigger, and then dragged him through the snake's hole down to the swamp; she is intent on evil, and hates some we love. Result . . .'

'Yes, the result you arrive at?'

'First, Mimi Watford should be taken away at once – I should suggest West Australia. And then –'

'Yes?'

'The monster must be destroyed.'

'Bravo! That is a true and fearless conclusion. At whatever cost, it must be carried out.'

'At once?'

'Soon, at all events. That creature's very existence is a danger. Her presence in this neighbourhood makes the danger immediate.'

As he spoke, Sir Nathaniel's mouth hardened and his eyebrows came down till they met. There was no doubting his concurrence in the resolution, or his readiness to help in carrying it out. But he was an elderly man with much experience and knowledge of law and diplomacy. It seemed to him to be a stern duty to prevent anything irrevocable taking place till it had been thought out and all was ready. There were all sorts of legal cruxes to be thought out, not only regarding the taking of life, even of a monstrosity in human form, but also of property. Lady Arabella, be she woman or snake or devil, owned the ground she moved in, according to British law, and the law is jealous and swift to avenge wrongs done within its ken. Within three hundred years the law has accepted facts and evidence that would not be received in later years by school children. All such difficulties should be – must be – avoided for Mr Salton's sake, for Adam's own sake, and, most of all, for Mimi Watford's sake. Before he spoke again, Sir Nathaniel had made up his mind that he must try to postpone decisive action until the circumstances depended on – which, after all, were only problematical – should have been tested satisfactorily, one way or another. When he did speak, Adam at first thought that his friend was wavering in his intention, or 'funking' the responsibility. He could have no such thought regarding Adam. That young man's strong, mobile face was now as set as flint. His eyes were full of fire, non-blazing fire, but slumbrous, which is much more indicative of danger. His brows were in a straight line across his face, and his eyes in parallel course. As to purpose, he was fixed; the only question with him was – when! However, his respect for Sir Nathaniel was so great that he would not act or even come to a conclusion on a vital point without his sanction.

He came close and almost whispered in his ear:

'Will you speak with me of this again – say, when my uncle has gone to bed, and we shall be undisturbed?'

Sir Nathaniel nodded. They had both determined to wait.

XXVI

A Living Barbette

When Mr Salton had retired for the night, Adam and Sir Nathaniel with one accord moved to the study. Things went with great regularity at Lesser Hill, so they knew that there would be no interruption to their talk.

When their cigars were lighted, Sir Nathaniel said:

'I hope, Adam, that you do not think me either slack or changeable of purpose. I really am not so, and I mean to go through this business to the bitter end – whatever it may be. Be satisfied that my first care is, and shall be, the protection of Mimi Watford. To that I am pledged; my dear boy, we who are interested are all in some form of the same danger. That monster out of the pit hates and means to destroy us all – you and me certainly, and probably your uncle. We are just on the verge of stormy times for us all. I wanted especially to talk with you to-night, for I cannot help thinking that the time is fast coming – if it has not come already – when we must take your uncle into confidence. It was one thing when fancied evils threatened, but now he as well as the rest of us is marked for death; and it is only right that he should know all.'

'I am with you, sir. Things have changed since we agreed to keep him out of the trouble. Now we dare not; consideration for his feelings might cost him his life. It is a duty we have – and no light or pleasant one, either. I have not a shadow of doubt that he will want to be one with us in this. But remember, we are his guests, in his house; and his name, his honour have to be thought of as well as his safety.

'I am still with you – to the death. Only, if there be any

special danger to him, let me bear, or at any rate share it.'

'All shall be as you wish, Adam. We need say no more of that. We are at one. And now as to practicability. What are we to do? We cannot manifestly take and murder Lady Arabella off-hand. Therefore we shall have to put things in order for the killing, and in such a way that we may not be taxed with a base crime. That is why I suggested waiting till we have some definite and complete proof.'

Adam stood up, and his voice rang as he said heartily:

'You are quite right, sir, as usual. We must be at least as exact as if we were in a law court. I see that.'

Sir Nathaniel acquiesced in such a hearty way as to set his young companion's mind at rest.

Adam sat down again and resumed the conversation, using an even, reflective tone which made the deliberation altogether useful:

'It seems to me, sir, that we are in an exceedingly tight place. Our first difficulty is to know where to begin. Our opponent has pretty well all the trumps. I never thought this fighting an antediluvian monster was such a complicated job. This one is a woman, with all a woman's wisdom and wit, combined with the heartlessness of a *cocotte* and the want of principle of a suffragette. She has the reserved strength and impregnability of a diplodocus. We may be sure that in the fight that is before us there will be no semblance of fair-play. Also that our unscrupulous opponent will not betray herself!'

Sir Nathaniel commented on this:

'That is so. But being of feminine species, she probably will over-reach herself. That is much more likely – more in woman's way. Now, Adam, it strikes me that, as we have to protect ourselves and others against feminine nature, our strong game will be to play our masculine against her feminine. Men can wait better than women.'

He laughed a mirthless laugh that was all from the brain and had no heart at all, and went on:

147

'You must remember that this female has had thousands of years' experience in waiting. As she stands, she will beat us at that game.'

For answer Adam began preparing his revolver, which was at half-cock:

'There is always a quick way of settling differences of that kind!' was all he said; but Sir Nathaniel understood and again uttered a warning:

'How are differences to be settled with a creature of that kind? We might as well fight with a barbette; she is invulnerable so far as physical harm at our hands is concerned.'

'Even barbettes get occasionally blown up!' said Adam.

'Ah! barbettes aren't alive all over and, so far as we know, self-recuperative. No! we must think out some plan to have ready if all else should fail. We had better sleep on it. She is a thing of the night; and the night may give us some ideas.'

So they both turned in.

Adam knocked at Sir Nathaniel's door in the gray of the morning, and, on being bidden, came into the room. He had several letters unclosed in his hand. Sir Nathaniel sat up in bed.

'Well!'

'I should like to read you a few letters, but, of course, shall not send them unless you approve. In fact' – this with a smile and a blush – 'there are several things which I want to do; but I hold my hand and my tongue till I have your approval.'

'Go on!' said the other kindly. 'Tell me all, and count at any rate on my sympathy and on my approval and help if I can see my way.'

Accordingly Adam proceeded:

'When I told you the conclusions I had arrived at, I put in the foreground that Mimi Watford should for the sake of her own safety be removed – to West Australia, I suggested, – and that the monster which had wrought all the harm should be destroyed.'

'Yes, I remember.'

'To carry this into practice, sir, one preliminary is required – unless harm of another kind is to be faced.'

Sir Nathaniel looked as if he had on his reflecting cap. Then he proceeded, taking up the other's argument:

'Before she goes to West Australia, or indeed to anywhere else, Mimi should have some protector which all the world would recognise. The only form of this safety recognised by convention is marriage!'

'Yes, sir. I see you realise!'

Sir Nathaniel smiled in a fatherly way.

'To marry, a husband is required. And that husband should be you.'

'Yes, yes.'

'And that marriage should be immediate and secret – or, at least, not spoken of outside ourselves . . . And now I must ask you a somewhat delicate question! Would the young lady be agreeable to that proceeding?'

'I do not know, sir!'

'You do not know? Then how are we to proceed?'

'I suppose we – or one of us – must ask her. That one must be myself – and I am ready.'

'Is this a sudden idea, Adam, a sudden resolution?'

'A sudden resolution, sir, but not a sudden idea. The resolution is sudden because the need is sudden and imperative. If I were to speak in hyperbole, I could say that the idea is as old as Fate, and that the resolution was waiting before the beginning of the world!'

'I am glad to hear it. I hope it will turn out that the coming of the White Worm has been a blessing in disguise. But now, if things have to be hurried on like this, what is to be the sequence of events?'

'First, that Mimi should be asked to marry me. If she agrees, all is well and good. The sequence is obvious.'

'And is to be kept a secret amongst ourselves?'

Adam answered at once:

'I want no secret, sir, except for Mimi's good. For myself, I should like to go and shout it out on the house-tops! But I see that we must be discreet. Untimely knowledge to our enemy might work incalculable harm.'

'And how would you suggest, Adam, that we could combine the momentous question with secrecy?'

Here Adam grew red and moved uneasily. Then with a sudden rush he spoke:

'Someone must ask her – as soon as possible!'

'And that someone?'

'I have been thinking the matter over, sir, since we have been here. It requires expedition to achieve safety, and we shall all have to do as duty requires.'

'Certainly. And I trust that none of us shall shirk such a duty. But this is a concrete thing. We may consider and propose in the abstract, but the action is concrete – who, again, is to be the "someone"? Who is to ask her?'

'I thought that you, sir, would be so good!'

'God bless my soul! This is a new kind of duty to take on one – at my time of life. Adam, I hope you know that you can count on me to help in any way I can!'

'I have counted on you, sir, when I ventured to make such a suggestion. I can only ask, sir,' he added, 'that you will be more than ever kind to me – to us, and look on the painful duty as a voluntary act of grace prompted by kindness and affection.'

Sir Nathaniel said in a meek but not a doubting voice:

'Painful duty!'

'Yes,' said Adam boldly. 'Painful to you, though to me it would be all joyful.'

'Yes, I understand!' said the other kindly.

Then he went on: 'It is a strange job for an early morning! Well, we all live and learn. I suppose the sooner I go the better. Remember, I am in your hands and shall do just what you wish, and shall try to do it just as you wish. Now you had better write a line for me to take with me. For, you see, this is to be a somewhat unusual transaction, and it may be embarrassing to the lady, even to myself. So we ought to have some sort of warrant, something to show on after-thought, that we have been all along mindful of her feelings. It will not do to take acquiescence for granted – although we act for her good. You had better write the letter to have ready, and I had better not know what is in it – except the main purpose of the introducing the subject. I shall explain fully as we go along anything that she may wish.'

'Sir Nathaniel, you are a true friend; and I am right sure that both Mimi and I shall be grateful to you for all our lives – however long or however short they may be!'

So the two talked it over and agreed as to points to be borne in mind by the ambassador. It was striking six when Sir Nathaniel left the house, Adam seeing him quietly off.

As the young man followed him with wistful eyes – almost jealous of the privilege which his kind deed was about to bring him, he felt that his own heart was in his friend's breast.

XXVII

Green Light

The memory of that morning was like a dream to all those concerned in it. Sir Nathaniel had a confused recollection of detail and sequence, though the main facts stood out in his memory boldly and clearly. Adam Salton's recollection was of an illimitable time filled with anxiety, hope, and chagrin, all unified and dominated by a sense of the slow passage of time and accompanied by vague nebulous fears. Mimi could not for a long time think at all or recollect anything, except that Adam loved her and was saving her from a terrible danger. In the bitter time itself, whilst she was learning those truths she found her own heart. When she had time to think, later on, she wondered how or when she had any ignorance of the facts that Adam loved her and that she loved him with all her heart. Everything, every recollection however small, every feeling, seemed to fit into those elemental facts as though they had all been moulded together. The main and crowning recollection was her saying goodbye to Sir Nathaniel and entrusting to him loving messages straight from her heart to Adam Salton, and of his bearing when with an impulse which she could not check – and did not want to – she put her lips to his and kissed him. Later, when she was alone and had time to think, it was a passing grief to her that she would have to be silent, for a time, to Lilla on the happy events of that strange early morning mission.

She had, of course, agreed to keep all secret until Adam should give her leave to speak.

The advice and assistance of Sir Nathaniel de Salis was a great help to Adam Salton in carrying out his idea of marrying Mimi Watford without publicity. He went with him to London, and, with his knowledge and influence, the young man got the licence of the Archbishop of Canterbury for a private marriage. Sir Nathaniel then took him to live in his own house till the marriage should have been solemnised. All this was duly done, and, the formalities having been fixed, Adam and Mimi were married at Doom.

Adam had tried to arrange that he and his wife should start for Australia at once; but the first ship to suit them did not start for ten days. So he took his bride off to the Isle of Man for the interim. He wished to place a stretch of sea between Mimi and the White Worm, that being the only way to ensure protection for his wife. When the day for departure arrived, they went from Douglas in the *King Orrey* to Liverpool. On arrival at the landing-stage, they drove to Congleton, where Sir Nathaniel met them and drove them at once to Doom, taking care to avoid any one that he knew on the journey. They travelled at a great pace and arrived before dusk at Doom Tower.

Sir Nathaniel had taken care to have the doors and windows shut and locked – all but the door used for their entry. The shutters were up and the blinds down. Moreover, heavy curtains were drawn across the windows. When Adam commented on this, Sir Nathaniel said in a whisper:

'Wait till we are alone, and I shall tell you why this is done; in the meantime not a word or a sign. You will approve when we have had a talk together.'

They said no more on the subject till, when after dinner, they were ensconced alone in Sir Nathaniel's study, which was on the top storey of the tower. Doom Tower was a lofty structure, seated on an eminence high up in the Peak. The top of the tower commanded a wide prospect ranging from the hills above the Ribble to the near side of the Brow, which marked the northern bound of ancient Mercia. It was of the early Norman period, less than a century younger than Castra Regis. The windows of the study were barred and locked, and heavy dark curtains closed them in. When this was done not a gleam of light from the tower was seen from outside.

When they were alone Sir Nathaniel spoke, keeping his voice to just above a whisper:

'It is well to be more than careful. In spite of the fact that your marriage was kept secret, as also your temporary absence, both are known.'

'How? To whom?'

'How, I know not; but I am beginning to have an idea. To whom is it the worst? Where it is most dangerous.'

'To her?' asked Adam in momentary consternation.

Sir Nathaniel shivered perceptibly as he answered:

'The White Worm – yes!'

Adam noticed that from thence on he never spoke amongst themselves of Lady Arabella otherwise, except when he wished to divert the suspicion of others or cover up his own. Then, having opened the door, looked outside it and closed it again, he put his lips to Adam's ear and whispered even more softly:

'Not a word, not a sound to disturb your wife. Her ignorance may be yet her protection. You and I know all and shall watch. At all costs, she must have no suspicion!'

Adam hardly dared to breathe. He put his finger to his lips and at last said under his breath:

'I shall do whatever you tell me to, and all the thanks of my heart are to you!'

Sir Nathaniel switched off the electric light, and when the room was pitch dark he came to Adam, took him by the hand, and led him to a seat set in the southern window. Then he softly drew back a piece of the curtain and motioned his companion to look out.

Adam did so, and immediately shrank back as though his eyes had opened on pressing danger. His companion set his mind at rest by saying in a low voice, not a whisper:

'It is all right; you may speak, but speak low. There is no danger here – at present!'

Adam leaned forward, taking care, however, not to press his face against the glass. What he saw would not under ordinary circumstances have caused concern to anybody but to him. With his knowledge, it was simply appalling – though the night was now so dark that in reality there was little to be seen.

On the western side of the tower stood a grove of old trees of forest dimensions. They were not grouped closely, but stood a little apart from each other, producing the effect of a row widely planted. Over the tops of them was seen a green light, something like the danger signal at a railway-crossing. At the height of the tower, the light was not enough to see anything even close to it. It seemed at first quite still; but presently, when Adam's eye became accustomed to it, he could see that it moved a little as if trembling. This at once recalled to Adam's mind all that had been. He seemed to see again the same duplicate light quivering above the well-hole in the darkness of that inner room at Diana's Grove – to hear again Oolanga's prolonged shriek, and to see the hideous black face, now grown gray with terror, disappear into the impenetrable gloom of the mysterious orifice. Instinctively he laid his hand on his revolver, and stood up ready to protect his wife. Then, seeing that nothing happened, and that the light and all outside the tower remained the same, he softly pulled the curtain over the window, and, rising up, came and sat down beside Sir Nathaniel who looked up for a moment with a sharp glance, and said in an even voice:

'I see you understand. I need say nothing.'

'I understand!' he replied in the same quiet tone.

Sir Nathaniel switched on the light again, and in its comforting glow they began to talk freely.

XXVIII

At Close Quarters

'She has diabolical cunning,' said Sir Nathaniel. 'Ever since you left, she has ranged along the Brow and wherever you were accustomed to frequent. I have not heard whence the knowledge of your movements came to her, nor have I been able to learn any data whereon I have been able to found an opinion. She seems to have heard both of your marriage and your absence; but I gather, by inference, that she does not know where you and your wife are, or of your return. So soon as the dusk falls, she goes out on her rounds, and before dawn covers the whole ground round the Brow, and away up into the heart of the Peak. I presume she doesn't condescend to rest or to eat. This is not to be wondered at in a lady who has been in the habit of sleeping for a thousand years at a time, and of consuming an amount of food at a sitting which would make a moderate-sized elephant kick the beam. However, be all that as it may, her ladyship is now nightly on the prowl, and in her own proper shape that she used before the time of the Romans. It certainly has great facilities for the business on which she is now engaged. She can look into windows of any ordinary kind. Happily, this house is beyond her reach, especially if she wishes – as she manifestly does – to remain unrecognised. But, even at this height, it is wise to show no lights, lest she might learn something of even our presence or absence.'

Here Adam stood up again and spoke out.

'Would it not be well, sir, if some one of us should see this monster in her real shape at close quarters? I am willing to run the risk – for I take it there would be no slight risk in the doing. I don't suppose anyone of our time has seen her close and lived to tell the tale.'

Sir Nathaniel rose and held up an expostulatory hand as he said:

'Good God, lad! what are you suggesting? Think of your wife and all that is at stake.'

Adam interrupted:

'It is of my wife that I think, for her sake that I am willing to risk whatever is to be risked. But be assured I shall not drag her into it – or even tell her anything to frighten her. When I go out she shall not know of it.'

'But if you mention the matter at all she will suspect.'

'The fact of the snake being on the look-out must be told to her to warn her, but I will do it in such a way as not to create any undue suspicion regarding herself. Indeed, I had made up my mind as to what to say some time ago, when it was borne in on me to warn her about keeping the place dark. With your permission, I shall go now and tell her of that, and then when I return here you might lend me a key so that I can let myself in.'

'But do you mean to go alone?'

'Certainly. It is surely enough for one person to run the risk.'

'That may be, Adam, but there will be two.'

'How so! You surely don't mean that Mimi should come with me?'

'Lord, no! But if she knew you were going she would be sure to want to go too; so be careful not to give her a hint.'

'Be sure I shall not. Then who is to be the other?'

'Myself! You do not know the ground; and so would be sure to get into trouble. Now, I know every inch of it, and can guide you how to go safely to any place you want. Adam, this is an exceptional thing – yielding to no law of action that any of us ever heard of. As to danger! what of that to you and me when your wife's safety is concerned! I tell you, no forlorn hope that either of us ever heard of has a hundredth part of the danger we are running into. Yet I do it with all my heart – even as you do.'

Adam made a low bow as to one worthy of all honour, but he said no word more on the subject. After he had switched off the light he then peeped out again through the window and saw where the green light still hung tremblingly above the trees. Before the curtain was drawn and the lights put up again, Sir Nathaniel said:

'So long as her ladyship does not know whereabout we are, we shall have as much safety as remains to us; so, then, bear in mind that we cannot be too careful.'

When the two men slipped out by the back door of the house, they walked cautiously along the avenue which trended towards the west. Everything was pitch dark – so dark that at times they had to feel their way by the borders and palings and tree-trunks. They could still see, seemingly far in front of them and high up, the baleful dual light which at the height and distance seemed like a faint line. As they were now on the level of the ground, the light seemed infinitely higher than it had looked from the top of the tower; it actually seemed now, when it trembled, to move amongst the stars. At the sight Adam's heart fell; the whole danger of the desperate enterprise which he had undertaken burst upon him. But shortly this feeling was followed by another which restored him to himself – a fierce hate and loathing, and a desire to kill, such as he had never experienced or even dreamt of.

They went on for some distance on a level road fairly wide, from which the green light was still visible. Here Sir Nathaniel spoke softly again, placing his lips to Adam's ear for safety:

'We must be very silent. We know nothing whatever of this creature's power of either hearing or smelling, though we presume that both are of no great strength. As to seeing, we may presume the opposite, but in any case we must try to keep in the shade or hidden behind the tree-trunks. The slightest error would be fatal to us.'

Adam made no answer. He only nodded, in case there should be any chance of the monster seeing the movement.

After a time, that seemed interminable, they emerged from the circling wood. It was like coming out into sunlight by comparison with the misty blackness which had been around them. There was actually some light – enough to see by, though not sufficient to distinguish things at a distance or minutely. Naturally Adam's eyes sought the green light in the sky. It was still in about the same place, but its surroundings were more visible. It now was at the summit of what seemed to be a long white pole, near the top of which were two pendant white masses like rudimentary arms. The green light, strangely enough, did not seem lessened by the surrounding starlight, but had a clearer effect and a deeper green. Whilst they were carefully regarding this – Adam with the aid of a folding opera-glass – their nostrils were assailed by a horrid stench – something like that which rose from the well-hole in Diana's Grove. This put them in mind of the White Worm, and they tried to examine its position as seen against the sky in the faint starlight. By degrees, as their eyes got and held the right focus, they saw an immense towering mass that seemed snowy white. It was tall and wonderfully thin. The lower part was hidden by the trees which lay between, but they could follow the tall white shaft and the duplicate green lights which topped it. As they looked there was a movement: the shaft seemed to bend and the line of green light descended amongst the trees. They could see the green light twinkle as it passed through the obstructing branches. Seeing where the head of the monster was, the two men ventured a little further forward, and, a propitious ray of moonlight helping, saw that the hidden mass at the base of the shaft was composed of vast coils of the great serpent's body, forming a substratum or base from which the upright mass rose. As still they looked, this lower mass moved, the glistening folds catching the moonlight, and they could see the monster's progress was along the ground. It was coming towards them at a swift pace, so instinctively they both turned and ran, taking care as they went to make as little noise as possible, either by their footfalls or by disturbing the undergrowth close to them. They never stopped or paused till they saw before them the high dark tower of Doom. Quickly they entered, locking the door behind them. They did not need to talk, with such a horrid memory behind them and still accompanying them. So in the dark they found their separate rooms and went to bed.

XXIX

In the Enemy's House

Sir Nathaniel was in the library next morning after breakfast when Adam came to him carrying a letter. As he entered the room he said:

'Her ladyship doesn't lose any time. She has begun work already!'

Sir Nathaniel, who was writing at a table near the window, looked up.

'What is it?' said he.

Adam held out to him the letter he was carrying. It was in a blazoned envelope.

'Ha!' said Sir Nathaniel, 'from Lady Arabella! I expected something of the kind.'

'But, sir,' said Adam, 'how could she have known we were here? She didn't know last night.'

'I don't think we need trouble about that, Adam. There is much we do not and cannot understand. This is only another mystery. Suffice it that she does now know. It is all the better and safer for us.'

'Better and safer?' replied Adam, amazed.

'Certainly. It is better to know the danger before us; and this is a warning, though it was not intended so. Let me see it. Addressed to Mr Adam Salton! Then she knows everything. All the better.'

'How,' said Adam with a puzzled look. 'How is it all the better?'

'General process of reasoning, my boy; and the experience of some years in the diplomatic world. Just that we are all the safer with a creature that follows its own instincts. This creature is a monster without heart or consideration for anything or anyone. She is not nearly so dangerous in the open as when she has the dark to protect her. Besides, we know, by our own experience of her movements, that for some reason she shuns publicity. Perhaps it is that she knows it won't interfere in her designs on Caswall – or rather, on Caswall's estate. In spite of her vast bulk and abnormal strength, she is afraid to attack openly. After all, vast as she is, she is only a snake and with a snake's nature, which is to keep low and squirm and proceed by stealth and cunning. She will never attack when she can run away, although she knows well that running away would probably be fatal to her. What is the letter about?'

Sir Nathaniel's voice was calm and self-possessed. When he was engaged in any struggle of wits he was all diplomatist.

'It is asking Mimi and me to tea this afternoon at Diana's Grove, and hoping that you also will favour her.'

Sir Nathaniel smiled as he answered directly:

'Please ask Mrs Salton to accept for us all.'

'Accept? To go there? She means some deadly mischief. Surely – surely it would be wiser not.'

'It is an old trick that we learn early in diplomacy, Adam: to fight on ground of your own choice. It is true that she initiated the place on this occasion; but by accepting it we make it ours. Moreover, she will not be able to understand our reason or any reason for our doing so, and her own bad conscience – if she has any bad or good – and her own fears and doubts will play our game for us. No, my dear boy, let us accept, by all means.'

'Must we accept for you too, sir? I am loth that you should run such a risk. Surely you are better out of it.'

'No! It is better that I should be with you. In the first place, it will be less suspicious – you know you are my guests, and it will be better to preserve convention than to break it. In the next place, and the main reason for my going, there will be two of us to protect your wife in case of necessity. As to fear for me, do not count that. In any case, I am not a timorous man. And in this case I should accept all the danger that could be heaped on me.'

Adam said nothing, but he silently held out his hand, which the other shook: no words were necessary.

When it was getting near tea-time, Mimi asked Sir Nathaniel:

'Shall we walk over? It is only a step.'

'No, my dear,' he answered. 'We must make a point of going in state. We want all publicity.' She looked at him inquiringly. 'Certainly, my dear. In the present circumstances publicity is a part of safety. Do not be surprised if, whilst we are at Diana's Grove, occasional messages come for you – for all or any of us.'

'I see!' said Mrs Salton. 'You are taking no chances.'

'None, my dear. All I have learned at foreign courts and amongst civilised and uncivilised people is going to be utilised within the next couple of hours.'

'I shall gladly learn,' she said: 'it may help me on other occasions.'

'I hope to God it will not!'

Sir Nathaniel's voice was full of seriousness, which made the look grave also. Somehow it brought to her in a convincing way the awful gravity of the occasion. Before they came to the gate, Sir Nathaniel said to her:

'I have arranged with Adam certain signals which may be necessary if certain eventualities occur. These need be nothing to do with you directly. Only bear in mind that if I ask you or Adam to do anything, please do not lose a second in the doing of it. We shall all try to pass off such moments with an appearance of unconcern. In all probability nothing requiring such care shall occur. She will not try force though she has so much of it to spare. Whatever she may attempt to-day of harm to any of us will be in the way of secret plot. Some other time she may try force, but – if I am able to prognosticate such a thing – not to-day. The messengers who may ask for you or any of us shall not be witnesses only: they may help to stave off danger.' Seeing query in her face he went on. 'Of what kind the danger may be I know not, and cannot guess. It will doubtless be some ordinary circumstance of triviality; but none the less dangerous on that account. Here we are at the gate. Now, be self-possessed and careful in all matters, however small. To keep your head is half the battle.'

There were quite a lot of servant men in livery in the hall. The doors of the green drawing-room were thrown open, and Lady Arabella came forth and offered them cordial welcome. This having been got over, Lady Arabella went into the other room, where a servant was holding a salver on which was laid a large letter sealed. The instant her back was turned, Sir Nathaniel whispered to Adam:

'Careful! I remember just such a cloud of servants at the Summer Palace in the Kremlin the day the Grand Duke Alexipof was assassinated at the reception given to the Khan of Bokhara.'

With a slight motion of his left hand, he put the matter aside, enjoining silence. At that moment a servant in plain clothes came and bowed to Lady Arabella, saying:

'Tea is served, your ladyship, in the atrium.'

The doors of a suite of rooms were thrown partially open, the farthest of them showing the lines and colours of a Roman villa. Adam, who was acutely watchful and was suspicious of everything, saw on the far side of this newly disclosed room a panelled iron door of the same colour and configuration as the outer door of the inner room where was the well-hole wherein Oolanga had disappeared. Something in the sight alarmed him, and he quietly went forward and stood near the door. He made no movement even of his eyes, but he could see that Sir Nathaniel was watching him intently and, he fancied, with approval.

They all sat near the table spread for tea, Adam still keeping near the door. Lady Arabella had taken Mimi with her, the two men following, and sat facing the iron door. She fanned herself, impressively complaining of heat, and told one of the footmen to throw all the outer doors open. Tea was in progress when Mimi suddenly started up with a look of fright on her face; at the same moment, the men became cognisant of a thick smoke which began to spread through the room – a smoke which made those who experienced it gasp and choke. The men – even the footmen – began to edge uneasily towards the inner door. Lady Arabella alone was unmoved. She sat still in her seat at the table, with a look of unconcern on her face which disturbed all present, except Sir Nathaniel – and later, Adam, so soon as he caught Sir Nathaniel's eye. Denser and denser grew the smoke, and more acrid its smell. Presently, Mimi, towards whom the draught from the open door wafted the smoke, rose up choking, and ran to the door, which she threw open to its fullest extent, disclosing on the outside of it a curtain of thin silk fixed not to the door but the doorposts. As the door opened more freely the draught from the open door swayed the thin silk towards her, enveloping her in a sort of cloud. In her fright, she tore down the curtain, which enveloped her from head to foot. Then she ran towards the open outer door, unconscious or heedless of the fact that she could not see where she was going. At this moment, Adam, followed by Sir Nathaniel, rushed forward and joined her – Adam catching her by the upper arm and holding her tight. It was well that he did so, for just before her lay the black orifice of the well-hole, which, of course, she could not see with the silk curtain round her head. The floor was extremely slippery; something like thick oil had been spilled where she had to pass; and close to the edge of the hole her feet shot from under her, and she stumbled forward towards the well-hole.

XXX

A Race for Life

When Adam saw Mimi slip, he sprang forward, still holding her arm, so, as they both moved forward at equal rate of speed, there was no unnecessary shock. Instinctively he flung himself backward, still holding her. His weight here told, and, as his grip held her fast, he dragged her up from the hole and they fell together on the floor outside the zone of slipperiness. In a moment he had sprung to his feet and raised her up, so that together they rushed out through the open door into the sunlight, Sir Nathaniel coming close behind them. They were all pale except the old diplomatist, who looked both calm and cool. It sustained and cheered both Adam and his wife to see him thus master of himself. Both Mr and Mrs Salton managed to follow his example, to the wonderment of the footmen, who saw the three who had just escaped a terrible danger walking together gaily, as under the guiding pressure of Sir Nathaniel's hand they turned to re-enter the house. When they were out of earshot of the servants, Sir Nathaniel whispered softly:

'Hush – not a sound. Do not appear to notice that anything has happened. We are not safe yet – not out of this ordeal.'

And so chatting and laughing they re-entered the atrium where Lady Arabella still sat in her place as motionless as a statue of marble. In fact, all those in the room remained so still as to give the newcomers the impression that they were looking at an instantaneous photograph. In a few seconds, however, normal sound and movement were renewed. Lady Arabella, whose face had blanched to a deadly white, now appeared to be in great spirits, and resumed her ministrations at the tea-board as though nothing unusual had happened. The slop-basin was full of half-burned brown paper over which tea had been poured.

Sir Nathaniel, who had been narrowly observing his hostess, took the first opportunity afforded him of whispering to Adam:

'More than ever be careful. The real attack is to come yet. She is too quiet for reality. When I give my hand to your wife to lead her out – by whatever door, – I don't know which yet, – come with us – quick, and caution her to hurry. Don't lose a second, even if you have to make a scene. Hs-s-s-h!'

Then they resumed their places close to the table, and the servants, in obedience to Lady Arabella's order, brought in fresh tea.

Thence on, that tea-party seemed to Adam, whose faculties were at their utmost intensity, like a terrible dream. As for poor Mimi, she was so overwrought both with present and future fear, and with horror at the danger she had escaped, that her faculties were numb. However, she was braced up for a trial, and she felt assured that whatever might come she would be able to go through with it. Sir Nathaniel seemed just as usual – suave, dignified, and thoughtful – perfect master of himself and his intentions. To her husband it was evident that Mimi was ill at ease. The mere way she kept constantly turning her head to look around her, the quick coming and going of the colour of her face, her hurried breathing, alternating with periods of suspicious calm, were to those who had power to discern subtle evidence of mental perturbation. To her, the attitude of Lady Arabella seemed compounded of social sweetness and personal consideration. It would be hard to imagine any more thoughtful and tender kindness towards an honoured guest. Even Adam seemed touched with it, though he never relaxed his vigilance or took his eyes off the lady's movements. When tea was over and the servants had come to clear away the cups, Lady Arabella, putting her arms round Mimi's waist, strolled with her into the adjoining room, where she collected a number of photographs which were scattered about, and, sitting down beside her guest, began to show them to her. While she was doing this, the servants closed all the doors of the suite of rooms and that which opened from the room outside, – that of the well-hole into the avenue. Presently she came back to the room where Adam and Sir Nathaniel were, and sat on a sofa on which Mimi had already taken her seat. Suddenly, without any seeming cause, the light in the room began to grow dim. The light outside seemed to become similarly affected, even the glass of the window becoming obscure. Sir Nathaniel, who was sitting close to Mimi, rose to his feet, and, crying, 'Quick!' caught hold of her right hand and began to drag her from the room. Adam caught her other hand, and between them they drew her through the outer door which the servants were beginning to close. It was difficult at first to find the way, the darkness was so great; but to their relief a multitude of the cowled birds rushed through the open door, and then, falling back, formed a lane-way through the air which there was no mistaking. In seemingly frantic haste they rushed through the avenue towards the gate, Adam whistling shrilly. Mr Salton's double carriage with the four horses and two postillions, which had been waiting quite still in the angle of the avenue, dashed up. Her husband and Sir Nathaniel lifted – almost threw – Mimi into the carriage. The postillions plied whip and spur, and the vehicle, rocking with its speed, swept through the gate and tore up the road. Behind them was a hubbub – servants rushing about, orders being called out, doors shutting, and somewhere, seemingly far back in the house, a strange noise like a lumbering cart moving on thin ice. There was no slackening of pace. Every nerve of the men, and even of the horses, was strained as they dashed recklessly along the road. The two men held Mimi between them, the arms of both of them round her as though protectingly. As they went, there was a sudden rise in the ground; but the horses, breathing heavily as if mad, dashed up it at racing speed, not even slackening their pace when the hill fell away again leaving them to hurry along the downgrade. At the utmost speed of which the horses were capable, they made for Macclesfield. Thence on to Congleton. Having passed the latter place, as they looked back they saw a great shapeless mass behind them, its white showing through the creeping dusk, all form lost in its swift passage. From Congleton they headed for Runcorn, where there were clusters of lights at the bridge and a stream of single lights, or small groups of lights, along by the ship canal. The horses tore madly on, seemingly in the extremity of terror, and followed in their course by a sickening smell such as had arisen through the well-hole. At Runcorn they headed for Liverpool, joyous, even in the midst of their terror, when they saw the blaze of lights at the landing-stage and extending down the river till they disappeared in the line of the piers and floating buoys. As they drew near they heard with glad ears the hooting of a great steamer, ablaze with many lights from stem to stern.

'We are in time!' said Adam, but made no other remark. At Runcorn they saw a white mass slip down the slope from the roadway to the Mersey, and heard the wash of a great body that slid into the tide-way. The postillions, with their goal in sight, redoubled their exertions, and they tore along the streets at reckless pace, careless of the shouted warnings and threats of the police and the many drivers of various vehicles. They tore down the steep movable way to the landing-stage – just in time to see the great vessel move into the river, and to hear the throb of the engines.

The hearts of Adam and his wife grew cold, for their last chance seemed gone. But at the foot of the movable bridge stood Davenport, watch in hand. The moment the carriage drove up he raised his hand in signal to the captain of a great Isle of Man steamer, who was evidently looking out for him. When he saw the hand raised, he worked the engine telegraph, and the great paddle-wheels began to revolve. The

Manx Maid was the fastest boat sailing from Liverpool; and from the instant the flanges to her paddles struck the water, she began to overhaul the Australian boat. They had not got far down the river when she overtook the latter and ranged alongside without slackening speed. Affairs had already been arranged between the two boats with a time to be reckoned by seconds. Adam and his wife, Sir Nathaniel, and Davenport were transferred to the ocean steamship whilst going at as full speed as was allowable at this point of the river, and the latter swept on her way. Davenport went down to his cabin with Adam, telling him on the way what arrangements had been made and how he had received the message from Diana's Grove; and that the voyagers would be able to get off at Queenstown as they might desire.

XXXI

Back to Doom

There seemed to be a great and unusual excitement on the river and along both banks as the *Manx Maid* swept on her way. From the tops of the lighthouses and the pleasure towers; from the yards of every big ship going out or coming in, spy-glasses were projected and binoculars in use; there was rushing to and fro on all the docks, and many shots were heard. Sir Nathaniel went about the deck trying to find the cause; at last a quartermaster told him that, so far as they could make out from semaphore signals, a great whale had come down the river and was heading out to sea. It had been first noticed at Runcorn, he said, going downstream; but where it had come from no one knew, for it had been unnoticed before that time. For Sir Nathaniel and his friends this was quite sufficient. The danger was not over yet. Adam went straight to the captain and made a request that the searchlight with which the ship was equipped should be kept on the alleged whale day and night, as long as it might be within sight. This was attended to at once, and so long as there was anything to be seen there were constant reports. Adam and his friends had many opportunities of seeing the monster, and more than once recognised the contours of its head and the green flash of its eyes. Just before midnight the report came that the whale had been seen to turn, and was now heading towards the Mersey. Then all was darkness, and reports ceased. The pursuit had been given over.

Adam and Mimi and Sir Nathaniel slept sound that night.

Refreshed with sleep, which had for many nights been a

stranger to them all, the party rose with renewed courage and the brave intentions which come with it.

When Queenstown was in sight, Adam, leaving his wife in their cabin, took Sir Nathaniel to the saloon, then empty, and astonished him by telling him that he was going off when the ship stopped, and was returning to the Brow at once.

'But what about your wife?' the latter asked. 'Does she go on alone?'

'No, sir; she comes back with me,' was the startling reply.

Sir Nathaniel walked back and forwards several times before he spoke:

'I presume, my dear boy, that you have thought well over what you are about to do, and weighed up the possible consequences. I am not given to interfere with my neighbour's affairs, and such a thing as this is a man's own responsibility to be decided entirely by himself. Of course when he has a wife her wishes are paramount. What does she say?'

'We are quite agreed, Sir Nathaniel. We both see it as a duty which we owe to other people to be on the spot and do what we can.'

'But,' expostulated Sir Nathaniel, 'with the terrible experiences you have had – the recollection of the terrible dangers which you have escaped – is it wise to place such an awful burden as a possible repetition, or even extension of these things, on the shoulders of a young girl just entering – and happily entering – life? Forgive my interference. I shall not press my views unduly on either of you; but to bring the view before your notice is also a duty, a very sacred duty which I must not forgo.'

'I know that, sir, and with all our heart Mimi and I thank you for your kindness. But it is just because of that experience which is already had, and perhaps paid for, that our power to help others has grown – and our responsibility in equal proportion.'

Sir Nathaniel said solemnly:

'God forbid that I should come between any man – or woman – and a duty. Remember that I am with you, heart and soul. I shared the trouble and the risk with you at the beginning, and, please God, I shall do so to the end – whatever that may be!'

Sir Nathaniel said no more, but he was helpful in all ways, loyally accepting the wishes of his friends and supporting them. Mimi thanked him in the warmth of her handclasp, for his sharing the risk, and for his devoted friendship. Then they three settled all matters so far as they could foresee.

When the ship arrived in the roads at Queenstown they debarked in the tender and set out in the first train towards Liverpool. There, in obedience to instructions telegraphed to him by Davenport, they were met with the carriage with four horses and the postillions just as when they had left Diana's Grove. The postillions, who were well-plucked men, had volunteered to come though they knew the terrible risk they ran. But the horses had been changed – wisely – for they could not easily get over the fright in the prolonged race against the monster.

Mr Salton had been advised that they were not returning to Lesser Hill, so did not expect to see them. All was prepared at Doom with locks and bolts and curtains as when they left.

It would be foolish to say that neither Adam nor Mimi had fears in returning. On the contrary, the road from Liverpool and Congleton was a *via dolorosa*. Of course Mimi felt it more keenly than her husband, whose nerves were harder, and who was more inured to danger. Still she bore up bravely, and as usual the effort was helpful to her. When once she was in the study in the top of the turret, she almost forgot the terrors which lay outside in the dark. She did not attempt even a peep out of the window; but Adam did – and saw nothing. The full moonlight showed all the surrounding country, but nowhere was to be observed that tremulous line of green light or the thin white tower rising up beyond the woods.

The peaceful night had good effect on them all; danger, being unseen, seemed afar off. At times it was hard to realise that it had ever been. With courage quite restored, Adam rose early and walked all along the Brow, seeing no change in the signs of life in Castra Regis. What he did see, to his wonder and concern, on his returning homeward, was Lady Arabella in her tight-fitting white dress and ermine collar, but without her emeralds, emerging from the gate of Diana's Grove and walking towards the Castle. Pondering on this and trying to find some meaning in it, occupied his thoughts till he joined Mimi and Sir Nathaniel at breakfast. They were all silent during the meal, simply because none of them had anything to say. What had been had been, and was known to them all. Moreover, it was not a pleasant topic. One experience they had – at least Adam and Mimi had, for Sir Nathaniel had long ago learned all that it could teach – that is, that memory of even the most stirring or exciting or mournful time soon passes; the humdrum of life is beyond all episodes, and swamps them. A fillip was given to the conversation when Adam told of his seeing Lady Arabella, and her being on her way to Castra Regis. They each had something to say of her, and of what her wishes or intentions were towards Edgar Caswall. Mimi spoke bitterly of her in every aspect. She had not forgotten – and never would – never could – the occasion when to Lilla's harm she consorted even with the nigger. As a social matter, she was disgusted with her over following up of the rich landowner – 'throwing herself at his head so shamelessly,' was how she expressed it. She was interested to know that the great kite still flew from Caswall's tower. But beyond such matters she did not try to go. Indeed, for such she had no data. She was really surprised – in a quiet way – to hear how fully the old order of things had been already restored. The only comments she made in this connection were of strongly expressed surprise at her ladyship's 'cheek' in ignoring her own criminal acts, and her impudence in taking it for granted that others had overlooked them also. Adam had tried unsuccessfully to find any report of the alleged whale in the Mersey, so he remained silent on that subject. Perhaps he had a vague hope that the monster had been unable to sustain her maritime adventures, and had perished. He was well content that this should be so, though he had already made up his mind that he would spare neither time nor effort, or indeed life itself, to root out Diana's Grove and all it contained. He had already expressed his intention to Sir Nathaniel and to Mimi. The former thoroughly approved his intention and pledged himself to support him in his efforts. Mimi agreed with him, but woman-like advised caution.

XXXII

A Startling Proposition

The more Mimi thought over the late events, the more puzzled she was. Adam had actually seen Lady Arabella coming from her own house on the Brow, yet he – and she too – had last seen the monster in the guise in which she had occasionally appeared wallowing in the Irish Sea. What did it all mean – what could it mean? except that there was an error of fact somewhere. Could it be possible that some of them – all of them had been mistaken? That there had been no White Worm at all? That the eyes of Adam and Sir Nathaniel had deceived them? She was all at sea! On either side of her was a belief impossible of reception. Not to believe in what seemed apparent was to destroy the very foundations of belief . . . And yet . . . and yet in old days there had been monsters on the earth, and certainly some people had believed in just such mysterious changes of identity . . . It was all very strange. Perhaps, indeed, it was that she herself was mad. Yes, that must be it! Something had upset her brain. She was dreaming untruths based on reality. Just fancy how any stranger – say a doctor – would regard her if she were to calmly tell him that she had been to a tea-party with an antediluvian monster, and that they had been waited on by up-to-date men-servants. From this she went into all sorts of wild fancies. What sort of tea did dragons prefer? What was it that essentially tickled their palates? Who did the washing for dragons' servants? Did they use starch? If, in the privacy of their houses – homes – lairs, were dragons accustomed to use knives and forks and teaspoons? Yes, that at any rate was true; she had seen them used herself. Here she got into such a state of intellectual confusion that even the upside-down reasoning of the border-land between waking and sleeping would not account for it. She set herself to thinking deeply. Here she was in her own bed in the house of Sir Nathaniel de Salis, Doom Tower – that at any rate was a fact; and to that she would hold on. She would keep quiet and think of nothing – certainly not of any of these strange things – till Adam was with her. He would tell her the truth. She could believe all that he would say. Therefore, till he came she would remain quiet and try not to think at all. This was a wise and dutiful resolution; and it had its reward. Gradually thoughts, true or false, ceased to trouble her. The warmth and peace of her body began to have effect; and after she had left a message for Adam to come up to her when he returned, she sank into a deep sleep.

Adam returned, exhilarated by his walk, and more settled in his mind than he had been for some time. He, too, had been feeling the reaction from the high pressure which he had been experiencing ever since the intentions of Lady Arabella had been manifested. Like Mimi, he had gone through the phase of doubt and inability to believe in the reality of things, though it had not affected him to the same extent. The idea, however, that his wife was suffering ill-effects from her terrible ordeal braced him up, and when he came into her room and waked her, he was at his intellectual and nervous best. He remained with her till she had quite recovered her nerve, and in this condition had gone again into a peaceful sleep. Then he sought Sir Nathaniel in order to talk over the matter with him. He knew that the calm common-sense and self-reliance of the old man, as well as his experience, would be helpful to them all. Sir Nathaniel had by now come to the conclusion that for some reason which he did not understand, or indeed try to, Lady Arabella had entirely changed her plans, and, for the present at all events, was entirely pacific. Later on, when the ideas of the morning were in farther perspective, he was inclined to attribute her changed demeanour to the fact that her influence over Edgar Caswall was so far increased as to justify a more fixed belief in his submission to her charms. She had seen him that morning when she visited Castra Regis, and they had had a long talk together, during which the possibility of their union had been discussed. Caswall, without being enthusiastic on the subject, had been courteous and attentive; as she had walked back to Diana's Grove she almost congratulated herself on her new settlement in life. That the idea was becoming fixed in her mind, and was even beginning to materialise, was shown by a letter which she wrote later in the day to Adam Salton and had sent to him by hand. It ran as follows:

'DEAR MR SALTON, – I wonder if you would kindly advise and, if possible, help me in a matter of business. I have no aptitude or experience in such matters, and am inclined to lean on a friend. Briefly, it is this. I have been for some time trying to make up my mind to sell this place (Diana's Grove), but so many difficulties have been suggested about so doing, that I have put off and put off the doing of it till now. The place is entirely my own property, and no one has to be consulted with regard to what I may wish to do about it. It was bought by my late husband, Captain Adolphus Ranger March, who then had a residence, The Crest, Appleby. He acquired all rights of all kinds, including mining and sporting. When he died he left his whole property to me. Now my father wants me to live with him, and I feel it a call of duty to do so. I am his only child, and he is beginning to be an old, a very old man. Moreover, he has certain official duties to perform and dignities to support. He is, as perhaps you know, Lord Lieutenant of the County, and he feels the want of a female relative to take the head of the table. I am, he says, the only one for the post. He is too old to marry again, and, besides help in the duties named, he wants the comfort of a companion. I shall feel the leaving this place, which has become endeared to me by many sacred memories and affections – the recollection of many happy days of my young married life and the more than happy memories of the man I loved and who loved me so much. I should be glad to sell the place for any kind of fair price – so long, of course, as the purchaser was one I liked and of whom I approved. May I say that you yourself would be the ideal person. But I dare not hope for so much. It strikes me, however, that among your Australian friends may be someone who wishes to make a settlement in the Old Country, and would, in such case, care to fix the spot in one of the most historic regions in England, full of romance and legend, and with a never-ending vista of historical interest – an estate which, though small, is in perfect condition and with illimitable possibilities of development, and many doubtful – or unsettled – rights which have existed before the time of the Romans or even Celts, who were the original possessors. In addition, the house is one of the oldest in England, and kept up to the dernier cri for the last two thousand years. Of all this, immediate possession is to be had. My lawyers can provide you, or whoever you may suggest, with all business and historical details. A word from you of acceptance or refusal is all that is necessary, and we can leave details to be thrashed out by our agents. Forgive me, won't you, for troubling you in the matter, and believe me, yours very sincerely,

'ARABELLA MARCH.'

Adam read this over several times, and then, his mind being made up – though not with inflexible finality, – he went to Mimi and asked if she had any objection. She answered – though after a shudder – that she was in this, as in all things, willing to do whatever he might wish. She added as he was leaving the room:

'Dear, I am willing you should judge what is best for us both. Be quite free to act as you see your duty, and as your inclination calls. We are in the hands of God, and He has hitherto guided us, and will to His own end.'

XXXIII

War à l'Outrance

From his wife's room Adam Salton went straight to the study in the tower, where he knew Sir Nathaniel would be at that hour. The old man was alone, so, when he had entered in obedience to the 'Come in,' which answered his query, he closed the door and came and sat down beside him. He began at once:

'Do you think, sir, it would be well for me to buy Diana's Grove?'

'God bless my soul!' said the old man, startled, 'what on earth would you want to do that for?'

'Well, sir, I have vowed to destroy that White Worm, and my being able to do whatever I may choose with the Lair would facilitate matters and avoid complications.'

Sir Nathaniel hesitated longer than usual before speaking. He was thinking deeply.

'Thank you, Adam, for telling me – though, indeed, I had almost taken so much for granted. But it is well to have accurate knowledge if one is going to advise. I think that, for all reasons, you would do well to buy the property and to have the conveyance settled at once. If you should want more money than is immediately convenient, let me know, so that I may be your banker.'

'Thank you, sir, most heartily; but, indeed, I have more money at immediate call than I can want. I am glad you approve.'

'More than approve. You are doing a wise thing in a financial way. The property is historic, and as time goes on it will increase in value. Moreover, I may tell you something which indeed is only a surmise, but which, if I am right, will add great value to the place.'

Adam listened. He went on:

'Has it ever struck you why the old name, "The Lair of the White Worm," was given? Imagine the word "white" in italics. We know now that there was a snake which in early days was called a worm; but why white?'

'I really don't know, sir; I never thought of it. I simply took it for granted.'

'So did I at first – long ago. But later I puzzled my brain for a reason.'

'And what was the reason, sir?'

'Simply and solely because the snake or worm *was* white.'

'How was that? There must have been a reason. Tradition did not give it a colour without *some* reason.'

'Evidently what people saw was white. I puzzled over it till I saw some light on the subject.'

'Won't you let me follow your reasoning, sir?'

'Certainly. We are in the county of Stafford, where the great industry of china-burning was originated and grew. Stafford owes much of its wealth to the large deposits of the rare china clay found in it from time to time. These deposits became in time pretty well exhausted; but for centuries Stafford adventurers looked for the special clay as Ohio and Pennsylvania farmers and explorers looked for oil. Anyone owning real estate on which clay can be discovered strikes a sort of gold mine.'

'Yes, and then – ?' The young man looked puzzled.

The old man continued:

'The original "Worm" so-called, from which the name of the place came, had to find a direct way down to the marshes and the mud-holes. Now, the clay is easily penetrable, and the original hole probably pierced the bed of china clay. When once the way was made it became a sort of highway for the Worm. But as much movement was necessary to ascend such a great and steep height, some of the clay got attached to his rough skin by attrition. The downway must have been easy work, and there was little attrition; but the ascent was different, and when the monster came to view in the upper world, he was fresh from contact with the white clay. Hence the name, which has no cryptic significance but only fact. Now, if that surmise be true – and I do not see why it is not – there must be a deposit of valuable clay of immense depth. And there is no reason why it is not of equally large superficies.'

Adam's comment pleased the old gentleman.

'I have it in my bones, sir, that you have struck – or rather reasoned out – a great truth.'

Sir Nathaniel went on cheerfully. 'When the world of commerce and manufacture wakes up to the value of your find, it will be as well that your title to ownership has been perfectly secured. If anyone ever deserved such a gain, it is you.'

With his friend's aid, Adam secured the property without loss of time. Then he went to see his uncle, and told him about it. Mr Salton was delighted to find his young relative already constructively the owner of so fine an estate – and one which gave him an important status in the county.

The next morning, when Adam went in to his host in the smoking-room, the latter asked him how he purposed to proceed with regard to keeping his vow.

'It is a difficult matter which you have undertaken. To destroy such a monster is something like one of the labours of Hercules, in that not only its size and weight and power of using them in little-known ways are against you, but the occult side is alone an unsurpassable difficulty. The Worm is already master of all the elements except fire. And I do not see how fire can be used for the attack. It has only to sink into the earth in its charted way, and you could not overtake it if you had the resources of the biggest coal-mine in existence. But I daresay you have mapped out some plan in your mind,' he added courteously.

'I have, sir. But, of course, it is purely theoretical and may not stand the test of practice.'

'May I know the idea you formed?'

'Well, sir, this was my argument: This old lady is fairly experienced. I suppose, by the way, that there is no offence in calling her an old lady, considering that she has been disporting herself in her own way for some thousands of years. So there is no use in trying means that were familiar to her at the time of the Flood. I have been turning my brain inside out and upside down to hit on a new scheme. We hear in Ecclesiastes that there is nothing new under the sun, and as she antedated that work, I daresay she is up to everything which has been popularly known ever since. So at last I decided to try a new adaptation of an old scheme. It is about a century old. But what is a century to her? At the time of the Chartist trouble an idea spread amongst financial circles that an attack was going to be made on the Bank of England. Accordingly, the directors of that institution consulted many persons who were supposed to know what steps should be taken, and it was finally decided that the best protection against fire – which is what was feared – was not water but sand. To carry the scheme into practice great store of fine sea-sand – the kind that blows about and is used to fill hour-glasses – was provided throughout the building, especially at the points liable to attack, from which it could be brought into use.

'I propose to follow the example. I shall provide at Diana's Grove, as soon as it comes into my possession, an enormous amount of such sand, and shall take an early occasion of pouring it into the well-hole, which it will in time choke. Thus Lady Arabella, in her guise of the White Worm, will find herself cut off from her refuge. The hole is a narrow one, and is some hundreds of feet deep. The weight of the sand this can contain would not in itself be sufficient to obstruct; but the friction of such a body working up against it would be tremendous.'

'One moment. What use, then, would the sand there be for destruction?'

'None, directly; but it would hold the struggling body in place till the rest of the scheme came into practice.'

'And what is the rest?'

'As the sand is being poured into the well-hole at intervals, large quantities of dynamite can also be thrown in!'

'Good. But how would the dynamite explode – for, of course, that is what you intend. Would not some sort of wire or fuse be required for each parcel of dynamite?'

Adam smiled.

'Not in these days, sir. That was proved in the second and greater explosion at Hell Gate in New York.Before the explosion a hundred thousand pounds of dynamite in sealed canisters was placed about the miles of workings. At the last a charge of gunpowder was fired – a ton or so. And the concussion exploded all the dynamite. It was most successful. Those who were non-experts in high explosives expected that every pane of glass in New York would be shattered. But, in reality, the explosive did no harm outside the area intended, although sixteen acres of rock had been mined and only the supporting walls and pillars had been left intact. The whole of the rocks which made the whirlpool in East River were simply shattered into the size of matches.'

Sir Nathaniel nodded approval.

'That seems a good plan – a very excellent one. But if it has to tear down so many feet of precipice it may wreck the whole neighbourhood.'

'And free it for ever from a monster,' added Adam, as he left the room to find his wife.

XXXIV

Apprehension

Lady Arabella had instructed her solicitors to hurry on with the conveyance of Diana's Grove, so no time was lost in letting Adam Salton have formal possession of the estate. After his interview with Sir Nathaniel, he had taken steps to begin putting his plan into action. In order to accumulate the necessary amount of fine sea-sand, he had ordered the steward to prepare for an elaborate system of top-dressing all the grounds. A great heap of the chosen sand, which Mr Salton's carts had brought from bays on the Welsh coast, began to grow at the back of the Grove. No one seemed to suspect that it was there for any purpose other than what had been given out. Lady Arabella, who alone could have guessed, was now so absorbed in her matrimonial pursuit of Edgar Caswall, that she had neither time nor inclination for thought extraneous to this. Adam, as a member of the Australian Committee for Defence and a crack gunner in the West Australian Volunteer Artillery, had, of course, plenty of opportunities for purchasing and storing war material; so he put up a rough corrugated-iron shed behind the Grove, in which he had stored his explosives and also a couple of field pieces which he thought it well to have near him in case of emergency. Even the White Worm would have to yield to the explosive shells which they could carry. All being ready for his great attempt whenever the time should come, he was now content to wait, and, in order to pass the time, was content to interest himself in other things – even in Caswall's great kite, which still flew from the high tower of Castra Regis. Strange to say, he took a real interest, beyond the advantage to his own schemes, in Caswall's childish play with the runners. It may, of course, have been that in such puerile matters, which in reality did not matter how they eventuated, he found a solace, or at any rate a relief, from things which were naturally more trying. At any rate, however intended, the effect was there, and the time passed without any harm being done by its passage. The mount of fine sand grew to proportions so vast as to puzzle the bailiffs and farmers round the Brow. The hour of the intended cataclysm was approaching apace. Adam wished – but in vain – for an opportunity, which would appear to be natural, of visiting Caswall in the turret of Castra Regis. At last he got up early one morning, and when he saw Lady Arabella moving towards the Castle, took his courage *à deux mains* and asked to be allowed to accompany her. She was glad, for her own purposes, to comply with his wishes. So together they entered, unobserved at that early hour, and found their way to the turret-room. Caswall was much surprised to see Adam come to his house in such a way, but lent himself to the task of seeming to be pleased. He played the host so well as to deceive even Adam. They all went out on the turret roof, where he explained to his guests the mechanism for raising and lowering the kite, taking also the opportunity of testing the movements of the multitudes of birds, how they answered almost instantaneously to the lowering or raising of the kite. After a little while, Adam's stock of knowledge of this was so increased that he was glad that he had ventured on the visit.

As Lady Arabella walked home with Adam from Castra Regis, she asked him if she might make a request. Permission having been accorded, she explained that before she finally left Diana's Grove, where she had lived so long, she had a desire to know the depth of the well-hole. Adam was really happy to meet her wishes, not from any sentiment, but because he wished to give some valid and ostensible reason for examining the passage of the Worm, which would obviate any suspicion resulting from his being on the premises.

This exactly suited him, and he made full use of his opportunities. He brought from London a Kelvin sounding apparatus with an adequate length of piano-wire for testing any depth, however great. The wire passed over the easily-running wheel, and when this was once fixed over the hole, he was satisfied to wait till the most advantageous time to make his final experiment. He was absolutely satisfied with the way things were going. It seemed to him almost an impossibility that there should be any hitch or disturbance in his carefully arranged plans. It often amazed Adam to see how thoroughly Lady Arabella seemed to enjoy the sounding of the well-hole, despite the sickening stench exhaled by the fissure. Sometimes he would have to go out into the outer air to get free from it for a little while. It really was not merely an evil smell; it rather seemed to partake of some of the qualities of some noxious chemical waste. But she seemed never to tire in the work, but went on as though unconscious that anything disagreeable at all existed. Adam tried to find relief by interesting her in the experiments with the kite. The top of the Castle, at any rate, was free from the foul breath of the pit, and whilst he was engaged there he did not feel as if his actual life was being imperilled by the noxious smell. One thing he longed for, a little artillery practice, though indeed there was a solace to him in the thought that he was the crack shot in the West Australian Artillery.

In the meantime, affairs had been going quietly at Mercy Farm. Lilla, of course, felt lonely at the absence of her cousin, but the even tenor of life went on for her as for others. After the first shock of parting was over, things went back to their accustomed routine. In one respect, however, there was a marked difference. So long as home conditions had remained unchanged, Lilla was content to put ambition far from her and to settle down to the life which had been hers as long as she could remember. But Mimi's marriage set her thinking; naturally, she came to the conclusion that she too might have a mate. There was not for her much choice – there was little movement in the matrimonial direction at the farmhouse. But there was a counter-balancing advantage that one man had already shown his preference for her in an unmistakable way. True, she did not approve of the personality of Edgar Caswall, and his struggle with Mimi had frightened her; but he was unmistakably an excellent *parti*, much better than she could ever have any right to expect. This weighs much with a woman, and more particularly one of her class. So, on the whole, she was content to let things take their course, and to abide by the issue. As time had gone on, she had reason to secretly believe that things did not point to happiness. But here again was a state of things purely feminine, which was easily got over. The happiness which is, so to speak, 'in the bush,' is at best vague, and the opposite is more vague still. It is hard for a young person, specially of the female sex, to believe that things may not turn out eventually as well as they had originally promised. She could not shut her eyes to certain disturbing facts, amongst which were the existence of Lady Arabella and her growing intimacy with Edgar Caswall; his own cold and haughty nature, so little in accord with the love which is the foundation of a young maid's dreams of happiness; and, finally, that the companion of her youth – her life – would, by her marriage to Adam, be taken away to the other side of the earth, where she was to make her home. How things would of necessity alter if she were to marry herself, she was afraid to think. All told, the prospect was not happy for her, and she had a secret longing that *something* might occur to upset the order of things as at present arranged. She had a feeling that she would be happy to accept whatever might happen in consequence of the change. She had also a sort of foreknowledge that the time was coming with startling rapidity when Mr Caswall would come to pay another visit at the farm – a thing which she was quite unable to contemplate with any unmixed pleasure, more especially as Mimi would not be with her to help her in bearing the trial. She dreaded lest there should be another struggle of wills in which she would have to be the shuttle-cock. The result of her pondering over the subject was that she saw the beginning of the end of her happy life, and felt as if she was looking into a cold fog in which everything was concealed from her. And so she was filled with many unrelieved apprehensions.

XXXV

The Last Battle

When Lilla Watford got Edgar Caswall's note asking if he might come to tea on the following afternoon, her heart sank within her. If it was only for her father's sake, she must not refuse him or show any disinclination which he might construe into incivility. She missed Mimi more than she could say or even dared to think. Hitherto, she had always looked to her for sympathy, for understanding, for loyal support. Now she and all these things, and a thousand others – gentle, assuring, supporting – were gone. And instead there was a horrible aching void. In matters of affection for both sexes, and overcoming timorousness for woman, want ceases to be a negative and becomes positive. For the whole afternoon and evening, and for the following forenoon, poor Lilla's loneliness grew to be a positive agony. For the first time she began to realise the sense of her loss as though all the previous suffering had been merely a preparation. Everything she looked at, everything she remembered or thought of, became laden with poignant memory. Then on the top of all was a new sense of dread. The reaction from the sense of security, which had surrounded her all her life, to a never-quieted apprehension was at times almost more than she could bear. It so filled her with fear that she had a haunting feeling that she would as soon die as live. However, whatever might be her own feelings, duty had to be done. And as she had been brought up to consider duty as first, she braced herself to go through, to the very best of her ability, what was before her. Still, the severe and prolonged struggle for self-control told upon her. She looked as she felt, ill and weak. She was really in a nerveless and prostrate condition, with black circles round her eyes, pale even to her lips, and with an instinctive trembling which she was quite unable to repress. It was for her a sad mischance that Mimi was away, for her love would have seen through all obscuring causes, and have brought to light the girl's unhappy condition of health. Lilla was utterly unable to do anything to escape from the ordeal before her; but her cousin, with the experience of her former struggles with Mr Caswall and of the condition in which these left her, would have taken steps – even peremptory ones, if necessary – to prevent a repetition.

Edgar arrived punctually to the time appointed by herself. When Lilla, through the great window, saw him approaching the house, her condition of nervous upset was pitiable. She braced herself up, however, and managed to meet and go on with the interview in its preliminary stages without any perceptible change in her normal appearance and bearing. It had been to her an added terror that the black shadow of Oolanga, whom she dreaded, should follow hard on his master. A load was lifted from her mind when he did not make his usual stealthy approach. She had also feared, though in lesser degree, lest Lady Arabella should be present to make trouble for her as before. The absence of her, too, made at least the beginning of the interview less intolerable. With a woman's natural forethought in a difficult position, she had provided the furnishing of the tea-table as a subtle indication of the social difference between her and her guest. She had chosen the implements of service, as well as all the provender set forth, of the humblest kind. Instead of arranging the silver teapot and china cups, she had set out an earthen teapot such as was in common use in the farm kitchen. The same idea was carried out in the cups and saucers of thick homely delft, and in the cream-jug of similar kind. The bread was of simple whole-meal, home-baked. The butter was of course good, since she had made it herself, and the preserves and honey came from her own garden. Her face beamed with satisfaction when the guest eyed the appointments with a supercilious glance. It was all a shock to the poor girl herself, who enjoyed offering to a guest the little hospitalities possible to her; but that had to be sacrificed with other pleasures. Caswall's face was more set and iron-clad than ever – his piercing eyes seemed from the very beginning to look her through and through. Her heart quailed when she thought of what would follow – of what would be the end, when this was only the beginning. As some protection, though it could be only of a sentimental kind, she brought from her own room the photographs of Mimi, of her grandfather, and of Adam Salton, whom by now she had grown to look on with reliance, as a brother whom she could trust. She kept the pictures near her heart, to which her hand naturally strayed when her feelings of constraint, distrust, or fear became so poignant as to interfere with the calm which she felt was necessary to help her through her ordeal. At first Edgar Caswall was courteous and polite, even thoughtful; but after a little while, when he found her resistance to his domination grow, he abandoned all forms of self-control and appeared in the same dominance as he had previously shown. She was prepared, however, for this, both by her former experience and the natural fighting instinct within her. By this means, as the minutes went on, both developed the power and preserved the equality in which they had begun.

Without warning or any cogent cause, the psychic battle between the two individualities began afresh. This time both the positive and negative causes were all in the favour of the man. The woman was alone and in bad spirits, unsupported; and nothing at all was in her favour except the memory of the two victorious contests; whereas the man, though unaided, as before, by either Lady Arabella or Oolanga, was in full strength, well rested, and in flourishing circumstances. It was not, therefore, to be wondered at that his native dominance of character had full opportunity of asserting itself. He began his preliminary stare with a conscious sense of power, and, as it appeared to have immediate effect on the girl, he felt an ever-growing conviction of ultimate victory. After a little Lilla's resolution began to flag. She felt that the contest was unequal – that she was unable to put forth her best efforts. As she was an unselfish, unegotistical person, she could not fight so well in her own battle as in that of someone whom she loved and to whom she was devoted. Edgar saw the relaxing of the muscles of face and brow, and the almost collapse of the heavy eyelids which seemed tumbling downward in sleep. She made gallant efforts to brace her dwindling powers, but for a time unsuccessfully. At length there came an interruption, which seemed like a powerful stimulant. Through the wide window she saw Lady Arabella enter the plain gateway of the farm and advance towards the hall door. She was clad as usual in tight-fitting white, which accentuated her thin, sinuous figure. The sight did for Lilla what no voluntary effort could. Her eyes flashed, and in an instant she felt as though a new life had suddenly developed within her. Lady Arabella's entry, in her usual unconcerned, haughty, supercilious way, heightened the effect, so that when the two stood close to each other battle was joined. Mr Caswall, too, took new courage from her coming, and all his masterfulness and power came back to him. His looks, intensified, had more obvious effect than had been noticeable that day. Lilla seemed at last overcome by his dominance. Her face became red and pale – violently red and ghastly pale by rapid turns. Her strength seemed gone. Her knees collapsed, and she was actually sinking on the floor, when to her surprise and joy Mimi came into the room, running hurriedly and breathing heavily. Lilla rushed to her, and the two clasped hands. With that, a new sense of power, greater than Lilla had ever seen in her, seemed to quicken her cousin. Her further hand swept the air in front of Edgar Caswall, seeming to drive him backward more and more by each movement, till at last he seemed to be actually hurled through the door which Mimi's entrance had left open, and fell on his back at full length on the gravel path without. Then came the final and complete collapse of Lilla, who, without a sound, sank down pale as death on the floor.

XXXVI

Face to Face

Mimi was greatly distressed when she saw her cousin lying prone. She had a few times in her life seen Lilla on the verge of fainting, but never senseless; and now she was frightened. She threw herself on her knees beside Lilla, and tried, by rubbing her hands and such measures commonly known, to restore her. But all her efforts were unavailing. Lilla still lay white and senseless. In fact, each moment she looked worse; her breast, that had been heaving with the stress, became still, and the pallor of her face grew like marble. At these succeeding changes Mimi's fright grew, till it altogether mastered her. She succeeded in controlling herself only to the extent that she did not scream. Lady Arabella followed Caswall, when he had recovered sufficiently to get up and walk – though stumblingly – in the direction of Castra Regis. When Mimi was quite alone with Lilla and the need for effort had ceased, she felt weak and trembled. In her own mind, she attributed it to a sudden change in the weather. It was momentarily becoming apparent that a storm was coming on. The sky was covered with flying clouds. The silence was so marked as to become a positive quality. There was in the air that creaking sound that shows that electricity is gathering. For a little while she noticed that though the great kite still flew from the turret, the birds were beginning to gather as they had done when the kite had fallen. But now they began to disappear in some mysterious way: first singly, and then in increasing numbers till the whole world without seemed a widespread desolation. Something struck her when she had become cognizant of this, and with wild affright in her face she again stooped over Lilla.

And then came a wild cry of despair. She raised Lilla's white face and laid it on her warm young breast, but all in vain. The cold of the white face thrilled through her, and she utterly collapsed when it was borne in on her that Lilla had passed away.

The dusk gradually deepened and the shades of evening closed in, but she did not seem to notice or to care. She sat still on the floor with her arms round the body of the girl whom she loved. Darker and blacker grew the sky as the coming storm and the closing night joined forces. Still she sat on – alone – tearless – unable to think. Slowly the evening merged in night. Mimi did not know how long she sat there. Though it seemed to her that ages had passed, it could not have been more than a few minutes. She suddenly came to herself, and was surprised to find herself in almost absolute darkness. For a while she lay quiet, thinking of the immediate past. Lilla's hand was still in hers, and to her surprise it was still warm. Somehow this helped her consciousness, and without any special act of will she stood up. She lit a lamp and looked at her cousin. There was no doubt that Lilla was dead; but the death must have been recent. Though her face was of set white, the flesh was still soft to the touch. When the lamplight fell on her eyes, they seemed to look at her with intent – with meaning. She put out the light and sat still in the darkness, feeling as though she were seeing with Lilla's eyes. The blackness which surrounded her allowed of no disturbing influence on her own consciousness: the gloom of the sky, of which there was an occasional glimpse as some flying cloud seemed to carry light with it, was in a way tuned to her own gloomy thoughts. For her all was dark, both within and without. Her hope seemed as dead as her cousin's body. And over and behind all was a sense of unutterable loneliness and sorrow. She felt that nothing in the world could ever come right again. In this state of dark isolation a new resolution came to her, and grew and grew until it became a fixed definite purpose. She would face Caswall and call him to account for his murder of Lilla – that was what she called it to herself. She would also take steps – she knew not what or how – to avenge the part taken by Lady Arabella. In this frame of mind she lit all the lamps in the room, got water and linen from her room, and set about the decent ordering of Lilla's body. This took some time; but when it was finished, she put on her hat and cloak, put out the light, and, locking the door behind her, set out quietly and at even pace for Castra Regis. As she drew near the Castle, she saw no lights except those in and around the tower room. The lights showed her that Mr Caswall was there, and so she entered by the hall door, which as usual was open, and felt her way in the darkness up the staircase to the lobby of the room. The door was ajar, and the light from within showed brilliantly through the opening. She saw Edgar Caswall walking restlessly to and fro in the room with his hands clasped behind his back. She opened the door without knocking, and walked right into the room. As she entered, he ceased walking, and stared at her in surprise. She made no remark, no comment, but continued the fixed look which he had seen on her entrance.

For a time silence reigned, and the two stood looking fixedly at each other. Caswall was the first to speak.

'I had the pleasure of seeing your cousin, Miss Watford, to-day.'

'Yes,' she answered, her head up, looking him straight between the eyes, which made even him flinch. 'It was an ill day for her that you did see her.'

'Why so?' he asked in a weak way.

'Because it cost her her life. She is dead!'

'Dead! Good God! When did she die? What of?'

'She died this evening just after you left her.'

'Are you sure?'

'Yes – and so are you – or you ought to be. You killed her!'

'I killed her! Be careful what you say! Why do you say such a thing?'

'Because, as God sees us, it is true; and you know it. You came to Mercy Farm on purpose to kill her – if you could. And the accomplice of your guilt, Lady Arabella March, came for the same purpose.'

'Be careful, woman,' he said hotly. 'Do not use such names in that way, or you shall suffer for it.'

'I am suffering for it – have suffered for it – shall suffer for it. Not for speaking the truth as I have done, but because you two with devilish malignity did my darling to death. It is you and your accomplice who have to dread punishment, not I.'

'Take care!' he said again.

'Oh, I am not afraid of you or your accomplice,' she answered spiritedly. 'I am content to stand by every word I have said, every act I have done. Moreover, I believe in God's justice. I fear not the grinding of His mills. If needed, I shall set the wheels in motion myself. But you don't care even for God, or believe in Him. Your god is your great kite, which cows the birds of a whole district. But be sure that His hand, when it rises, always falls at the appointed time. His voice speaks in thunder, and not only for the rich who scorn their poorer neighbours. The voices that call on Him come from the furrow and the workshop, from grinding toil and unrelieved stress and strain. Those voices He always hears, however frail and feeble they may be. His thunder is their echo, His lightning the menace that is borne. Be careful! I say even as you have spoken. It may be that your name is being called even at this very moment at the Great Assize. Repent while there is still time. Happy you if you may be allowed to enter those mighty halls in the company of the pure-souled angel whose voice has only to whisper one word of justice and you thenceforth disappear for ever into everlasting torment.'

XXXVII

Eritis Sicut Deus

For the last two days most of those concerned had been
especially busy. Adam, leaving his wife free to follow her own
desires with regard to Lilla and her grandfather, had busied
himself with filling the well-hole with the fine sand prepared
for the purpose, taking care to have lowered at stated intervals
quantities of the store of dynamite so as to be ready for the
final explosion. He had under his immediate supervision a
corps of workmen, and was assisted in their superintendency
by Sir Nathaniel, who had come over for the purpose and
was staying at Lesser Hill. Mr Salton, too, showed much
interest in the job, and was eternally coming in and out,
nothing escaping his observation. Lady Arabella was staying
at her father's place in the Peak. Her visit to Mercy Farm was
unknown to any one but herself and Mimi, and she had kept
her own counsel with regard to its unhappy conclusion. She
had, in fact, been at some pains to keep the knowledge from
Edgar. The Kelvin sounding apparatus was in good working
order, and it seemed to be a perpetual pleasure to her, despite
the horrible effluvium, to measure again and again the depth
of the well-hole. This appeared to have some strange fascination for her which no one employed in the work shared.
When any of the workmen made complaint of the stench to
which they were subjected, she did not hesitate to tell them
roundly that she believed it was a 'try on' on their part to
get an immoderate quantity of strong drink. Naturally, Adam
did not hear of Lilla's death. There was no one to tell him
except Mimi, who did not wish to give him pain, and who,
in addition, was so thoroughly occupied with many affairs,

some of which we are aware of, that she lacked the opportunity of broaching the matter – even to her husband.

When Mimi returned to Sir Nathaniel's after her interview with Edgar Caswall, she felt the new freedom as to her movements. Since her marriage to Adam and their coming to stay at Doom Tower, she had been always fettered by fear of the horrible monster at Diana's Grove. But now she dreaded it no longer. She had accepted the fact of its assuming at will the form of Lady Arabella and *vice versa*, and had been perhaps equally afraid whichever form it took. But now she did not concern herself about one or the other. True, she wanted to meet Lady Arabella, but this was for militant purposes. She had still to tax and upbraid her for her part in the unhappiness which had been wrought on Lilla and for her share in her death. As for the monster, it had been last seen in the channel, forging a way out to sea, and, so far as she knew or cared, had not been seen since and might never be seen again. Now she could once more wander at will along the breezy heights of the Brow or under the spreading oaks of Diana's Grove unfearful of the hateful presence of either the Lady or her *alter ego*, the Worm. She dared not compare what the place had been to her before the hateful revelation, but she could – and she thanked God for that – enjoy the beauties as they were, what they had been, and might be again were they once free. When she left Castra Regis after her interview with Edgar Caswall, she walked home to Doom, making a long detour along the top of the Brow. She wanted time to get calm and be once more master of herself before she should meet her husband. Her nerves were in a raw condition, and she felt more even than at first the shock of her cousin's death, which still completely overwhelmed her. The walk did her good. In the many changes of scene and the bracing exercise, she felt her nervous strength as well as her spirits restored. She was almost her old self again when she had entered the gates of Doom and saw the lights of her own room shining out into the gloom.

When she entered her own room, her first act was to run to the window and throw an eager look round the whole circle of sight. This was instructive – an unconscious effort to clear her mind of any apprehension that the Worm was still at hand rearing its vast height above the trees. A single glance satisfied her that at any rate the Worm *in propria persona* was not visible. So she sat down for a little in the window-seat and enjoyed the pleasure of full view from which she had been so long cut off. The maid who waited on her had told her that Mr Salton had not yet returned home, so that she felt free to enjoy the luxury of peace and quiet.

As she looked out of the window of the high tower, which she had opened, she saw something thin and white move along the avenue far below her. She thought she recognised the figure of Lady Arabella, and instinctively drew back behind the drawn curtain. When she had ascertained by peeping out several times that the Lady did not see her, she watched more carefully, all her instinctive hatred of Lady Arabella flooding back at the sight of her. Lady Arabella was moving swiftly and stealthily, looking back and around her at intervals as if she feared to be followed. This opportunity of seeing her, as she did not wish to be seen, gave Mimi an idea that she was up to no good, and so she determined to seize the occasion of watching her in more detail. Hastily putting on a dark cloak and hat, she ran downstairs and out into the avenue. Lady Arabella had moved, but the sheen of her white dress was still to be seen among the young oaks around the gate-way. Keeping herself in shadow, Mimi followed, taking care not to come so close as to awake the other's suspicion. The abnormal blackness of the sky aided her, and, herself unnoticed and unnoticeable, she watched her quarry pass along the road in the direction of Castra Regis.

She followed on steadily through the gloom of the trees, depending on the glint of the white dress to keep her right. The little wood began to thicken, and presently, when the road widened and the trees grew closer to each other though they stood farther back, she lost sight of any indication of her whereabouts. Under the present conditions it was impossible for her to do any more, so, after waiting for a while, still hidden in the shadow to see if she could catch another glimpse of the white frock, she determined to go on slowly towards Castra Regis and trust to the chapter of accidents to pick up the trail again. She went on slowly, taking advantage of every obstacle and shadow to keep herself concealed. At last she entered on the grounds of the Castle at a spot from which the windows of the turret were dimly visible, without having seen again any sign of Lady Arabella. In the exceeding blackness of the night, the light in the turret chamber seemed by comparison bright, though it was indeed dim, for Edgar Caswall had only a couple of candles alight. The gloom seemed to suit his own state of mind.

All the time that she, Mimi Salton, had been coming from Doom, following as she thought Lady Arabella March, she was in reality being followed by Lady Arabella, who, having the power of seeing in the darkness, had caught sight of her leaving Doom Tower and had never again lost sight of her. It was a rarely complete case of the hunter being hunted, and, strange to say, in a manner true of both parties to the chase. For a time Mimi's many turnings, with the natural obstacles that were perpetually intervening, kept Mimi disappearing and reappearing; but when she was close to Castra Regis there was no more possibility of concealment, and the strange double following went swiftly on. At this period of the chase, the disposition of those concerned was this: Mimi, still searching in vain for Lady Arabella, was ahead; and close behind her, though herself keeping well concealed, came the other, who saw everything as well as though it were daylight. The natural darkness of the night and the blackness of the storm-laden sky had no difficulties for her. When she saw Mimi come close to the hall door of Castra Regis and ascend the steps, she followed. When Mimi entered the dark hall and felt her way up the still darker staircase, still, as she believed, following Lady Arabella, the latter still kept on her way. When they had reached the lobby of the turret-rooms, neither searched actively for the other, each being content to go on, believing that the object of her search was ahead of her.

Edgar Caswall sat thinking in the gloom of the great room, occasionally stirred to curiosity when the drifting clouds allowed a little light to fall from the storm-swept sky. But nothing really interested him now. Since he had heard of Lilla's death, the gloom of his poignant remorse, emphasised by Mimi's upbraiding, had made more hopeless even the darkness of his own cruel, selfish, saturnine nature. He heard no sound. In the first place, his normal faculties seemed benumbed by his inward thought. Then the sounds made by the two women were in themselves difficult to hear. Mimi was light of weight, and in the full tide of her youth and strength her movements were as light and as well measured and without waste as an animal of the forest.

As to Lady Arabella, her movements were at all times as stealthy and as silent as those of her pristine race, the first thousands of whose years was occupied, not in direct going to and fro, but on crawling on their bellies without notice and without noise.

Mimi, when she came to the door, still a little ajar, gave with the instinct of decorum a light tap. So light it was that it did not reach Caswall's ears. Then, taking her courage in both hands, she boldly but noiselessly pushed the door and entered. As she did so, her heart sank, for now she was face to face with a difficulty which had not, in her state of mental perturbation, occurred to her.

XXXVIII

On the Turret Roof

The storm which was coming was already making itself manifest, not only in the wide scope of nature, but in the hearts and natures of human beings. Electrical disturbance in the sky and the air is reproduced in animals of all kinds, and particularly in the highest type of them all – the most receptive – the most electrical themselves – the most recuperative of their natural qualities, the widest sweeping with their net of interests. So it was with Edgar Caswall, despite his selfish nature and coldness of blood. So it was with Mimi Salton, despite her unselfish, unchanging devotion for those she loved. So it was even with Lady Arabella, who, under the instincts of a primeval serpent, carried the ever-varying indestructible wishes and customs of womanhood, which is always old – and always new. Edgar, after he had once turned his eyes on Mimi, resumed his apathetic position and sullen silence. Mimi quietly took a seat a little way apart from Edgar, whence she could look on the progress of the coming storm and study its appearance throughout the whole visible circle of the neighbourhood. She was in brighter and better spirits than she had been all day – or for many days past. Lady Arabella tried to efface herself behind the now open door. At every movement she appeared as if trying to squeeze herself into each little irregularity in the flooring beside her. Without, the clouds grew thicker and blacker as the storm-centre came closer. As yet the forces, from whose linking the lightning springs, were held apart, and the silence of nature proclaimed the calm before the storm. Caswall felt the effect of the gathering electric force. A sort of wild exultation grew upon him such as he had sometimes felt just before the breaking of a tropical storm. As he became conscious of this he instinctively raised his head and caught the eye of Mimi. He was in the grip of an emotion greater than himself; in the mood in which he was he felt the need upon him of doing some desperate deed. He was now absolutely reckless, and as Mimi was associated with him in the memory which drove him on, he wished that she too should be engaged in this enterprise. Of course, he had no knowledge of the proximity of Lady Arabella. He thought that he was alone, far removed from all he knew and whose interests he shared – alone with the wild elements, which were being lashed to fury, and with the woman who had struggled with him and vanquished him, and on whom he would shower, though in secret, the full measure of his hate.

The fact was that Edgar Caswall was, if not mad, something akin to it. His always eccentric nature, fed by the dominance possible to one in his condition in life, had made him oblivious to the relative proportions of things. That way madness lies. A person who is either unable or unwilling to distinguish true proportions is apt to get further afield intellectually with each new experience. From inability to realise the true proportions of many things, there is but one step to a fatal confusion. Madness in its first stage – monomania – is a lack of proportion. So long as this is general, it is not always noticeable, for the uninspired onlooker is without the necessary base of comparison. The realisation only comes with an occasion, when the person in the seat of judgment has some recognised standard with which to compare the chimerical ideas of the disordered brain. Monomania gives the opportunity. Men do not usually have at hand a number, or even a choice of standards. It is the one thing which is contrary to our experience which sets us thinking; and when once the process of thought is established it becomes applicable to all the ordinary things of life; and then discovery of the truth is only a matter of time. It is because imperfections of the brain are usually of a character or scope which in itself makes difficult a differentiation of irregularities that discovery is not usually made quickly. But in monomania the errant faculty protrudes itself in a way that may not be denied. It puts aside, obscures, or takes the place of something else – just as the head of a pin placed before the centre of the iris will block out the whole scope of vision. The most usual form of monomania has commonly the same beginning as that from which Edgar Caswall suffered – an overlarge idea of self-importance. Alienists, who study the matter exactly, probably know more of human vanity and its effects than do ordinary men. Their knowledge of the intellectual weakness of an individual seldom comes quickly. It is in itself an intellectual process, and, if the beginnings can at all be traced, the cure – if cure be possible – has already begun. Caswall's mental disturbance was not hard to identify. Every asylum is full of such cases – men and women who, naturally selfish and egotistical, so appraise to themselves their own importance that every other circumstance in life becomes subservient to it. The declension is rapid. The disease supplies in itself the material for self-magnification. The same often modest, religious, unselfish individual who has walked perhaps for years in all good ways, passing stainless through temptations which wreck most persons of abilities superior to his own, develops – by a process so gradual that at its first recognition it appears almost to be sudden – into a self-engrossed, lawless, dishonest, cruel, unfaithful person who cannot be trusted any more than he can be restrained. When the same decadence attacks a nature naturally proud and selfish and vain, and lacking both the aptitude and habit of self-restraint, the development of the disease is more swift, and ranges to farther limits. It is such persons who become imbued with the idea that they have the attributes of the Almighty – even that they themselves are the Almighty. Vanity, the beginning, is also the disintegrating process and also the melancholy end. A close investigation shows that there is no new factor in this chaos.

It is all exact and logical. It is only a development and not a re-creation: the germs were there already; all that has happened is that they have ripened and perhaps fructified. Caswall's was just such a case. He did not become cruel or lawless or dishonest or unfaithful; those qualities were there already, wrapped up in one or other of the many disguises of selfishness.

Character – of whatever kind it be, of whatever measure, either good or bad – is bound in the long run to justify itself according to its lights. The whole measure of drama is in the development of character. Grapes do not grow on thorns nor figs on thistles. This is true of every phase of nature, and, above all, true of character which is simply logic in episodical form. The hand that fashioned Edgar Caswall's physiognomy in aquiline form, and the mind that ordained it, did not err. Up to the last he maintained the strength and the weakness of aquiline nature. And in this final hour, when the sands were running low, he, his intentions, and his acts – the whole variations and complexities of his individuality – were in essence the very same as those which marked him in his earliest days. He had ripened; that was all.

Mimi had a suspicion – or rather, perhaps, an intuition – of the true state of things when she heard him speak, and at the same time noticed the abnormal flush on his face, and his rolling eyes. There was a certain want of fixedness of purpose which she had certainly not noticed before – a quick, spasmodic utterance which belongs rather to the insane than to those of intellectual equilibrium. She was a little astonished, not only by his thoughts but by his staccato way of expressing them. The manner remained almost longer in her memory than the words. When, later, thinking the matter over, she took into account certain matters of which at the time she had not borne in mind: the odd hour of her visit – it was now after midnight – close on dawn; the wild storm which was now close at hand; the previous nervous upset, of her own struggle with him, of his hearing the news of Lilla's death, of her own untimely visit so fraught with unpleasant experiences and memories. When in a calmer state she weighed all these things in the balance, the doing so not only made for toleration of errors and excesses, but also for that serener mental condition in which correctness of judgment is alone attainable.

As Caswall rose up and began to move to the door leading to the turret stair by which the roof was reached, he said in a peremptory way, whose tone alone made her feel defiant:

'Come! I want you.'

She instinctively drew back – she was not accustomed to such words, more especially to such tone. Her answer was indicative of a new contest:

'Where to? Why should I go? What for?'

He did not at once reply – another indication of his overwhelming egotism. He was now fast approaching the attitude of conscious Final Cause. She repeated her questions. He seemed a little startled; but habit reasserted itself, and he spoke without thinking the words which were in his heart.

'I want you, if you will be so good, to come with me to the turret roof. I know I have no right to ask you, or to expect you to come. It would be a kindness to me. I am much interested in certain experiments with the kite which would be, if not a pleasure, at least a novel experience to you. You would see something not easily seen otherwise. The experience *may* be of use some time, though I cannot guarantee that.'

'I will come,' she answered simply; Edgar moved in the direction of the stair, she following close behind him.

She did not like to be left alone at such a height, in such a place, in the darkness, with a storm about to break. Of himself she had no fear; all that had been seemed to have passed away with her two victories over him in the struggle of wills. Moreover, the more recent apprehension – that of his madness – had also ceased. In the conversation of the last few minutes he seemed so rational, so clear, so unaggressive, that she no longer saw reason even for doubt. So satisfied was she that even when he put out a hand to guide her to the steep, narrow stairway, she took it without thought in the most conventional way. Lady Arabella, crouching in the lobby behind the door, heard every word that had been said, and formed her own opinion of it. It was evident to her that there had been some *rapprochement* between the two, who had so lately been hostile to each other, and that made her furiously angry. It was not jealousy, but only that Mimi was interfering with her plans. She had by now made certain of her capture of Edgar Caswall, and she could not tolerate even the lightest and most contemptuous fancy on his part which might divert him from the main issue. When she became aware that he wished Mimi to come with him to the roof and that she had acquiesced, her rage got beyond bounds. She became oblivious to any danger that might be in the visit to such an exposed place at such a time, and to all lesser considerations, and made up her mind to forestall them. By now she knew well the turns and difficulties of the turret stair, and could use it in darkness as well as in light, – this, independent of her inherited ophidian power of seeing without light. When she had come to the lobby this evening, she had seen that the steel wicket, usually kept locked, that forbade entrance on the stairway, had been left open. So, when she was aware of the visit of the two others to the roof, she stealthily and noiselessly crept through the wicket, and, ascending the stair, stepped out on the roof. It was bitterly cold, for the fierce gusts of the storm which swept round the turret drove in through every unimpeded way, whistling at the sharp corners and singing round the trembling flagstaff. The kite-string and the wire which controlled the runners made a concourse of weird sounds which somehow, perhaps from the violence which surrounded them, acting on their length, resolved themselves into some kind of harmony – a fitting accompaniment to the tragedy which seemed about to begin.

Lady Arabella scorned all such thoughts, putting them behind her as she did fear. Still moving swiftly and stealthily, she glided across the stone roof and concealed herself behind one of the machicolations of the tower. She was already safely ensconced when the heads of Edgar and Mimi, whom he guided, appeared against the distant sky-line as they came up the steep stair. Mimi's heart beat heavily. Just before leaving the turret-chamber she had got a fright which she could not shake off. The lights of the room had momentarily revealed to her, as they passed out, Edgar's face concentrated as it did whenever he intended to use his mesmeric power. Now the black eyebrows made a thick line across his face, under which his eyes shone and glittered ominously. Mimi recognised the danger, and assumed the defiance that had twice already served her so well. She had a fear that the circumstances and the place were against her, and she wanted to be fore-armed.

The sky was now somewhat lighter than it had been. Either there was lightning afar off, whose reflections were carried by the rolling clouds, or else the gathered force, though not yet breaking into lightning, had an incipient power of light. It seemed to affect both the man and the woman. Edgar seemed altogether under its influence. His spirits were bois-terous, his mind exalted. He was now at his worst; madder even than he had been earlier in the night. Mimi, trying to keep as far from him as possible, moved across the stone floor of the turret roof, and found a niche which concealed her. It was not far from Lady Arabella's place of hiding, but the angle of the machicolation stood between them, separating them. It was fortunate for Mimi that she could not see the other's face. Those burning eyes concentrated in deadly hate would have certainly unnerved her just as she wanted the full of her will power to help her in extremity.

Edgar, left thus alone on the centre of the turret roof, found himself altogether his own master in a way which tended to increase his madness. He knew that Mimi was close at hand, though he had lost sight of her. He spoke loudly, and the sound of his own voice, though it was carried from him on the sweeping wind as fast as the words were spoken, seemed to exalt him still more. Even the raging of the elements round him seemed to add to his exaltation. To him it seemed that these manifestations were obedient to his own will. He had reached the sublime of his madness; he was now in his own mind actually the Almighty, and whatever might happen would be the direct carrying out of his own commands. As he could not see Mimi nor fix whereabout she was, he shouted loudly:

'Come to me. You shall see now what you are despising, what you are warring against. All that you see is mine – the darkness as well as the light. I tell you that I am greater than any other who is, or was, or shall be. Look you now and learn. When the Master of Evil took Him up on a high place and showed Him all the kingdoms of the earth, he was doing what he thought no other could do. He was wrong. He forgot *Me*. You shall see. I shall send you light to see by. I shall send it up to the very ramparts of heaven. A light so great that it shall dissipate those black clouds that are rushing up and piling around us. Look! Look! At the very touch of my hand that light springs into being and mounts up – and up – and up!'

He made his way whilst he was speaking to the corner of the turret whence flew the giant kite, and from which the runners ascended. Mimi looked on, appalled and afraid to speak lest she should precipitate some calamity. Within the machicolated niche Lady Arabella, quiet and still as death, cowered in a paroxysm of fear. Edgar took from his pocket a small wooden box, through a hole in which the wire of the runner ran. This evidently set some machinery in motion, for a sound as of whirring came. From one side of the box floated what looked like a piece of stiff ribbon, which snapped and crackled as the wind took it. For a few seconds Mimi saw it as it rushed along the sagging line to the kite. When close to it, there was a loud crack, like a minor explosion, and a sudden light appeared to issue from every chink in the box. Then a quick flame flashed along the snapping ribbon, which glowed with an intense light – a light so great that the whole of the countryside around stood out against the background of black driving clouds. For a few seconds the light remained, then suddenly disappeared in the blackness around. That light had no mystery for either Mimi or Lady Arabella, both of whom had often seen manifestations of the same thing. It was simply a magnesium light which had been fired by the mechanism within the box carried up to the kite. Edgar was in a state of tumultuous excitement, shouting and yelling at the top of his voice and dancing about like a violent lunatic. But the others were quiet, Mimi nestling in her niche and avoiding observation as well as she could. Once the sagging string, caught in a wind-flurry, was thrown across the back of her hand. Its trembling had an extraordinary effect on her, bracing her up to the full of her emotional power. She felt, on the instant, that the spirit of Lilla was beside her, and that it was Lilla's touch which she had felt. Lady Arabella had evidently made up her mind what to do; the inspiration how to do it came to her with the sight of Mimi's look of power evident to her ophidian sight. On the instant she glided through the darkness to the wheel whereon the string of the kite was wound. With deft fingers she found where the wheel of the Kelvin sounding apparatus was fixed to it, and, unshipping this, took it with her, reeling out the wire as she went, and so keeping, in a way, in touch with the kite. Then she glided swiftly to the wicket, through which she passed, locking the gate behind her as she went. Down the turret stair she flew quickly, letting the wire run from the wheel which she carried carefully, and, passing out of the hall door, ran down the avenue with all her speed. She soon reached her own gate, ran down the avenue, and with her small key opened the iron door leading to the atrium. The fine wire passed easily under the door. In the room beside the atrium, where was the well-hole, she sat down panting, unknown to all, for in the coming she had escaped observation. She felt that she was excited, and in order to calm herself began a new form of experiment with regard to her observation of the hole. She fastened the lamp which was ready for lowering to the end of the wire, whose end came into the room. Then she began quietly and methodically lowering the two by means of the Kelvin sounding apparatus, intending to fire at the right time the new supply of magnesium ribbon which she had brought from the turret. She felt well satisfied with herself. All her plans were maturing, or had already matured. Castra Regis was within her grasp. The woman whose interference she feared, Lilla Watford, was dead. Diana's Grove and all its hideous secrets was now in other hands, an accident to whom would cause her no concern. Truly, all was well, and she felt that she might pause a while and rest. She lay down on a sofa close to the well-hole so that she could see it without moving when she had lit the lamp. In a state of blissful content she sank into a gentle sleep.

XXXIX

The Breaking of the Storm

When Lady Arabella had gone away in her usual noiseless fashion, the two others remained for a while quite still in their places on the turret roof: Caswall because he had nothing to say and could not think of anything; Mimi because she had much to say and wished to put her thoughts in order. For quite a while – which seemed interminable – silence reigned between them. At last Mimi made a beginning – she had made up her mind how to act.

'Mr Caswall,' she said loudly, so as to make sure of being heard through the blustering of the wind and the perpetual cracking of the electricity.

Caswall said something in reply which she understood to be: 'I am listening.'

His words were carried away on the storm as they came from his mouth. However, one of her objects was effected: she knew now exactly whereabout on the roof he was. So she moved close to the spot before she spoke again, raising her voice almost to a shout:

'The wicket is shut. Please to open it. I can't get out.'

As she spoke she was quietly fingering the revolver which Adam had given to her when she got back to Liverpool, and which now lay in her breast. She felt that she was caged like a rat in a trap, but did not mean to be taken at a disadvantage, whatever happened. By this time Caswall also was making up his mind what his own attitude would be. He, too, felt trapped, and all the brute in him rose to the emergency. He never had been counted – even by himself – as chivalrous;

but now, when he was at a loss, even decency of thought had no appeal for him. In a voice which was raucous and brutal – much like that which is heard when a wife is being beaten by her husband in a slum – he hissed out, his syllables cutting through the roaring of the storm:

'I didn't let you in here. You came of your own accord – without permission, or even asking it. Now you stay or go as you choose. But you must manage it for yourself; I'll have nothing to do with it.'

She answered, woman-like, with a query:

'It was Lady Arabella who shut and locked it. Was it by your wish?'

'I had no wish one way or the other. I didn't even know that she was here.'

Then suddenly he added: 'How did you know it?'

'By her white dress and the green gleam of her eyes. Her figure is not hard to distinguish, even in the dark.'

He gave some kind of snort of disagreement. Taking additional umbrage at this, she went on in words which she thought would annoy him most:

'When a woman is gifted with a figure like hers, it is easy to tell her even in a rope-walk or a bundle of hop-poles.'

He even improved on her affronting speech:

'Every woman in the eastern counties seems to think that she has a right to walk into my house at any hour of the day or night, and into every room in the house whether I am there or not. I suppose I'll have to get watch-dogs and police to keep them out, and spring guns and man-traps to deal with them if they get in.' He went on more roughly as if he had been wound up to it.

'Well, why don't you go?'

Her answer was spoken with dangerous suavity:

'I am going. Blame yourself if you do not like the time and manner of it. I daresay Adam – my husband – Mr Salton, will have a word to say to you about it!'

'Let him say, and be damned to him, and to you too! I'll show you a light. You shan't be able to say that you could not see what you were doing.'

As he spoke he was lighting another piece of the magnesium ribbon, which made a blinding glare in which everything was plainly discernible, down to the smallest detail. This exactly suited her. She took accurate note of the wicket and its fastening before the glare had died away. She took her revolver out and had fired into the lock, which was shivered on the instant, the pieces flying round in all directions, but happily without causing hurt to anyone. Then she pushed the wicket open and ran down the narrow stair and so to the hall door. Opening this also, she ran down the avenue, never lessening her speed till she stood outside the door of Doom Tower. The household was all awake, and the door was opened at once on her ringing.

She asked: 'Is Mr Salton in?'

'He has just come in, a few minutes ago. He has gone up to the study.'

She ran upstairs at once and joined him. He seemed relieved when he saw her, but scrutinised her face keenly. He saw that she had been in some concern, so led her over to the sofa in the window and sat down beside her.

'Now, dear, tell me all about it!' he said.

She rushed breathlessly through all the details of her adventure on the turret roof. Adam listened attentively, helping her all he could, both positively and negatively, nor embarrassing her by any questioning or surprise. His thoughtful silence was a great help to her, for it allowed her to collect and organise her thoughts. When she had done he gave her his story without unnecessary delay:

'I kept out of your way so as to leave you unhampered in anything you might wish to attend to. But when the dark came and you were still out, I was a little frightened about you. So I went to where I thought you might be. First to Mercy; but no one there knew where you were. Then to Diana's Grove.

216

There, too, no one could tell me anything. But when the footman who opened the door went to the atrium, looking if you were about, I caught a glimpse of the room where the well-hole is. Beside the hole, and almost over it, was a sofa on which lay Lady Arabella quietly sleeping. So I went on to Castra Regis, but no one there had seen you either. When that magnesium light flared out from close to the kite, I thought I saw you on the turret. I tried to ascend, and actually got to the wicket at foot of the turret stair. But that was locked, so I turned back and went round the Brow on the chance of meeting or seeing you; then I came on here. I only knew you had come home when Braithwait came up to the study to tell me. I must go and see Caswall to-morrow or next day to hear what he has to say on the subject. You won't mind, will you?'

She answered quickly, a new fear in her heart:

'Oh no, dear, I wouldn't and won't mind anything you think it right to do. But, dear, for my sake, don't have any quarrel with Mr Caswall. I have had too much trial and pain lately to wish it increased by any anxiety regarding you.'

'You shall not, dear – if I can help it – please God,' he said solemnly, and he kissed her.

Then, in order to keep her interested so that she might forget the fears and anxieties that had disturbed her, he began to talk over details of her adventure, making shrewd comments which attracted and held her attention. Presently, *inter alia*, he said:

'That's a dangerous game Caswall is up to. It seems to me that that young man – though he doesn't appear to know it – is riding for a fall!'

'How, dear? I don't understand.'

'Kite flying on a night like this from a place like the tower of Castra Regis is, to say the least of it, dangerous. It is not merely courting death or other accident from lightning, but it is bringing the lightning into where he lives.'

'Oh, do explain to me, Adam. I am very ignorant on such subjects.'

'Well, you see, Mimi, the air all around is charged and impregnated with electricity, which is simply undeveloped lightning. Every cloud that is blowing up here – and they all make for the highest point – is bound to develop into a flash of lightning. That kite is up in the air about a mile high and is bound to attract the lightning. Its very string makes a road for it on which to travel to earth. When it does come, it will strike the top of the tower with a weight a hundred times greater than a whole park of artillery. It will knock Castra Regis into matches. Where it will go after that, no one can tell. If there be any metal by which it can travel, such will not only point the road, but be the road itself. If anything of that sort *should* happen, it may – probably will – wreck the whole neighbourhood!'

'Would it be dangerous to be out in the open air when such a thing is taking place?' she asked.

'No, little girl. It would be the safest possible place – so long as one was not in the line of the electric current.'

'Then, do let us go outside. I don't want to run into any foolish danger – or, far more, to ask you to do so. But surely if the open is safest, that is the place to be. We can easily keep out of electric currents – if we know where they are. By the way, I suppose these are carried and marked by wires, or by something which can attract? If so, we can look for such. I had my electric torch that you gave me recharged the day I was in Wolverhampton with Sir Nathaniel.'

'I have my torch too, all fit,' interposed Adam.

Without another word, she put on again the cloak she had thrown off, and a small, tight-fitting cap. Adam too put on his cap, and, after looking that his revolver was all right, gave her his hand, and they left the house together. When they had come to the door, which lay quite open, Adam said:

'I think the best thing we can do will be to go round all the places which are mixed up in this affair.'

'All right, dear, I am ready. But, if you don't mind, we might go first to Mercy. I am anxious about grandfather, and

218

we might see that – as yet, at all events – nothing has happened there.'

'Good idea. Let us go at once, Mimi.'

So they went on the high-hung road along the top of the Brow. The wind here was of great force, and made a strange booming noise as it swept high overhead; though not the sound of cracking and tearing as it passed through woods of high slender trees which grew on either side of the road. Mimi could hardly keep her feet. She was not afraid; but the force to which she was opposed gave her a good excuse to hold on to her husband extra tight.

At Mercy there was no one up. At least, all the lights were out. But to Mimi, accustomed to the nightly routine of the house, there were manifest signs that all was well, except in the little room on the first floor, where the blinds were down. Mimi could not bear to look at that, to think of it. Adam understood her pain. He bent over and kissed her, and then took her hand and held it hard. And thus they passed on together, returning to the high road towards Castra Regis. They had now got ready their electric torches, depressing the lens of each towards the ground so that henceforth on their journey two little circles of bright light ran ahead of them, and, moving from side to side as they went, kept the ground in front of them and at either side well disclosed.

At the gate of Castra Regis they were, if possible, extra careful. When drawing near, Adam had asked his wife several questions as to what signs, if any, had been left of Lady Arabella's presence in the tower. So she told him, but with greater detail, of the wire from the Kelvin sounder, which, taking its origin from the spot whence the kite flew, marked the way through the wicket, down the stairs and along the avenue.

Adam drew his breath at this, and said in a low, earnest whisper:

'I don't want to frighten you, Mimi, dear, but wherever that wire is there is danger.'

'Danger! How?'

'That is the track where the lightning will go; any moment, even now whilst we are speaking and searching, a fearful force may be loosed upon us. You run on, dear; you know the way down to where the avenue joins the high road. Keep your torch moving, and if you see any sign of the wire keep away from it, for God's sake. I shall join you at the gateway.'

She said in a low voice:

'Are you going to find or to follow that wire alone?'

'Yes, dear. One is sufficient for that work. I shall not lose a moment till I am with you.'

'Adam, when I came with you into the open, when we both feared what might happen, my main wish was that we should be together when the end came. You wouldn't deny me that right, would you, dear?'

'No, dear, not that or any right. Thank God that my wife has such a wish. Come; we will go together. We are in the hands of God. If He wishes, we shall be together at the end, whenever or wherever that may be. Kiss me, dear – even if it be for the last time. Give me your hand. Now, I am ready.'

And so, hand in hand, they went to find the new danger together. They picked up the trail of the wire on the steps of the entrance and followed it down the avenue, taking especial care not to touch it with their feet. It was easy enough to follow, for the wire, if not bright, was self-coloured, and showed at once when the roving lights of the electric torches exposed it. They followed it out of the gateway and into the avenue of Diana's Grove. Here a new gravity clouded over Adam's face, though Mimi saw no cause for fresh concern. This was easily enough explained. Adam knew of the explosive works in progress regarding the well-hole, but the matter had been studiously kept from his wife. As they came near the house, Adam sent back his wife to the road, ostensibly to watch the course of the wire, telling her that there might be a branch wire leading to somewhere else. She was to search the under-growth which the wire went through, and, if she found it, was to warn him by the Australian native 'Coo-ee!' which had been arranged between them as the means of signalling. When Mimi had disappeared in the avenue, Adam examined the wire inch by inch, taking special note of where it disappeared under the iron door at the back of the house. When he was satisfied that he was quite alone, he went round to the front of the house and gently shoved the hall door, thinking that perhaps it was unlocked and unbolted, after the usual custom. It yielded, so he stole into the hall, keeping his torch playing the light all over the floor, both to avoid danger and to try to pick the wire up again. When he came to the iron door he saw the glint of the wire as it passed under it. He traced it into the room with the well-hole, taking care to move as noiselessly as possible. He saw Lady Arabella sleeping on the sofa close to the hole into which the continuation of the wire disappeared. As he did so he heard a whispered 'H-ss-h!' at the door, and, looking up, saw Mimi, who signalled him to come out. He joined her, and together they passed into the avenue.

Mimi whispered to him:

'Would it not be possible to give someone here warning? They are in danger.'

He put his lips close to her ear and whispered his reply:

'We could, but it would not be safe. Lady Arabella has brought the wire here herself for some purpose of her own. If she were to suspect that we knew or guessed her reason, she would take other steps which might be still more danger-ous. It is not our doing, any of it. We had better not interfere.'

Mimi, who had spoken from duty, far from any wish or fear of her own, was only too glad to be silent, and to get away, both safe. So her husband, taking her by the hand, led her away from the wire.

When they were in the wide part of the avenue, he whis-pered again:

'We must be careful, Mimi, what we do. We are surrounded with unknown dangers on every side, and we may, in trying to do good in some way, do the very thing which we should most avoid.'

Under the trees, which cracked as the puff of wind clashed their branches and the slender shafts swayed to and from the upright, he went on:

'We know that if the lightning comes it will take the course of the kite string. We also know that if it strikes Castra Regis it will still follow the wire, which we have just seen running along the avenue. But we don't know to where else that wire may lead the danger. It may be to *Mercy* – or to *Lesser Hill*; in fact, to anywhere in the neighbourhood. Moreover, we do not know when the stroke may fall. There will be no warning, be sure of that. It will, or may, come when we least expect it. If we cut off the possibilities of the lightning finding its own course, we may do irreparable harm where we should least wish. In fact, the Doom is probably spoken already. We can only wait in what safety, or possibility of safety, we can achieve till the moment sounds.'

Mimi was silent, but she stood very close to him and held his hand tight. After a few moments she spoke:

'Then let the Doom fall when it may. We are ready. At least, we shall die together!'

With the belief that death was hovering over them, as was shown in the resignation which they expressed to each other, it was little wonder that Adam and Mimi were restless and practically unable to remain quiet or even in one place. They spent the dark hours of the night wandering along the top of the Brow, and waiting for – they knew not what. Strange to say, they both enjoyed, or thought they did, the tumult of Nature's forces around them. Had their nervous strain been less, the sense of æstheticism which they shared would have had more scope. Even as it was, the dark beauties of sky and landscape appealed to them; the careering of the inky-black clouds; the glimpses of the wind-swept sky; the rush and roar of the tempest amongst the trees; the never-ceasing crackle of electricity; the distant booming of the storm as it rushed over the Mercian highlands, and ever mingling its roar with the scream of the waves on the pebble beaches of the eastern sea; the round, big waves breaking on the iron-bound marge of the ocean; the distant lights, which grew bright as the storm swept past, and now and again seemed to melt into the driving mist – all these things claimed their interest and admiration, forming, as it were, a background of fitting grandeur and sublimity to the great tragedy of life which was being enacted in their very midst. When such a thought crossed Mimi's mind, it seemed to restore in an instant her nerve and courage. In the wild elemental warfare, such surface passions as fear and anger and greed seemed equally unworthy to the persons within their scope and to the occasion of their being. In those flying minutes, Adam and Mimi found themselves, and learned – did they not know it already? – to value personal worthiness.

As the dawn grew nearer, the violence of the storm increased. The wind raged even more tumultuously. The flying clouds grew denser and blacker, and occasionally flashes of lightning, though yet far-distant, cut through the oppressive gloom. The tentative growling of thunder changed, at instants, to the rolling majesty of heaven's artillery. Then came a time when not seconds elapsed between the white flash and the thunder-burst, which ended in a prolonged roll which seemed to shake the whole structure of the world.

But still through all the great kite, though assailed by all the forces of air, tugged strenuously but unconquered against its controlling string.

At length, when the sky to the east began to quicken there seemed a lull in the storm. Adam and Mimi had gone the whole length of the Brow, and had come so far on the return towards Castra Regis as to be level with Diana's Grove. The comparative silence of the lull gave both Adam and his wife the idea of coming again close to the house. In his secret heart Adam was somewhat impatient of the delay of the kite drawing down the lightning – and he was also not too well pleased at it. He had been so long thinking of the destruction of the Lair of the White Worm that the prolongation seemed undue and excessive – indeed, unfair. Nevertheless, he waited with an outward appearance of patience and even calm; but his heart was all the while raging. He wanted to know and to feel that he had seen the last of the White Worm. With the coming of the day the storm *seemed* less violent, simply because the eyes of the onlookers came to the aid of their ears. The black clouds seemed less black because the rest of the landscape was not swathed in impenetrable gloom. When any of our usual organs of sense are for any cause temporarily useless, we are deprived of the help of perspective in addition to any special deprivation. To both Adam and Mimi the promise of the dawn was of both help and comfort. Not only was the lifting of the pall of blackness – even if light only came through rents in the wind-torn sky – hopeful, but the hope that came along with light brought consolation and renewing of spirit. Together they moved on the road to Diana's Grove. Adam had taken his wife's arm in that familiar way which a woman loves when she loves the man, and, without speaking, guided her down the avenue towards the house.

The top of the hill on which Diana's Grove was seated had, from time immemorial, been kept free from trees or other obstruction which might hide the view. In early days this was not for any æsthetic reason, but simply to guard against the unseen approach of enemies. However, the result was the same; an uninterrupted view all round was obtained or preserved. Now, as the young people stood out in the open they could see most of the places in which for the time they were interested. Higher up on the Brow and crowning it rose Castra Regis, massive and stern – the very moral of a grey, massive frowning Norman fortress. Down the hill, half way to the level of the plain where lay the deep streams and marsh-ringed pools, Mercy Farm nestled among protecting woods. Half hidden among stately forest trees, and so seeming far away, Lesser Hill reared its look-out tower. Adam took Mimi's hand, and instinctively they moved down close to the house of Diana's Grove, noticing, as they went, its inhospitable appearance. Never a window, a door, or chimney seemed to have any living force behind it. It was all cold and massive as a Roman temple, with neither prospect nor promise of welcome or comfort. Adam could not help recalling to his mind the last glimpse he had of its mistress – looking thinner even than usual in her white frock, drawn tight to her as it had been to resist the wind pressure. Calmly sleeping, she lay on the sofa close to the horrible well-hole – so close to it that it seemed as if the slightest shock or even shake would hurl her into the abyss. The idea seemed to get hold of him; he could not shake it off. For a few moments it seemed to him as if the walls had faded away like mist, and as if, in a vision of second sight, there was a dim adumbration of a phase of the future – a kind of prophecy. Mimi's touch on his arm as if to suggest moving from the spot, recalled him to himself. Together they moved round to the back of the house, and stood where the wind was less fierce in the shelter of the iron door.

Whilst they were standing there, there came a blinding flash of lightning which lit up for several seconds the whole area of earth and sky. It was only the first note of the celestial prelude, for it was followed in quick succession by numerous flashes, whilst the crash and roll of thunder seemed continuous. Adam, appalled, drew his wife to him and held her close. As far as he could estimate by the interval between lightning and thunder-clap, the heart of the storm was still some distance off, and so he felt no present concern for their safety. Still, it was apparent that the course of the storm was moving swiftly in their direction. The lightning flashes came faster and faster and closer together; the thunder-roll was almost continuous, not stopping for a moment – a new crash beginning before the old one had ceased. Adam kept looking up in the direction where the kite strained and struggled at its detaining cord, but, of course, the dawn was not yet sufficiently advanced to permit of his seeing it in a glance.

At length there came a flash so appallingly bright that in its glare nature seemed to be standing still. So long did it last that there was time to distinguish its configuration. It seemed like a mighty tree inverted, pendent from the sky. The roots overhead were articulated. The whole country around within the angle of vision was lit up till it seemed to glow. Then a broad ribbon of fire seemed to drop on the tower of Castra Regis just as the thunder crashed. By the glare of the lightning he could see the tower shake and tremble and finally fall to pieces like a house of cards. The passing of the lightning left the sky again dark, but a blue flame fell downward from the tower and, with inconceivable rapidity running along the ground in the direction of Diana's Grove, reached the dark silent house, which in the instant burst into flame at a hundred different points. At the same moment rose from the house a rending, crashing sound of woodwork, broken or thrown about, mixed with a quick yell so appalling that Adam, stout of heart as he undoubtedly was, felt his blood turned into ice. Instinctively, despite the danger and their consciousness of it, husband and wife took hands and listened, trembling. *Something* was going on close to them, mysterious, terrible, deadly. The shrieks continued, though less sharp in sound, as though muffled. In the midst of them was a terrific explosion, seemingly sounding from deep in the earth. They looked around. The flames from Castra Regis and also from Diana's Grove made all around almost as light as day, and now that the lightning had ceased to flash, their eyes, unblinded, were able to judge both perspective and detail. The heat of the burning house caused the iron doors either to warp and collapse or to force the hinges. Seemingly of their own accord, they flew or fell open, and exposed the interior. The Saltons could now look through the atrium and the room beyond

226

where the well-hole yawned, a deep narrow circular chasm. From this the agonised shrieks were rising, growing even more terrible with each second that passed. But it was not only the heart-rending sound that almost paralysed poor Mimi with terror. What she saw was alone sufficient to fill her with evil dreams for the remainder of her life. The whole place looked as if a sea of blood had been beating against it. Each of the explosions from below had thrown out from the well-hole, as if it had been the mouth of a cannon, a mass of fine sand mixed with blood, and a horrible repulsive slime in which were great red masses of rent and torn flesh and fat. As the explosions kept on, more and more of this repulsive mass was shot up, the great bulk of it falling back again. The mere amount of this mass was horrible to contemplate. Many of the awful fragments were of something which had lately been alive. They quivered and trembled and writhed as though they were still in torment, a supposition to which the unending scream gave a horrible credence. At moments some mountainous mass of flesh surged up through the narrow orifice as though it were forced by a measureless power through an opening infinitely smaller than itself. Some of these fragments were covered or partially covered with white skin as of a human being, and others – the largest and most numerous – with scaled skin as of a gigantic lizard or serpent. And now and again to these clung masses of long black hair which reminded Adam of a chest full of scalps which he had seen seized from a marauding party of Comanche Indians. Once, in a sort of lull or pause, the seething contents of the hole rose after the manner of a bubbling spring, and Adam saw part of the thin form of Lady Arabella forced up to the top amid a mass of blood and slime and what looked as if it had been the entrails of a monster torn in shreds. Several times some masses of enormous bulk were forced up through the well-hole with inconceivable violence, and, suddenly expanding as they came into larger space, disclosed great sections of the White Worm which Adam and Sir Nathaniel had seen looking over the great trees with its enormous eyes of emerald-green flickering like great lamps in a gale.

At last the explosive power, which was not yet exhausted, evidently reached the main store of dynamite which had been lowered into the worm hole. The result was appalling. The ground for far around quivered and opened in long deep chasms, whose edges shook and fell in, throwing up clouds of sand which fell back and hissed amongst the rising water. The heavily built house shook to its foundations. Great stones were thrown up as from a volcano, some of them, great masses of hard stone squared and grooved with implements wrought by human hands, breaking up and splitting in mid air as though riven by some infernal power. Trees near the house, and therefore presumably in some way above the hole, which sent up clouds of dust and steam and fine sand mingled, and which carried an appalling stench which sickened the spectators, were torn up by the roots and hurled into the air. By now, flames were bursting violently from all over the ruins, so dangerously that Adam caught up his wife in his arms and ran with her from the proximity of the flames.

Then almost as quickly as it had begun, the whole cataclysm ceased. A deep-down rumbling continued intermittently for some time. And then silence brooded over all – silence so complete that it seemed in itself a sentient thing – silence which seemed like incarnate darkness, and conveyed the same idea to all who came within its radius. To the young people who had suffered the long horror of that awful night, it brought relief – relief from the presence or the fear of all that was horrible – relief which seemed perfected when the red rays of sunrise shot up over the far eastern sea, bringing a promise of a new order of things with the coming day.

XL

Wreckage

His bed saw little of Adam Salton for the remainder of that night. He and Mimi walked hand in hand in the brightening dawn round by the Brow to Castra Regis and on to Doom Tower. They did so deliberately in an attempt to think as little as possible of the terrible experiences of the night. They both tried loyally to maintain the other's courage, and in helping the other to distract attention from the recollections of horror. The morning was bright and cheerful, as a morning sometimes is after a devastating storm. The air was full of sunshine. The clouds, of which there were plenty in evidence, brought no lingering idea of gloom. All nature was bright and joyous, being in striking contrast to the scenes of wreck and devastation, of the effects of obliterating fire and lasting ruin.

The only evidence of the once stately pile of Castra Regis was a shapeless huddle of shattered architecture dimly seen at moments as the sea-breeze swept aside the cloud of thin, bluish, acrid smoke which presently marked the site of the once lordly castle. As for Diana's Grove, they looked in vain for a sign which had a suggestion of permanence. The oak trees of the Grove were still to be seen – some of them – emerging from a haze of smoke, the great trunks solid and erect as ever, but the larger branches broken and twisted and rent, with bark stripped and chipped, and the smaller branches broken and dishevelled looking from the constant stress and threshing of the storm. Of the house as such, there was, even at the little distance from which they looked, no trace. With the resolution to which he had come – to keep from his wife as well as he could all sights which might cause her pain or horror or leave unpleasant memories – Adam resolutely turned his back on the area of the devastation and hurried on to Doom Tower. This, with the strength and cosiness of the place, its sense of welcome and the perfection of its thoughtful ordering, gave Mimi the best sense of security and peace which she had had since, on last evening, she had left its shelter. She was not only upset and shocked in many ways, but she was physically 'dog tired' and falling asleep on her feet. Adam took her to her room and made her undress and get into bed, taking care that the room was well lighted both by sunshine and lamps. The only obstruction was from a silk curtain drawn across the window to keep out the glare. When she was feeling sleep steal over her, he sat beside her holding her hand, well knowing that the comfort of his presence was the best restorative for her. He stayed with her in that way till sleep had overmastered her wearied body. Then he went softly away. He found Sir Nathaniel in the study having an early cup of tea, amplified to the dimensions of possible breakfast. After a little chat, the two agreed to go together to look at the ruins of Diana's Grove and Castra Regis. Adam explained that he had not told his wife that he was going over the horrible places again, lest it would frighten her, whilst the rest and sleep in ignorance would help her and make a gap of peacefulness between the horrors. Sir Nathaniel agreed in the wisdom of the proceeding, and the two went off together.

They visited Diana's Grove first, not only because it was nearer, but that it was the place where most description was required, and Adam felt that he could tell his story best on the spot. The absolute destruction of the place and everything in it seen in the broad daylight was almost inconceivable. To Sir Nathaniel it was as a story of horror full and complete. But to Adam it was, as it were, only on the fringes. He knew what was still to be seen when his friend had got over the knowledge of externals. As yet, Sir Nathaniel had only seen the outside of the house – or rather, where the outside of the house had been. The great horror lay within. However, age – and the experience of age – counts. Sir Nathaniel in his long and eventful life had seen too many terrible and horrible sights to be dismayed at a new one, even of the kind which lay close before him, though just beyond his vision. A strange, almost elemental, change in the aspect had taken place in the time which had elapsed since the dawn. It would almost seem as if Nature herself had tried to obliterate the evil signs of what had occurred, and to restore something of the æsthetic significance of the place. True, the utter ruin and destruction of the house was made even more manifest in the searching daylight; but the more appalling destruction which lay beneath was not visible. The rent, torn, and dislocated stone-work looked worse than before; the upheaved foundations, the piled-up fragments of masonry, the fissures in the torn earth – all were at the worst. The Worm's hole was still evident, a round fissure seemingly leading down into the very bowels of the earth. But all the horrid mass of blood and slime, of torn, evil-smelling flesh and the sickening remnants of violent death, were gone. Either some of the later explosions had thrown up from the deep quantities of water which, though foul and corrupt itself, had still some cleansing power left, or else the writhing mass which stirred from far down below had helped to drag down and obliterate the items of horror. A gray dust, partly of fine sand, partly of the waste of the falling ruin, covered everything, and, though ghastly itself, helped to mask in something still worse. After a few minutes of watching, it became apparent to both men that the turmoil far below had not yet quite ceased. At short irregular intervals the hell-broth in the hole seemed as if boiling up. It rose and fell again and turned over, showing in fresh form much of the nauseous detail which had been visible earlier. The worst parts to see were the great masses of the flesh of the monstrous Worm in all its red and sickening aspect. Such fragments had been naturally bad enough before, but now they were infinitely worse. Corruption comes with startling rapidity to beings whose destruction has been due wholly or in part to lightning. Now the whole mass seemed to have become all at once corrupt. But that corruption was not all. It seemed to have attracted every natural organism which was in itself obnoxious. The whole surface of the fragments, once alive, was covered with insects, worms, and vermin of all kinds. The sight was horrible enough, but, with the awful smell added, was simply unbearable. The Worm's hole appeared to breathe forth death in its most repulsive forms. Both Adam and Sir Nathaniel, with one impulse, turned and ran to the top of the Brow, where a fresh breeze from the eastern sea was blowing up.

At the top of the Brow, beneath them as they looked down, they saw a shining mass of white, which looked strangely out of place amongst such wreckage as they had been viewing. It appeared so strange that Adam suggested trying to find a way down so that they might see it closely.

Sir Nathaniel suddenly stopped and said:

'We need not go down. I know what it is. The explosions of last night have blown off the outside of the cliffs. That which we see is the vast bed of china clay through which the Worm originally found its way down to its lair. See, there is the hole going right down through it. We can catch the glint of the water of the deep quags far down below. Well, her ladyship didn't deserve such a funeral, or such a monument. But all's well that ends well. We had better hurry home. Your wife may be waking by now, and is sure to be frightened at first. Come home as soon as you can. I shall see that breakfast is ready. I think we all want it.'

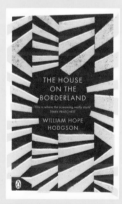

MORE
MACABRE
READS

THE LAIR OF THE
WHITE WORM

'A surreal and dark-humoured tale'
THE NEW YORK TIMES

BRAM STOKER